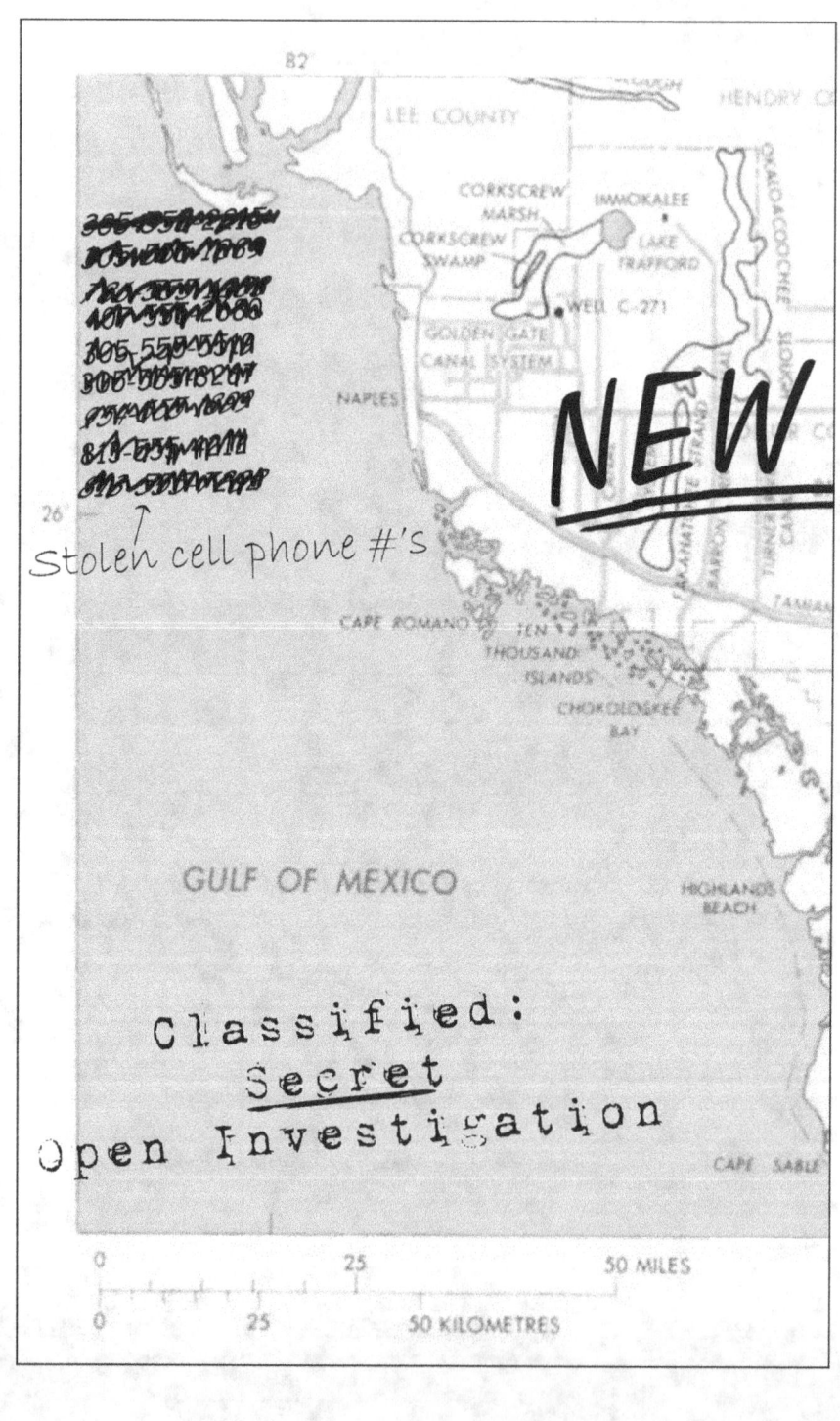

Stolen cell phone #'s

NEW

Classified:
Secret
Open Investigation

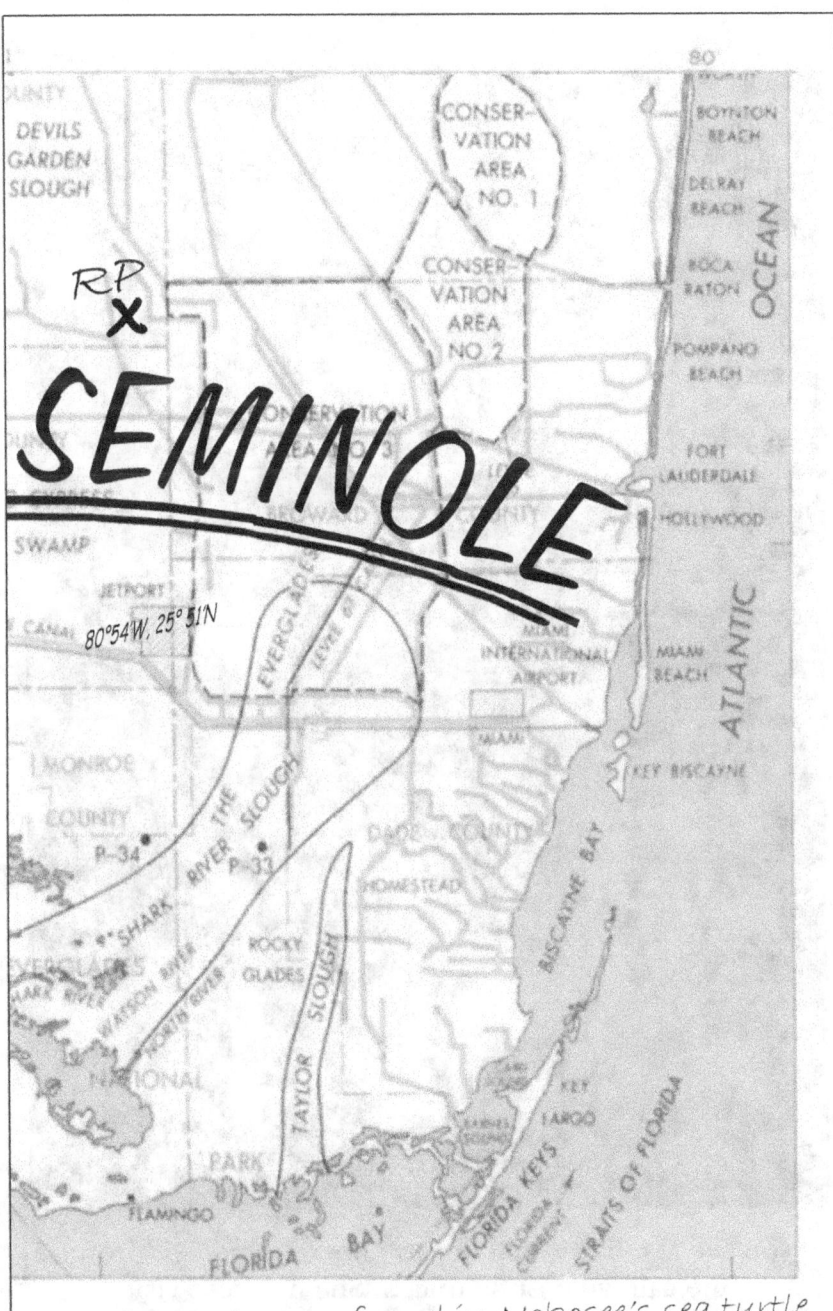

One of several maps found in Nokosee's sea turtle
shield. Note jet port coordinates and Raccoon
Point (RP) oil well location.

Stormy Jones
- Caucasian
- Blue eyes
- Blond hair (?)
- 5'-5"
- 17-years-old
- Multiple piercings
- May be wearing a Mohawk.
- Armed and Dangerous.
- Last seen: The Everglades.

DON'T START.

WANTED BY THE F.B.I

If you see Ms. Jones, tell her to phone home. We promise the call will not be traced. She may also visit
www.stormyphonehomenow.blogspot.com.

NOKOSEE

Rise of the New Seminole

by

Micco Mann

Palmetto Bug Books
Miami, FL

Inka Ochoski

This book is based on the notes taken from a secret FBI investigation. "Micco Mann" is the pseudonym of the Special Agent who interviewed Stormy Jones. Ms. Jones, as of this book's publication, is missing. She was last seen sporting a pink neon Mohawk while stealing J.T. Osceola's motorcycle and speeding west on Alligator Alley. Indian spears were tattooed on each side of her shaved head. If you should happen to see her or Nokosee Osceola, contact the nearest FBI office. Please note that the Bureau considers them "armed and dangerous."

www.fbi.gov/wanted.htm

Chapter 1

What are you, some kind of freaking flamingo?

I don't know when I fell in love with Nokosee. I know when we first met he scared the living bejesus out of me. Maybe it had something to do with his loincloth. You don't see many of them where I come from.

My name is Stormy Jones. "Stormy's" not my real name, of course, but it's better than the one my parents saddled me with and it suits me just fine. I'm seventeen-years-old, have blue eyes and today, spiked blond hair with pink flamingo highlights. Some people say I have an attitude, maybe so, but you would too if you had to spend your summers in the stinking Everglades. My parents are divorced and a judge "decreed" that I have to spend summers with my dad Sam. Unfortunately for me, he lives in the freaking Everglades. He's the head ranger for the park down there. Lives with the Indians, the Miccosukees and Seminoles. To me he's the "Great White Father" and he's used to getting things his way all year round so when I show up for the summers, his neat little world basically comes unglued because he doesn't know what to do with me. I think I make him nervous but that's all right, maybe he'll get enough of me and finally stop pretending he likes having me around for a couple of months and he'll let me stay with mom and my friends in Milltown, New Jersey. After what happened this summer, I'm pretty sure he will. Funny thing, though, I want to go back. Now. Not later. And it has nothing to do with my dad. It's Nokosee, my pagan caveman boyfriend. Well, he doesn't know he's my boyfriend anymore, but I'm pretty sure he misses me too and is going crazy down there without me.

I'd be lying if I told you we didn't hit it off. In the beginning it was pretty dicey, but by the end, it was pretty hot—in more ways than one, if you know what I mean. For one, the freaking Everglades is burning down around us most of the time, giant alligators are trying to eat us, body parts are popping up everywhere, my boyfriend uses me as gatorbait, my mom shoots my boyfriend, and some real mean, dumbass rednecks are trying to kill us, for crying out loud. And that's only half of it.

Let me start at the beginning, which was in Concourse D at MIA. I'm wearing this really hot outfit that's basically my only outfit because I love it the most. It starts with my lucky black "Korn" tee Eddie, my old boyfriend, bought for me at one of their concerts. On top of that, I'm wearing my to-die-for cropped black motorcycle jacket, which has tons of zippers. Because my dad hates seeing me in pants, I'm wearing the cutest red plaid mini skirt with matching Tartan peek-a-boo toe wedgies. I look absolutely adorable—in a dangerous sort of way. And, I feel really good about myself, like a model. At least I'm taller, thanks to the platforms and that's what I want to be when I see my dad this time. I want him to start seeing me like a woman instead of a little girl, his nice little girl. Anyway, as I'm lugging my backpack, I'm thinking about my spiked flamingo hair. It's already drooping in the Miami humidity—and this is inside the airport where there's air-conditioning!—when I hear my dad's voice.

"What are you, some kind of freaking flamingo?"

There's no smile on his face. If you can picture Jimmy Buffet with a crew cut, that's my dad—but in olive green "ranger" shorts and knee-length socks. I mean, he looks like a freaking Boy Scout standing in the middle of the airport. It is *so* embarrassing. He sees my latest piercings—I've got a slew of them on my ears, one on my nostril, and two over one eyebrow—and he just shakes his head like he's disgusted and disappointed. If he knew I had my tongue pierced too, I'm sure he would have gone apoplectic on me right there on the spot. That's why I left my tongue stud at home. I mean, who needs this, right? I'm taking a chance as it is with my belly button piercing. But I figure, as long as I keep it covered, he won't know a thing.

"That's right. I'm a freaking flamingo."

That's me. I don't know what to say. I mean, I'm lugging a backpack and my dad doesn't even offer to take it or say "Hi" or give me a hug.

"Figured. They're imports, too."

Talk about a hard ass, that's my dad. He glances at my two inch long air brushed glamour nails with rhinestones glued on the ends, shakes his head, turns around and walks away.

"C'mon, let's go," he says.

My eyes start tearing up but I promised I'd never cry again after the divorce and I haven't. Maybe if I were cuter he'd love me more. I don't know. I mean, I'm not bad looking. Maybe a little pudgy but I'm not so butt ugly I can't get a boyfriend. I had one back home when I met Nokosee. Eddie was on the football team. I was a cheerleader. It was perfect. Then he got cut from the team because he was a smart ass. Like me. So I quit being a cheerleader. It disappointed mom but I never really could get into that stuff anyway. Believe it or not, although he never said anything, I know it made my dad happy. He never liked the idea of me being "one of them," always "encouraging the prolonged adolescence of the American male" as if they were some sort of sub-human species to be studied. Anyway, I clench my jaw and follow him out of the airport.

Chapter 2

Lost and Found

Let's cut to the chase. This summer started out no different than the previous five summers. The Everglades is on fire. It's a joke. Despite everything my father does, the stupid Everglades catches on fire. He blames it on an "inordinate amount of conspicuously consuming water sucking yahoos" living there where the average South Floridian uses 179 gallons a day. At 3 million people, that's a lot of water. Anyway, he tells me the night I arrive at the compound, his headquarters and home on a Seminole reservation, that I'm old enough to fight the fires with the rest of his crew. I'm going like, "Are you kidding me? I'm not going anywhere near your stinking fire." There is no way I am going to risk chipping a nail out in the middle-of-nowhere fighting a stupid fire. I mean, they cost me some real dough. I worked hard to earn the money as a sales clerk at our local Hot Topic and there is no way I'm going to endanger these babies. You talk about "endangered species," well, as far as I'm concerned, my nails are more important than those stupid deer and things dad is always trying to save. Don't get me wrong. It's not like I don't care about things like that, but if it hadn't been for my father being a park ranger and all, I wouldn't even have to decide between the two. I'd still be a normal girl who works as a sales clerk in the local mall. But no-o-o, I have to be the kid that gets shuffled off every summer to a place that is constantly on fire and whose dad is in charge of trying to put it out. Un-freaking-believable.

Anyway, you can't argue with the old man. The next morning I'm putting on my makeup and getting my hair moussed up and he starts yelling at me from the kitchen to speed it up, that we don't have all day. Well, I'm not used to getting yelled at like that. Mom is pretty cool and laid back. She's never a hassle. So, instead of hopping to it, I light up a cigarette. I know, it's not good for you, but I basically don't care. By the time I show up for breakfast, dad's thrown my eggs and bacon out and is washing the dishes. I see this and I say, "So what's for breakfast?" He turns around and gives me the once over in the way only he can do. I immediately know I put together the wrong outfit. I think it's pretty cool —the cropped motorcycle jacket, my favorite tee, cut-off jeans, and some rolled down socks and Doc Martens. I figure if any snakes are around, the Docs ought to protect me. Dad, of course, doesn't see it that way.

"You gotta be kidding me," he says dryly as he wipes his hands on the dishcloth.

"What?" I stupidly reply.

"We're fighting a fire, not hanging out at the mall."

"Dad, I don't hang out at the mall. I work there."

"You might want to ditch the jacket. It's going to be pretty hot out there."

I shake my head and inhale on my cigarette.

"I don't recommend the shorts either. Your legs look like skeeter meat."

"Skeeters" are what dad calls mosquitoes. You'll find he has a unique vocabulary, something he insists I not copy since he doesn't want me sounding like I don't have "no edumacation." I look at the empty table.

"So where's breakfast?"

"Breakfast was half-an-hour-ago. We're late. Let's go."

He throws the towel down and walks past me.

"And ditch that cigarette," he says in passing. "We're trying to put out fires, not start new ones."

Welcome to my world.

##

We're in this unbelievably loud helicopter with no doors pop calls a Hughie. Another one is following us. It's like a low budget version of *Apocalypse Now.* One of the guys has cranked up his ghetto blaster so that we can have an accompanying soundtrack. Yeah, that's right, I'm hearing Wagner's *Ride of the Valkyries* in the background. Too much. We've been flying for only about ten minutes and we're already in the middle-of-freaking-nowhere. I can barely see the skyscrapers in downtown Miami as we rush further and further away from civilization- or at least what passes for it where dad lives. I wouldn't call it "civilized" where the Great White Father has taken up abode but at least it has air-conditioning. Barely. No central A/C, just a few noisy room units but without that, I'd probably go stark raving mad. I planned on spending all summer in my air-conditioned room where the humidity wouldn't wilt my punk pompadour—only going out occasionally at night to some club-- but that idea went out the open window on dad's *un*-air-conditioned old government issued pick-up truck the day he picked me up at MIA. It took us over an hour to get to No-wheres-ville. In all that time, I never said a word to him, which was easy since he never once made an attempt to talk to me. When he pulled up in front of his office-slash-home on the reservation, my slight hope that I might actually get through this last forced summer with my dad had fallen as flat as my Mohawk.

I'd be lying if I told you I wasn't nervous now. We're flying *into* a fire, for crying out loud. If mom knew this, she'd be all over him. But I can't squeal on him. This time. He means well. It's his way of bonding with me. Last summer he wanted me to "fell" a tree with him, carve it up, and turn it into a canoe—I'm sorry, a *bithlo*, that's what the Miccosukees and Seminoles call them. He figured if you took in account the time it took to fight the fires, it would take all summer to make one of them and he would have been right too because those things are long; we're talking about twenty-feet long! I was hoping the fire would burn every last tree down to the ground before that could happen but as it turned out, he caught holy hell from my mom when she found out about it from me and the "felling" and the carving never became a problem after that.

Poor guy, I really felt sorry for him. I could have told on him this time too, but it just isn't worth it seeing him mope around for two months. Maybe that's why he's quieter than usual this time. Maybe he's holding a grudge against me. Anyway, I figure I'll do such a bad job at putting out the fire he'll give up and let me atrophy back at the ranger shack all summer.

I can hardly formulate a plan to fail royally in front of him because I can't hear myself think in the Hughie much less hear what he's yelling at me to do. Before I know it, we're descending into a cloud of smoke, which the helicopter blades whip up into swirling vortexes, and I start coughing immediately. Tears are rolling out of my eyes because of the ash and soot in the air and I'm thinking, at least I won't have to worry about working at looking bad in front of my father since I'm coughing up a storm. In fact, I can't stop coughing.

The Hughie hits the ground hard and I see my dad leaning over towards me and I think he's going to pound my back to help me breathe or something but the next thing I know, the man has grabbed me by the back of my motorcycle jacket and is lifting me by one hand and carrying me out of the helicopter. He pushes my head down until the Hughie flies away and I find myself staring at the smoking, cracked and blackened mud.

"Put this on," he yells at me.

I look up and he's shoving a gas mask in my face. I must confess, at this point, I really think hard about calling my mom. But it wouldn't do any good. There isn't any cell phone service out there. Trust me, once that Hughie left, it was like we had taken a time machine back a thousand years.

I don't care what the gas mask does to my doo—hell, it wilted the moment I stepped out of the ranger shack—I just want to breathe. For the first time I can relate to my friend who has asthma. Talk about pain. Each deep breath through the gas mask sounds scary. In fact, I can't believe I'm making that sound, but I am. When I look up, I see my dad looking at me, like he cares or something. When he sees me looking at him, he turns away and yells some orders to his crew. They disperse and start setting fires around the perimeter of the clearing with something that looks like flamethrowers. At this point, I got to tell you, I think I'm in the middle of a freaking war. I understand the concept of starting new fires to control old fires by creating a barrier where there isn't anything for a fire to catch on to, but right now at this moment, it seems like an idea that still needs a little work.

"Follow me!"

Dad is grabbing me by the arm and yelling at me. Of course I do as he says. He sticks a shovel in my hand.

"Stay close and start shoveling!"

I don't realize it, but those are the last words I'll hear from him for quite some time.

I don't know when the fire got out of control but it probably happened when the fire and smoke separated my dad and me. I know my goose is cooked when I see the Hughies rise out of the smoke and fly off. I can't believe he didn't check to see if I was on board one of them. No wonder mom divorced him! My god, he's a complete idiot!

I scream my head off and hear the sound of my voice echoing in my gas mask. I throw it off and yell for all I'm worth—which isn't very much as I soon find out. Before I know it, I'm coughing and crawling along the hot, parched mud—and let me tell you, it is *hot*. I yank my hands away and it looks like they are that close to blistering. Worst yet, I can hardly breathe.

I hear a tree fall nearby. I can't see it because of the smoke but a ball of fire and hot cinders pops out and knocks me onto my back. All I can think about is whether or not my hair is on fire. My dad never liked my doo and he loved to remind me about Michael Jackson when his hair caught fire because of all the crap he had on it to hold it in place. So I grab my hair and start rolling and screaming across the parched Everglade bottom like some kind of crazy lady. Unfortunately, I'm only making things worse because I'm kicking up a cloud of hot dust and ash, which makes it even harder to breathe. Every time I take a deep breath it feels like someone is taking a blowtorch to my lungs. I have to get out of there. I know I must look pretty lame, but somehow I roll up onto my hands and knees and crawl like a demented baby on all fours across the hot ground. I don't have a clue where I'm going because I can't see a thing. My eyes are tearing up from the ash and soot and the smoke is hiding everything.

That's when I run into the sawgrass. Talk about pain. You gotta wonder what God was thinking when he came up with this stuff. Each blade is covered with little serrated teeth and the whole Everglades is *covered* with this freaking plant. "River of Grass," my ass— they should rename that book "River of Saws!" It'd be more truthful. This stuff has to be at least six-feet tall. I can't see over it and no matter what I try to do, it keeps cutting me up. I don't think it can get much worse until my sweat gets into the lacerations. I feel like my whole body is on fire. That's when my head starts spinning since I'm weak from hunger because my dad had to prove a point. I tell you, he's the Soup Nazi of fathers.

"Screw you, dad!"

Yeah, I'm a little P.O'd to say the least, maybe a little crazy too since I'm screaming out loud in the middle of nowhere but say what you will, getting angry gets me moving again which is better than waiting around to get shake and baked. Besides not seeing where I'm going, I don't know where I'm going. Maybe I'm not thinking clearly. I know I'm screaming. And thinking about my manicure. I know, that sounds stupid, but when I'm running like a chicken with its head cut off through the sawgrass, I keep my arms up in front of me and, well, I can't help but notice my manicure. Or what is left of it. I guess you never know what will go through your mind when you find yourself in a life and death situation like this. Anyway, it's kind of funny because I start thinking about my dad again, about how wrong he is this time: my Harley jacket is protecting my arms and upper body.

"Ha, dad," I hear myself thinking, *"you don't know everything."*

That's when the sawgrass catches my hair and yanks me to the ground. Tears are rolling out of my eyes from the pain when I twist around and see my pink locks stuck to the sawgrass.

There goes my punk pride and joy.

Mom calls it my "pink badge of courage." Yeah, you guessed it, I'm thinking about my mom this time— and maybe Stephen Crane, which is really weird-- until I feel the heat and it literally lights a fire under my ass. I grab my hair close to the scalp, reach back with my other arm and bring it down across the sawgrass. I'm free but that stupid grass has swiped nine inches of my pink-tipped hair. I leave it dangling from the sawgrass and start running again.

"Oh, my God," I shout out loud, "I can't believe this is happening to me!"

I can't see over the sawgrass. I can't see the sun because it's hidden behind thick smoke and ash, which is rolling over the tips of the sawgrass down on top of me. When something grazes my leg, I scream, fall into the sawgrass and nearly have a conniption fit. All I see are the legs of a white tail deer leaping through the sawgrass.

Another one crashes through and stops short when it sees me and I swear we both scream at the same time. Before I can cover my face, the deer jumps over me but its hooves glance off the side of my head. I'm like seeing stars and everything is spinning around me. I try to hold onto something to keep from falling over. Unfortunately, the thing I grab is hot, rough, and moving.

Snake!

Trust me, I let go of that thing quicker than you can say, "Snake!" Unfortunately, again, it was a millisecond too late. The snake, a black water moccasin, is already in my face. Its mouth is opened impossibly wide and its extended gleaming, needle sharp fangs are hurtling toward me when the hoof of another deer careening through the sawgrass suddenly flattens it.

I roll into a ball and try to protect my head as more deer jump over my body. They shake the earth and kick up more hot dust, which gets me coughing again. I can hear their cries and pray they won't trample me but it doesn't do any good. A deer digs its sharp hoof into my back and knocks the wind out of me. I can't believe the sounds I'm making as I struggle to suck in air. With each painful breath I inhale more smoke, ash, and *more pain*. Blood from my head wound is flowing into my eyes and, along with the sweat and tears, begins to roll uncontrollably down my cheeks. My lungs are crying out for air but when I try to give them what they want, the smoke, ash, and soot get me coughing so hard I fall against the hot, parched mud and start kicking up more clouds of dust, ash and soot. I lift my head and trail a long strand of saliva. It looks like I am coughing up blood.

This is the first time I really think I'm going to die. If I knew this would be the first of many near death experiences I will have over the next few days, maybe I wouldn't have bothered to lift my head to look for a miracle. In any event, I do and there it is in front of me: an opening in the sawgrass. I can't believe my tear-filled eyes but the deer have beaten down the grasses and cleared a path for me. I start crying like a big baby but cut myself short. I take a deep, screeching breath and somehow roll over onto my knees. When I try to straighten my back, pain shoots through my shoulder and buckles me at the waist. My head hits the hot earth. I know immediately the hoof has cut through my leather jacket. I can feel my t-shirt sticking to the cut and pulling at the lacerated skin with each movement of my body. I almost pass out from the pain and probably will until I hear a high-pitched scratching sound. I think something else is rushing through the sawgrass and make an attempt to get out of its way. And then, with each painful breath, I know that thing I hear racing through the jungle is only me trying to breathe and that it's enough to get me up on my feet. Half smiling, I look for the opening. It's still there and I find myself staggering towards it with what I'm sure is a stupid grin on my face.

The beaten path leads to a canal.

Say what? I ask myself.

My tortured synapses aren't making any sense of it right away. It's like I have stumbled onto crop circles in the middle of the Everglades. But this is a straight line carved across the middle-of-nowhere that goes on for miles, as far as the eye can see. But thanks to Dad, explanations are soon forthcoming from brain cells that have been smoked silly like a beehive.

UFOs have nothing to do with this. It was the Army Corp of Engineers. They have been working diligently for nearly a hundred years to drain the Everglades by slicing and dicing it up into chunks to grow mostly sugar cane and people. These canals are partially responsible for the yearly droughts. My dad says it forces an unnatural water management program on an ecosystem that doesn't need any managing unless, of course, you need land to farm or land for homes. Since you're limited to how much you can do with the east coast what with the Atlantic Ocean beating up against its sandy shores and all, the only land available is to the west stretching all the way to the Gulf of Mexico. The only problem, of course, is that it's mostly underwater, a shallow "sea of grass." But, hey, that's no problem; just call in the Army Corp of Engineers. If they can dig the Panama Canal, they can sure as hell drain the Everglades. And for much of south Florida, that's exactly what they did.

When I get closer, I notice the water has an unusual color, a swirling mixture of red and gray. I'm thinking about how that doesn't make any sense when a root catches my Docs and trips me up. In that instance, a Florida panther leaps out of the sawgrass and lands next to me. I swear to you our eyes lock. I'm so scared I can't breathe or move but you know what, it's scared too. Not of me, mind you, because it can easily kill me and have a nice meal of a New Jersey raised, free-range babe. No, I can tell from its desperate eyes it's only thinking about escaping the fire. Without its sawgrass cover, the cat knows it is vulnerable to attack from gators, bears or the thing it fears most, man. Before I have a chance to react, the panther snarls and leaps into the canal. The moment it's gone I suck in the whole universe.

When I get up and stumble toward the canal bank I can see that the land on the other side is untouched by the fire. Hammocks, which are pockets of higher ground where seedlings from live oak, gumbo-limbo, sable palm and other trees have set down roots, dot the Everglades. Most of them are now on fire. These aren't. I can't take my eyes off them and almost step right into the canal. Thank God I don't. When I look down I see that poor panther again, only this time it's in the jaws of a gator who is violently shaking that gorgeous, fearsome cat from side to side and, dammit, our eyes meet again and I can tell he knows he's going to die. He has given up and has accepted his fate. We are still looking at each other when the gator takes it beneath the water to hold it there until it drowns. I can't watch and I feel so useless because I can't help that panther. And I'm scared too. I think I have been thrown into a living nightmare where nothing makes sense and something evil is lying behind every shadow. I have to turn away and when I do, the nightmare only gets worse.

Deer bodies, at least ten of them, are floating in the canal, future meals for the gators who are in a feeding frenzy below me. Some of the deer have been ripped apart, their thin legs torn off and strewn in the bloody, frothing stream. I can still see them shaking and shuddering in the crimson water. I cover my ears so I don't have to hear their high-pitched screams but even to this day, their terrible deaths won't go away. I look back at the fire.

The fire, in one long line parallel to the canal, is nearly upon me. I look up and down the canal bank. I don't know which way to go. I start running away from the flow of the water, hoping to find a place where it isn't tainted with blood and death and pray I'm not running into the fire.

The smoke is getting thicker. I pause to catch my breath and hold onto a branch. It's hot. I look up. The branch is on fire. I let go and start to run again, looking for a place to jump into the water, a place where the blood hasn't flowed and the gators and the body parts haven't gathered.

But where is that place?

I can't find it. I look back at the fire. The flames are marching like giants across the sawgrass horizon, the smoke is blotting out the mid-afternoon sun and I swear I can hear the burning grass screaming. I turn to the sound.

What is that?

The shimmering heat waves are playing tricks with my eyes. It looks like a man silhouetted against the raging fire but he doesn't seem to have a nose. Instead, his face looks like a walrus.

Could it be Bigfoot, the legendary skunk ape of the Everglades? I've seen some dubious video of the creature and it doesn't look like that at all. *Maybe it's because the videos were faked*, I think. *Maybe this is the real thing.* I rub my eyes and look again.

No, it's a man— and he's horribly disfigured! He's screaming at the sky! At me! My god, he's only wearing a loincloth! Hell, why does this have to happen to me? I want to hide, but where? I've got the fire behind me. I can feel its heat. In front lies the horror in the canal.

Again, fate steps in: my boot slips down the embankment.

I'm in the water! I grab desperately at the rocky, blindingly white oolite sides and rip my palms open. I leave a trail of blood along the jagged face. Immediately I hear the "Jaws" theme and look down half expecting to see a Great White going for my Docs. I'm so repulsed by the thought of being in the blood soaked water with hungry alligators and the remains of their victims, that I find myself clawing and screaming up the canal wall. I catch an edge and try to hold on while bringing my boots up out of the nightmarish waters but my muscles are shaking with the effort and I don't know how long I can hold on.

I hear a splash and turn to see a twirling vortex in the bloody ash covered water.

Gator!

I try to pull myself up but the shaking gets worse. I turn toward the fire and see the man racing toward me, zigzagging in and out of the burning sawgrass.

Oh, God! He doesn't have a nose!

I'm such a shallow doofus I let go and fall into the water because I would rather face gators on a feeding frenzy than a man with a disfigurement. I deserve to die.

But that doesn't happen. Instead, I'm punished for my silliness with pain that is instant and extreme. It reverberates from the hoof cuts through my body and bounces off my temple wound and screams through every pore I own. I didn't know it was possible, but I even cry out under the water. I swallow the polluted, bloodstained, tannic tainted runoff. I want to heave. I surface gasping and vomiting. When I look up at the canal bank I see the man.

He's throwing a spear at me!

I scream like a little girl, duck and turn toward an alligator's open mouth. The spear pierces the mouth and lodges between the creature's eyes, penetrating the skull and entering its brain. I find myself staring in horror as the creature glides towards me and sinks beneath the dark water. I hear a splash and turn to look.

The man is gone.

He must have dove into the water!

I turn and start to swim toward the other side of the canal when I feel his hand trying to grab my boot under the water. I kick his hand with the steel toe of my Docs and he lets go. I kick away and continue to swim with each painful stroke toward the other side of the canal and begin to think about how dad's insistence that I learn to swim when I was little because of how easy it is to drown in all of the unguarded pools and canals in south Florida. In fact, according to him, it's the leading cause of death down here for young kids. Of course mom had to make it something competitive. Ten years on a swimming team made me fast and it all came to an end when I discovered boys and rock and roll. For the last two years I've been avoiding swimming because of my hair and makeup. I never thought I would ever swim again unless, of course, it became fashionable.

Or if I had to.

I can hear him swimming behind me. I'm too afraid to look back. Now I wish I hadn't worn the leather jacket or the boots. They're dragging me down, slowing my progress. A decade of perfecting my crawl stroke made me unintentionally open my eyes and look at him as if he's a competitor in the opposite lane. As my right hand goes down into the water, my head turns to the left side so my mouth can suck in its precious air and the eyes can see where the swimmer in the other lane is.

He's right beside me, swimming stroke for stroke, watching me.

He's horrible to look at. He doesn't have a nose. It seems to have been replaced by a large growth, maybe a tumor that is sprouting hair, so much hair that it droops over his mouth and trails in the water. I can't look. I swallow more blood and water, gasp and kick out at the hideous thing. I can see in a split second that his features are Indian although his hair is longer than any of the Seminoles or Miccosukees I know on the res.

The tribe probably exiled him because he's so ugly.

I kick him again. The mutant Miccosukee— if that's his tribe-- tries to hold onto my boot but I twist away and begin to swim the backstroke. I think this might be a better means of escape because this was my best event.

The Indian is startled for a moment and doesn't move. He takes a breath and dives underwater.

I reach backward even further until the pain becomes unbearable. My hand slaps the oolite canal wall. This porous coral rock-like stone lies just inches below the entire Everglades and it once again cuts my hands but I don't feel the pain this time. I flip around and look for something to grab onto, to pull myself out of the water. I can't find anything. My hands are clawing at the rocky embankment and leaving a bloody trail along the sides. I look back and see a line of bubbles popping up on the surface of the water, racing toward me.

He's got me around the waist and he's pulling me down!

I whip around and, without hesitation, as my dad has drilled it in to me over the years, kick the disfigured Indian squarely in his manhood with my steel tipped Docs.

The Indian never had a chance. He lets go immediately, grabs his balls and sinks slowly to the bottom dragging a trail of bubbles and a silent cry only the fish can hear.

I break the surface and devour the smoke filled air. I look back across the water.

The fire has reached the other side and is threatening to leap across the canal.

I turn to a sound in the water.

He's *baa-ck!*

The Indian sounds like a wounded animal. He shakes his head and his long hairy snout whips back and forth like an elephant's trunk. He sees me and screams a terrible, pore-opening scream. I lose my tenuous grip on the rocks and slide into the water. I see him start for me again.

I drag myself desperately along the embankment, hoping to find something to grab on to so I can pull myself out of the water. I see something protruding out over the canal bank and pull myself toward it. It's the Indian's bithlo, the thing my dad wanted me to carve out of a tree one summer and learned, when I wouldn't do it, that I wasn't going to be the son he never had, that I was his daughter with a mind of her own.

I reach up and grab the bow of the bithlo with one hand. My whole body begins to tremble from the effort and it is all I can do to hang on. I look back and see the injured, ugly Indian swimming slowly toward me. I breathe in deep another breath of the acrid smoke and pause for a moment before throwing my other arm up to grab the bithlo. I find my grip and, with an enormous effort on my part, pull myself out of the water.

The pain in my back tells me I'm tearing the cut, ripping the skin even further. My body quivers under the stress as I try to lift a leg out of the water. The shaking becomes so intense I fear losing my grip. I can see my arms trembling; I can feel my teeth rattling. The Doc is heavy to begin with but now, laden with water, it's almost impossible to lift. With a gut-wrenching grunt that scares even me, I manage to hook the boot over the edge of the bithlo.

Water pours out of the boot, down my leg and onto my bare stomach, a stomach I know isn't as rippled as it use to be. My other leg catches a foothold on the canal wall and I kick off. The effort pushes my body over the top of the bithlo but—

He's got my leg!

The man's touch unleashes a wave of adrenaline. I kick loose, pull my leg up and, on all fours, back away along the bithlo until my Docs slip out from underneath and I fall onto my stomach. Before I get a chance to cuss, I see them.

Evian water bottles, some still wrapped in plastic six-packs, scattered around me in the dugout.

The bithlo dips forward and I slide with the bottles toward the front. I look up.

The Indian's hand is grabbing the bow. And now the other hand has joined it. He's groaning as he pulls himself out of the water. His leg is over the side.

I roll off the bithlo and fall next to a giant sea turtle shell. I scream— you would too—and push it away. I look back at the bithlo.

It's bouncing up and down with the Indian's effort to climb out of the canal.

I get up and run toward the back of the bithlo and try to lift it up. It's a struggle but I manage to raise it about a foot. The Indian's weight on the other end and his sliding cargo of water bottles does the rest. Both he and his bithlo slide backward into the canal with a Muskogee curse, the language of the Seminoles. "The Chiefs," a Seminole street gang I belong to, would only teach me a few words but I'm pretty sure the Indian just cursed which is really a mouthful when you consider the language is polysyllabic up the wazoo.

I turn and run a few steps before stopping short.

Where? Which way?

The towering wall of sawgrass, aided by a wind pushed before the onrushing fire, seems to dare me with each swaying motion to try a different direction. I look back.

The Indian's hand is gripping the top of the oolite rim!

I turn quickly back to the imposing sawgrass barrier. I have to try to protect myself. I start to remove my Harley jacket. The bloody t-shirt has stuck to it and the pain is excruciating. I start to cry again, not just because of the pain, but because I'm afraid I can't hold him off.

The jacket is off but the pain takes me to my knees. I'm sure the skin has come with it. I look; it hasn't but there is a lot of blood inside the jacket. I start to cry until I hear the man grunt. I look back.

He's almost out of the canal.

I struggle to my feet and hold the jacket up in front of me so that it covers my face and shields my hands, arms, and stomach. My legs are a lost cause. I throw myself headlong into hell's garden.

What am I doing? I can't see where I'm going! I don't know where I'm going!

I look down at my legs. My thighs are slashed and bleeding and that once perfect tan is now a thing of the past. I want to cry but I'm so angry and so afraid I can't.

Why me?

All I ever wanted to do was to hang out with my friends back in Milltown: go to the movies, lie out in the sun, dance at the local teen club, maybe let Eddie "go all the way." Despite what my parents thought, I still hadn't crossed that threshold. Right then, though, I sure wish I had. I don't want to die a virgin.

But that's why I'm here in the first place, to get me away from Eddie.

Oh, how I wish I were in Eddie's arms right now, giving him what he always wanted. What a fool. I'm seventeen. Madonna was only sixteen when she left home. Why can't I be brave like her and just *do* it?

Before I can answer that question, I run straight into the towering trunk of a sable palm. Stunned, I fall backwards in a heap. I manage to get up on one elbow and try to focus on the thing I just ran into.

The state tree.

It's funny what will pop into your mind at odd moments. Dad has taught me well. I hear a footstep behind me and turn drunkenly around.

He's coming at me out of the shadows, breathing heavily. I can see the hair sprouting below his eyes where his nose should be, it's falling over his mouth and rises and drops with each labored breath. He crouches before me like some kind of wild animal. He's holding something in front of him.

It's the sea turtle shell.

I back away. *So that's how he walks through the sawgrass. He's painted something on it. Words.*

He tosses the shield aside and rises slowly, staring at me from under the dark shadows of the wet black hair covering his face. For the first time I can see that he is not a man-thing but a boy-thing about my age with the finest male body I've ever seen. *He's gotta have zero percent body fat.* Being an ex-swimmer, that's something I know a lot about.

My god, look at his abs! I can count every one of them! And his pecs! I have to turn away.

What are you thinking, you idiot? He's one butt ugly son-of-a-bitch.

He steps toward me and I turn quickly back.

"No you don't!" I shout unconvincingly. My voice is quivering as I push myself back up against the state tree. He stops and stares at me.

"Not a step closer!"

I'm almost crying. He doesn't move. I see the knife stuck in its sheath, which is tied to his loincloth. Both look dangerous. I don't have a chance. Either way, one or both of them is going to get me.

The hunky-horror reaches slowly across his body and draws the knife from its sheath. It will never reflect light because the blade is coated in black powder.

This is not a good sign. Thanks to my dad, the man who tries to impart everything he knows to me in the short time I'm with him every summer-- including how to drive an airboat and mark a trail-- I know a knife like that has been designed for somebody who doesn't want to be seen, for someone who is sneaking up on you and wants to slit your throat from behind.

"No, please."

I think I'm going to die. Again.

The knife is thrown so quickly that it strikes the tree just above my head before I can cry out. I look at the knife and then the Indian. He is holding his hands out to the sides, palms up as if to say he means no harm. But I don't believe him. I reach back and grab the knife but it won't come out of the tree. When I turn around, he's already on top of me. I try to kick him but he's a fast learner. He's learned the hard way the power of the Docs. Holding down one leg, he guides my kicking leg with just a slight movement of his hand toward the ground and holds both legs down.

My God, he's so strong!

Unable to move my legs I reach this time with both hands for the knife but I still can't remove it from the tree. When I turn around, the Indian is sitting on top of me. I lash out with my fists, but he grabs them and forces me onto my back with such ease it scares me even more. I shut my eyes and start to cry and try to struggle to free myself but I cannot. I feel his hand on my hair. I surprise myself when I open my eyes.

He was looking at my hair but when he sees my blue eyes, he drops the hair and sits back, startled.

I don't know what to think. I know my eyes are beautiful, that's what I've heard since I was a kid. Just like mom's.

God, I hope it doesn't turn him on.

Not waiting to find out, I throw a leg around his head but, although it's still pretty powerful from all that swimming, it's no match in strength for the Indian sitting on my stomach. He simply grabs it with one hand and pushes it slowly to the ground and, no matter how hard I fight to hold my shaking thigh up, I cannot compete against his overpowering strength. When he looks back to shift his body over my thighs, I take a swipe at his face with my free hand but he catches the blow just inches from his head, forces the arm down and then lays against me. I can feel his hairy tumor growth against my cheek and, maddened by the thought of this disfigured creature on top of me, I lunge toward the wet hair hanging from his scalp, bite onto it and shake it like a gator would its meal. He cries out and his howling inspires me to shake with even more ferocity.

He stops my thrashing by forcing the crown of his head up under my chin. As he does this, he moves my hands onto my breasts, grips them with one hand and reaches with his other hand for the knife. I see this and try to squirm free but the Indian won't allow me to move. So I sink my front teeth into his skull.

He cries out, rears back, yanks the knife out of the tree and, with one swift stroke, slices neatly through the hair between the short gap between my mouth and his scalp.

I fall back, eyes as wide as hubcaps, my mouth full of the deformed Indian's hair. I scream and the Indian's hair falls into my mouth. I gag.

He plunges the knife.

I grimace and turn away, choking and spitting up hair. I hear the knife strike the earth beside me. My eyes open and I see the knife only inches from my face. The numbers 72, 73, and 74 are scratched on the chipped black hilt. I turn swiftly back to the Indian. He's motioning with his free hand to calm down.

But I can't calm down and neither could you. His hand is moving toward my mouth.

My God, he's trying to strangle me.

I lurch forward and bite his hand. The Indian yells again and tries to shake loose but I won't let go even though I can taste the dirt— and I'm sure, the mutant DNA-- on his hand. My head rises up from the ground following his hand and returns just as quickly when he slams it back down. Stunned, I let go and look up at him through my bloodshot eyes. He's spinning over me, breathing heavily, looking at his hand. I try to head butt him, waiting for his head to come into range as it circles above me, but I misjudge the distance and he stiffens and my head bounces off his like a rubber ball against granite. The state tree is now spinning above me. The head butt opens up the gash across my forehead the deer had left behind and blood begins to flow over my eyebrow, into my eyes and across my cheek. The last thing I remember while struggling to keep my eyelids open, before unconsciousness, before the beginning of my new life, is his face. His hand is running gently across my forehead and he's looking into my eyes.

They are beautiful eyes.

Chapter 3

Into the Heart of Darkness

The rhythm of the five thousand-year-old stroke brings me out of a disturbing sleep. With each stroke of the Indian's long pole, I can feel the bithlo speed up and then slowly glide across the water until it almost stops; the first motion of man on water. I'm lying on the bottom of the bithlo on my side like a baby in her mother's womb. My hands are clasped as if I'm praying. I can tell my head is resting on the balled up motorcycle jacket because I can smell the wet leather. When my eyes flicker open, I see the water rolling by only inches away. And the reeds. And the sawgrass. I tense for a moment.

I don't want to see any ugly things.

I turn to stop the dream and feel the pain in my back. I look up. The Indian is standing over me in silhouette, the sun behind him. He's driving the long wooden pole into the water. I squint but can't see his face. The bithlo comes to a rough stop.

He's taking me somewhere. I want to go home.

He lifts me out of the bithlo without effort.

My God, he's so strong.

I try to look at him, but I'm too weak and my head falls back against his broad hairless chest. I hear him walking through the water and then out of the water. I open my eyes and look down past his brown, swimmer's smooth, sweat stained chest. The biggest gator I've ever seen is looking back up at me. It's walking beside the Indian and looking at me with its head cocked to the side. A jagged scar has creased its left eye and the eye itself is glazed over, frozen in blindness. It hisses at me. He kicks at it and I drift off to sleep.

##

When I awake my t-shirt has been removed and I'm lying on my stomach at the base of a large gumbo limbo tree.

My bra!

I feel for it. It's still on, still squeezing what I've got out of it, my Victoria's Secrets Secret Embrace™ push-up leopard skin print bra; my favorite.

Hey, they may not be that big, but pushed together I become one dangerous piece of jailbait.

Considering where I am, the leopard print is oh so apropos—not that anyone is going to see it except maybe my mom or Eddie, if he's real nice.

Or that crazy Indian!

The sun is setting. Is it still today?

I smell the wet deerskin under my body. I hear water splashing. I turn slowly, my back on fire. The Indian is wading in the water with a spear held high. He throws it at something in the water, runs after it, grabs it and brings up a fish. I smell something pungent and turn to it. The Indian has something cooking in a steel pot.

Coleman?

I'm surprised I can remember the name of the camping cookware. I see what is left of my t-shirt. It's hanging in shreds on a palmetto palm frond.

Why the hell did he go and do that? Man, that was a cool t-shirt.

When I turn back, he's standing next to me. I jump and try to slide back but the pain in my back stops me short. I cry out and pinch my eyes shut. When I open them, the Indian is kneeling beside me, his face hidden by his long straight, black hair.

His hair is dry now. How many hours have I been here? Is it still today? Please don't show me your face.

He takes me by the arms. I tighten.

Please don't hurt me.

He turns me gently onto my stomach.

I'm dreaming.

"Please don't hurt me," I hear myself saying out loud in someone else's voice.

He doesn't say anything. A moment passes but to me it seems like forever. He puts something warm and wet on my back. It sets it on fire. I arch up, grind my teeth and look. It's a strip of my t-shirt; he's dipped it in something. Then, just as quickly, the pain is gone. I relax and settle slowly onto the deerskin, savoring the release of pain and the soothing pleasure the ointment brings.

Thank you, thank you, thank you, I whisper to myself. *I don't think he's going to hurt me.*

A moment passes before he returns with a strip of cooked fish resting on his knife. He lightly touches my shoulder. I smell the fish first and reach out from my half-sleep, take the offering, put it in my mouth and chew it slowly. It's good, surprisingly good, better than I had ever expected. I offer a tired smile of thanks and fall asleep.

##

When I wake up, it's night and the world glows in the dark like a red-hot ember. A campfire is blazing nearby, its light reflecting off the orange glow of the water. Smoke and ash dance magically in the air all around me and reinforces the thought that I'm watching from afar, from the safety of my bedroom back home in Milltown.

I feel like I'm in a snow globe. I must be dreaming. This can't be happening to me.

The pain tells me differently. I close my eyes and begin to cry softly and, after awhile, fall asleep.

##

I smell something in the middle of the night and waken fitfully. A she-bear is looking at me. I can tell because its cub is next to her. Both are lying on the ground staring at me with red demon haunted eyes from the glow of the campfire.

"It's only a dream," a voice whispers to me and I fall back to sleep reassured.

##

Who's that?

I wake up again and catch a man looking at me from between the undergrowth. It's another Indian, older and just as ugly wearing war paint.

There must be a whole tribe of these mutant freaks out here.

I blink and he's gone and sleep returns.

##

I can hear the sound of a chopper.

They're coming to save me!

Even before my eyes are open, I know the nightmare is coming to an end. But then I see the Indian throwing sand on the fire.

Why is he doing that? I ask myself in a voice still half asleep.

Before I have an answer, I see him running toward me. He's picking me up and carrying me into the hammock.

Why are you doing this? I ask in a voice stuck between sleep and consciousness. *I wanna go home.*

The hammock is awash in light and wind and sound. The chopper is shining its search light down through the branches. The hammock is ripped apart under the chopper's wash. The sound is deafening. I want to see; want to be seen but the Indian won't let me go. I look at him and I'm surprised to see him looking upward and cowering like a trapped and frightened animal. I try to scream to get the chopper's attention but I'm so weak and scared that nothing comes out. I'm stuck in a dream and I can't get out. I'm so close to being rescued but I can't move. Everything is slowing down.

Suddenly, the chopper turns abruptly away-- "No! Stop! Please don't go!"— and all is quiet again except for my breathless hopeless sobbing.

Please, I pray in fevered silence, *let it all be a dream and let me wake up tomorrow in my bed back home in Milltown.*

##

The dream ends and the nightmare begins with a semi-conscious awareness of falling and a sudden snap. My eyes open and they see the open jaws of a gator. It snaps at my head but I don't scream because it still seems so unreal, something that's happening to someone else I'm watching in slow motion. I see myself being pulled back by my costly-- but always faithful-- bra and thrown into the bithlo.

"This would make a great commercial for Victoria's Secrets," I hear myself saying into my own ear— until I land hard in the bithlo and am shaken into an in-your-face consciousness that would make the most stoic Spartan scream out loud like a frightened child. My voice reaches out across a millennia and joins that long dead warrior's shameful cry as the gator that once was a hallucination becomes real and is multiplied by more snarling, frenzied monsters, all itching to reach up and eat me. My mind is racing with each new silent cry.

Where am I?

I look around. The snapping gators are below me.

Why?

They have surrounded the bithlo, which is moving back and forth and bumping up and down like some kind of cheap carnival ride. I see the bithlo is stuck between two branches in the burning gumbo-limbo tree.

The Indian must have put it here.

I look for him. He's behind me, standing and swinging the driving pole like Davey Crockett at the Alamo with flames leaping up behind him.

I turn quickly back to the gators. They must be starving because, despite the punishment they're receiving, they won't give up. One especially mean brute bites the pole and shakes it like a fresh capture. I see my fate and scream again. You would too.

The Indian won't let go of the pole. The bithlo is in danger of being pulled out of the burning tree. I instinctively push against the bithlo to get away and the bithlo rolls backward breaking the branch, tossing me and the Indian into the middle of the gators' fury. As I fall, I see him out of the corner of my eyes using the pole to vault over the beasts, driving the pole's sharpened end through a gator's tongue and jaw into the sand. He pulls it out and the creature's savage will explodes across my face and breasts in thick and small drops of ancient blood. The animal's peanut sized brain has never experienced pain like this. It rears its gaping maw and rolls across another gator toward the water, its tail wiping the sandy beach with its deep red blood.

I see the Indian continue the motion of yanking the pole and spinning with its energy to drive it straight down and through another gator's skull killing it instantly.

And then I see him looking at me; his eyes, so beautiful over his walrus snout, tell me I'm in trouble. I look around.

One of those bastards is up on its legs and racing towards me!

I try to back away but the gator suddenly falls to the sand and slides to a stop at my Docs. The Indian's knife is sticking out of its head. I turn to him. He's running toward me and screaming— I swear to God-- like Tarzan but I don't have time to process that thought because the Indian is jumping over me. I duck and turn to see them coming at us from behind the overturned bithlo, two at a time.

The Indian rips the knife out of the dead gator's skull and throws the pole with his other hand. It strikes a gator between the eyes and the beast's momentum carries it through the Indian's legs to a death again just inches from my Docs.

I attack the smoky, gritty air with short jerking breaths and can't turn away fast enough from the still twitching beast. My heart is banging hard against my breastbone and my eardrums and just when I think they're going to burst the Indian grabs the pole and yanks it out of the dead gator, splattering me with bone and jagged pieces of torn white flesh. I want to barf as the Indian jumps between me and another attacking gator. The gator stops its charge, opens its large deadly mouth and roars. I grab my ears and fall backward in surprise. I had heard them roar before when my dad had taken me out in the airboat, but they were always in the distance and never as loud.

The gator starts to circle the Indian and he keeps it at bay with the pole. I scramble across the sand to get closer to him. I peek around his body. There are three gators in front of us, none of which are the least bit impressed or frightened by the Indian's bravery.

I wish the Indian would stop yelling like Tarzan. What with the roaring gators and all, it's beginning to get on my nerves.

It sounds stupid. You gotta be crazy to act like that now.

Then it dawns on me.

*Oh, my God, he's crazy! I'm stuck between a mutant crazy man and a bunch of hungry gators! That's why he's running around in a loincloth! He's a freak **and** nuts!*

And then I hear the King Roar.

It's a sound so legendary, my dad told me, that few people have ever heard it— and lived to tell about it. But those who have will tell you that once heard, you know for the first time how vulnerable you are in the world outside the safety of your home, that there is nothing to save you from the unimaginable strength the beast possesses and that there is nothing you can do to reason with the creature because, quite possibly, its psychopathic, a trait ingrained in its DNA in a lineage that began before the age of dinosaurs.

And here it is, right in front of me, the thing of legends, the mighty bull gator, King Roar.

Seeing it coming out of the water and the morning fog and smoke and fire devouring the surrounding trees and shrubs sends chills down my spine for two reasons: its enormous size and because I've seen it before. It was in my dream and it is walking toward me now just as I had dreamed it; almost crablike to the side with its head angled in the opposite direction so that it can see with its one fierce eye.

I scoot back against the bithlo. The thing coming out of the water dwarfs the other gators. They start circling the new challenger when, without warning, one lunges and catches the giant monster just behind the head. King Roar whips its huge body violently around to try to bite its attacker and when it does, another gator lunges at it, catching it from behind on its right hindquarter. A third gator bites the giant beast's tail and won't let go despite the thrashing, which lifts it clear off the ground.

The Indian leaps into the deadly struggle and drives his sharp pole through the back of the gator on King Roar's tail. The gator falls back and knocks the Indian off of his feet with a swipe of its tail. He jumps to his feet, throws himself at the wounded gator and lands on top of its back. He pushes the impaled pole to the side and drives his knife through the top of the gator's skull.

Call me a wuss, but I find myself watching the dead gator's tail thrashing in the bloodstained sand instead of watching the mighty struggle happening before me.

What if he fails?

I can't look but I do.

The Indian is already on the second gator attacking King Roar. He drives his knife toward the skull but the gator lets go of King Roar at the last second and turns on the Indian. He holds on as the beast's momentum spins them across the burning shrubs, and down the sand into the now bloody water.

It's just like a Tarzan movie! They're rolling in the water just like they do in the movies!

I can see the Indian stabbing the gator repeatedly with each turn in the water but I wonder if he can hold on and kill it before it kills him.

"Kill the bastard! Kill it!"

I'm surprised to find myself standing and shouting. And crying. I know that if the Indian fails, it's all over for me. I jump over the burning branches and skip over the twitching tail of a dying gator before stopping at the water's edge.

What am I doing? Am I nuts? I can't help him.

I look for something— anything-- to throw at the gator.

Where are the coconuts?

Then I remember this island hammock is smack dab in the middle of the Everglades, far, far away from the nearest coconut palm.

No rocks?

Nada. I remember the pole sticking out of the gator's brainpan. To get to it, I will have to jump through the fire and go back toward the deadly struggle between King Roar and the alligators.

Oh, God, please help me.

I take a deep breath and choke on the ash and smoke in the air before stumbling up the embankment. I leap the fire and land in a heap in front of the dead gator. Its lifeless eye is staring back at me, its violent passion dripping with a tear to the sand and for a fleeting moment, my sigh betrays a subconscious bonding between my spirit and the ferocious life that once beat in the monster now lying motionless on the ground.

Still staring at the dead gator, I get to my feet and grab the pole. I can't pull it out of the gator's head. I look at the pole and without hesitation, step on the gator's head, twist and pop it loose, its laughably small brain clinging to the tip in long gooey yellow cottage cheese-like strands.

I throw up all over the gator and stumble backward, coughing and gagging and wiping the vomit from my mouth. Trying to catch my breath, I fall to my knees and use the pole to support myself when I hear what I think is a cry behind me. I look back.

The burning gumbo-limbo tree is falling in on itself in a crash of smoke and flame across the bithlo and the battling gators. The bull gator that had latched onto King Roar in a life and death struggle is on fire and running toward me. I have no time to react before it knocks me over on its smoking, fiery dash to the water. When I try to get up, King Roar slams me back down head first into the sand as he races after the gator. Spitting sand, I turn just in time to see the monster's flaming, flapping, dragon-like tail vanish in the encroaching smoke and ash.

I struggle to my feet in the smoke and look around. The bithlo has caught fire. I turn and try to find my way through the thickening smoke toward the water and stop short. I can't hear the fighting in the water. The splashing has stopped.

Oh, my God, what if he didn't kill the gator? What if it— they— are waiting for me?

I can't move but the smoke moves for me. King Roar is standing at the water's edge. The gator it had been fighting is lying at its feet, half in and out of the water; its head nearly ripped away from its smoking body. King Roar cocks its head to the side and looks up at me with bloody, steaming flesh hanging from its jaws.

I step back toward the fire and feel the heat. The super heated air is becoming more difficult to breathe because the fire is consuming the oxygen it needs to continue its own life. The smoke is descending around me now in wraith-like swirls intent on carrying me straight to hell.

Which way do I go? Where is the Indian?

My eyes are bloodshot and streaming tears but they can't hide what I see coming through the smoke. The Indian is walking toward me, beaten but not broken.

And new; totally transfigured into the most handsome boy I have ever seen. His hairy snout is gone. I'm thoroughly confused when, without pause, he walks up, grabs me around the waist and swings me across his shoulder like a sack of sugar. I try to straighten up but he won't have it. He slaps my bottom hard and I lurch further up in surprise until the pain in my back slaps me down across his back. Bouncing on his broad shoulder as he carries me toward the burning bithlo, my mind races trying to grab onto something that will explain everything-- especially the Indian's transformation into something to die for.

And then what do I do? I hurl more of last night's meal all over his back and his loincloth.

The Indian stops short.

Oh, my God, I scream silently. I'm so totally embarrassed.

But I'm not through yet, oh no, I still have one more thing to do: I fart; a good loud drawn-out one.

Blood rushes to my face, which isn't good since my stomach is above my head. I instinctively reach back to cover my butt and to apologize out loud but the Indian just shakes his head and continues walking. I can't make my mouth move fast enough to ask for eternal forgiveness because the rancid smell of my vomit and the bouncing up and down triggers another round of putrid projectile pitching and whatever dignity I try to hold onto by tightly squeezing my butt to bar the escape of another fart is running down his sculpted massive back past his narrow waist and clinging to his loincloth. With my face rolling back and forth in my own vomit, I gag and let slide another long, ground thumping fart. Its sound seems so far away to me but its smell catches me by surprise and when I open my eyes, the ground is spinning and I begin to moan.

The Indian, for his part, pays no mind and, without missing a beat, walks through the fire up to the bithlo, grabs its bow and starts pulling it out from under the burning branches of the fallen gumbo-limbo tree. I see his back muscles bulge when he picks up the bow and drags it across the sand. When my head flops to the side, I see King Roar appear out of the smoke, slipping up alongside, watching me in his own curious way.

The bithlo smokes and sizzles when it is slid into the water. The Indian splashes water onto the parts of the bithlo that are still burning and puts them out before laying me gently into it. When he walks back into the smoke, I try to sit up and almost roll out of the bithlo. I catch myself and fall back onto one elbow just as a burning branch falls across the stern. With my body shaking from fatigue, I look back across the rocking bithlo and see that the stern has caught fire again and the Indian is nowhere to be found.

Oh, man, where is that dude?

I decide to put the water out myself. Gathering what strength I still have, I scoot back against the side and slowly bend over the edge of the bithlo.

Man, I hope that creepy gator isn't there waiting for me to do something stupid.

It isn't but something else is: the water has turned to blood again.

I recoil and fall back into the bithlo. I look back up the beach. It looks like a battlefield with its fire and smoke and dead warriors fallen on the sand, staining it forever with their primordial blood. When I look again, I see the Indian stepping out of the smoke and that lost and savage time with the pole and the sea turtle shield and I think I have fallen through some kind of time warp.

He scoops up some water with the sea turtle shield, throws it on the fire at the back of the bithlo and puts it out. Holding the bithlo steady, he throws the shield into the shallow dugout and is about to jump in after it when he sees something floating on the water and picks it up.

It's his nose. Or, it's what I thought was his nose.

He shakes the water from it and wrings it between his hands and I see for the first time what it really is. It's something he made out of Spanish moss. The stuff looks like Castro's beard. It can be found on a lot of trees in the south. It looks like he's laced it through some kinda Velcro thing-ee he ties around his head. It's a mask. *But why?* I've never seen anything like it before. The history books my dad forced me to read about the Seminoles and the Miccosukees never depicted any of them looking like this guy. It's the most bizarre thing I've ever seen.

What sane person would want to look like that in public? I mean, in the right kind of light it's frightening as hell. Maybe that's it. It's like war paint. It's supposed to scare the crap out of you.

Smoke and ash are drifting in tightly around us and I begin to cough again. The Indian looks at me and pauses. Instead of placing the mask over his own face, he tries to put it on me. I back away and our eyes meet. I know you'll think this is silly, but something passes between us, something we can't put a finger on yet and I allow him to place the mask over my face.

God, I hope it doesn't have any bugs in it!

When he's finished putting it on me, I can't help but think I look like a damn fool and start laughing. Surprisingly, so does he.

Man, who the hell are you anyway? You're freakin' me out.

"Look, man," I find myself saying, "I'm sorry 'bout throwing up on you."

That didn't come out exactly the way I wanted it to. I know I look and sound like a drooling idiot and want to die right then and there in my own stinking vomit but I just can't shut up.

"I'm Stormy Jones."

I extend my hand to shake like some lame old white man and make an equally weak effort to smile so that he can see that I'm not trying to be some kind of wiseass, a reputation I know I've earned. But he can't see my smile because it's hidden behind the Spanish moss moustache.

Another tree falls victim to the fire with a long breaking cry and crashes through the smoke into the water just inches from the bithlo. I scream and turn toward the explosion of fire and water and would have rolled right out of the bithlo if it hadn't been for the Indian's quick reflexes. He catches my extended hand and, with effortless grace and without reply, pulls me back into the bithlo and jumps in behind me. He drives the pole into the water and pushes us onward into the smoke and the unknown.

I look up at him trying to think of something to say to gain back some self-respect when he looks down at the water and says something. I turn half in a daze to look and jump back. King Roar is gliding silently through the blood and water beside the bithlo, looking at me with its one good angry eye until the smoke engulfs it.

I grab my stomach and turn away. My stomach wants to betray me again. I panic and my cheeks flush and sweat beads up on my forehead.

God, I silently implore, *please, don't let me embarrass myself again.*

I can't see the bithlo's bow some fifteen feet in front of me because of the smoke.

How does he know where we're going? I ask myself in an effort to keep from thinking about my traitorous stomach. *Probably knows every inch of this damn place*, I answer.

With each stroke, the Indian sends us deeper into the smoke and ash until I can't see a thing. I look back. I can't see him, but I can feel the fast-slow rhythms of his poling.

I can't even hear the pole in the water. Smooth.

The stop-and-go motions of the bithlo have a soothing effect on my stomach and I begin to relax until the smoke and ash become so thick that my eyes begin to tear. I think about my mascara and then this thought rushes into my mind, pushing aside any anxiety I might have had about throwing up in the bithlo: *My god, I must look like some kinda freak to him too. It must be running all down my cheeks.*

I try to rub away whatever streaks might be there.

Maybe that's what he was looking at. It's not my eyes. I must look like Alice Cooper!

I put a hand in the water and then quickly pull it out. I try to look through the smoke to see if King Roar is around. I can't see anything. I look at my hands. They're covered with dirt, white ash, and pieces of a gator's brain. The reeking contents of my stomach take an express elevator up my esophagus, my mouth tightens and my cheeks blow outward like Dizzy Gillespie's did when he blew a high note on his broken trumpet but I manage somehow to keep what "cool" I have left by holding back the onrushing stomach acids and partially dissolved food particles with a well placed hand over the Spanish moss mask and my mouth and an act of will bordering on the heroic.

Swallowing it all back in, I throw my other arm aside to shake it clean, but it's no use, the vomit inducing flotsam clings to my body like a reoccurring nightmare. I look back at the water. I want to wash myself, to sip the water from between cupped, unsoiled hands to wash away the smell of my putrid breath but I don't want to die either.

When I hear the Indian cough for the first time somewhere in the smoke, it finally dawns on me what the mask is for.

So you can breathe, you idiot!

The mask is a filter against the smoke and ash and it works. I haven't coughed since I put it on. I see how perilous the situation is and that my appearance should be the least of my worries.

But he's so handsome.

Still cupping my mouth, I can't believe I'm thinking about him like that and become angry with myself.

You're right, dad, I got my priorities 'ass backwards.'

My dad's little colloquialism reminds me about one of the family arguments. Despite his rough edges, the guy was enlightened enough to know he didn't want his daughter defining herself by the man on her arm. "You don't need them, they need you," he'd say. Mom, on the other hand, encouraged that side of me that only wanted a boy to love me. Maybe it wasn't all that intentional, but why else would she let me go out "half dressed" as dad would say. Or support the thing that really got the old man going: cheerleading.

"Why encourage the prolonged adolescence of the American male?" he'd say. "After a while, they begin to think they're entitled to act like yahoos forever because some mindless twits in short skirts cheered them on when they were pimply-faced hormonally imbalanced idiots."

Probably the best thing I ever did in my old man's eyes was quitting cheerleading. You already know it was for all the wrong reasons. But as soon as I find myself around another macho man, what happens? I get all cheerleady. I want him to like me. I want to be his girlfriend. It's sickening. I ball my hands into fists and hit my knees.

What's wrong with me?

I don't even know this guy, but I'm thinking about doing it with him already like I'm in some kind of stupid romance novel.

What the hell's wrong with me? Am I really that easy?

I remember an Eddie Springer show. Some teenage girl was willing to do it for a bag of potato chips. At least I'm not that low. And then I think, *Right, I wouldn't do it for the potato chips because I know I'll get fat if I eat them. No, I'd hold out for love— whatever that is.*

After the divorce, my dad told me to hold out for something more than love because he didn't think it really existed. "It's something we invent," he said, "It doesn't last." Mom told me to hold out for money.

I'm thinking about how cynical my parents are when I hear the sound of a breaking branch high above my head. I look up just in time to see the flaming limb fall out of the smoke and crash onto the bithlo, showering me with red-hot cinders. I raise my arms to shield my face from the fiery onslaught. My polyester leopard skin bra catches on fire. I scream and try to slap the flames out but within seconds find myself being grabbed and thrown into the water. I come up choking and swallowing the long, curly strands of the Spanish moss mask. I reach into my mouth and start to pull the stuff out but my disloyal body, always quick to betray me with ill-timed periods and a delicate constitution, automatically vomits the strands along with the putrid water I swallowed and the contents of my treacherous stomach lying in wait just behind my mouth. I try to catch my breath and suck in the Spanish moss again. I feel like I'm drowning, my lungs on fire. I rip the mask off, throw it away and fall into the water. I'm surprised to find the water is only about two feet deep and that I haven't been eaten. With my next deep breath I open my eyes and see I'm no longer on fire but everything else is. I look for a place to run, but I can't find any openings in the fire. I hear another cracking sound. I know it's a tree, but I don't know where it is or where it will fall. I fear that at any second it will fall on me but it doesn't. It falls just in front of the bithlo, blocking its path and, it seems, stealing the air around us through the mouth of a smoking vortex. I can feel the very air in my lungs being vacuumed out.

I gag and fall into water that comes up to my neck. I hear a splash next to me and look to the side. The Indian has flipped the bithlo upside down. He grabs me, pulls me over to the bithlo and forces my head down into the ash-covered water. I choke and struggle to shake loose of his grip but cannot. He shoves me to the side with one hand and guides my head with the other up into the hollow space inside the overturned bithlo. I bump my head on the bottom, gasp for air and am surprised to find that I can breathe. It's dark inside but I can see a slight reddish glow in the water and know that the fire is just outside the bithlo. I feel the Indian crawl up from behind and know my butt is in his face and that makes me very nervous. I'm on all fours when I realize my hands are in the muddy bottom. I recoil— right into the Indian's face. He puts his hands on my butt and pushes hard against me, which sends me flying into the water. I emerge coughing and cursing.

"How dare you!"

I can't believe I'm talking to this guy like that. I wonder where this foolish bravado is coming from while I continue, no matter how much I want to stop, to lambaste him. Later, when I have time to reflect, I'll know it came out of anger and frustration and from my dad. He had embedded the notion in me from the time I was just a kid that no man could touch me without my permission.

In the burning world above and around the bithlo, my loud protestations are little more than a muffle as the fire races by charring the hull with its superheated air.

I finally shut up because it is requiring way too much effort to breathe and talk at the same time and the two of us, one a little bit punk, the other *way* too country, sit in the water up to our necks and listen in silence to the roaring inferno outside beating against the bithlo screaming for us to come out and die. And then, after what seems like forever, the fire, ever impatient, leaves us behind to find other living things to play with that aren't as resourceful. It's in that moment, in the silence, that the first bubble breaks the surface right beneath the Indian's nose.

"O-o-h man-n-n!" the Indian cries out in a long, slow deep voice that bounces off the dugout bottom. He lifts the bithlo, throws it to the side and stumbles out from underneath, falling into the water.

"I'm sorry! I'm sorry!" I yell as I lunge across the water toward him with supplicating hands. "It must be the fish! The spices you put on it— Wait a minute." I stop and stumble into the water. "You speak English!"

The Indian doesn't say anything as he sits in the water. He doesn't have to. His looks say it all as he makes a face and waves his hand in front of his nose.

"Don't pretend you don't know what I'm saying. I just heard you say 'Oh, man!'"

"Oh-man-no-mano-farte!" he says with a disgusted grimace. "Oh-man-no-mano-farte!"

I don't know what to think. When I pushed him and his bithlo into the canal and he cursed in Muskogee, he could have opted for the shorter one syllable English word, but didn't. Maybe he really doesn't know English.

The look he shoots me as he gets up out of the water is one of revulsion and it's enough to make me wince as he turns away, splashing through the ash covered, dark water.

I want to die all over again when I turn and happen to see the eerie world we've emerged into.

It's one of stark, blackened trees and smoldering debris. The sun is but a dull yellow disk in the gray sky. Smoke is rising off the now blackened bithlo bottom.

I look at the Indian.

He's digging through the shallow water into the Everglade
bottom and covering his body with mud. He turns to a tall
blackened, still smoldering cypress tree and begins to climb.
It's hot, but the mud coating allows him to climb high
enough above the flat horizon to see where the fire is going
and where it's been. Within moments he's back down and
clearing the bithlo of the burning debris. I help him flip the
bithlo over. He finds the turtle shield floating on the water,
throws it in and motions for me to help him put everything
back into the bithlo. He picks me up and sets me down in it
before jumping in and pushing off into another direction.
Within seconds, the thick smoke surrounds and devours us
and the sound of my coughing is the only thing that betrays
our hidden presence. That and, of course, my farts.

"Oh-man-no-mano-farte!"

##

I don't have to look at my pink plastic banded Swatch
watch to tell that it is nearly noon. The dim yellow orb is
almost straight above us when the bithlo comes to an abrupt
stop.

I'm thrown toward the bow over the turtle shield. When I
push up I happen to notice that the inside of the turtle
shield is lined with something that looks like a vinyl pouch. I
catch a stenciled imprint: *Body Armor, Inc.* Before I can
digest that implication, the Indian has grabbed me under my
arms and is lifting me out of the bithlo.

"Elichko!" he shouts, pointing to the stern. "Elichko!"

What's left of my mind is reeling. I don't know what is
going on. "What?"

The Indian takes me by the wrist and leads me to the back
of the bithlo and makes me grab one side. He grabs the
other side, lifts and pushes it forward. I slip and fall into the
shallow water. I hear him yelling something I can't
understand and look up.

He's standing with the bithlo's rear end on his shoulder
motioning me to join him. He looks like one of those

pictures I saw of Christ with the cross on his shoulder. Back then, Before the Divorce, or "B.D," as I like to classify it, when I was a kid and went to Sunday school, I remember the story about the guy who carried the cross near the end for Jesus because he couldn't do it anymore and how I would have volunteered if I'd been there. This childhood memory and the Indian's long hair, his god-like body and his fearless approach to the world convinces me to "take up the cross" without hesitation or question.

Although it isn't for a selfless cause, I know my effort at self-preservation would make my dad proud. Self-reliance was a big thing with the old man; something he tried to instill in me since my first days in scouting— and that was *Boy Scouting*. Dad was a scoutmaster back then and he insisted I was going to learn about the outdoors the way boys did right along side of him. I was the only girl in the troop for a long time until the troop started paying too much attention to me and I to them. Just when I could appreciate camping out with boys in tents, dad quit the scouts and took me with him. I remember how much Native American folklore is such an integral part of scouting and how ironic it is that I'm now smack in the middle of the "great outdoors" as dad likes to call it and helping a real live Indian cradle a real freakin' bithlo. You can't get more authentic than that.

It's not easy. The water has disappeared and the bithlo is too heavy to carry and has to be pushed along the parched and fissured Everglades bottom. The dugout has to be held at just the right angle or, if it is too high, it will dig into the bottom.

Progress is slow. My muscles are beginning to shake when the Indian stops and lowers the bithlo. I look at him for the first time in what seems hours. I like his profile with its strong jaw and its hawk-like nose. He's looking ahead, listening for something in the smoke. I turn and hear it too; the faint, high-pitched squeals of what I'm sure are animals in distress. Crouching close to the ground, the Indian steps cautiously forward into the smoke and disappears within seconds before my eyes. I look around and see ghostly shapes appearing and disappearing in the wafting and sifting smoke. The thought of being left alone there makes me uncomfortable. I feel vulnerable without the Indian's presence and decide to try to find him. Crouching, I place my hand on the bithlo and follow its length into the smoke.

He's waiting for me.

Before I can make a sound, the Indian slips his hand around my mouth. I struggle for a moment and want to scream but he turns me roughly around and looks into my eyes with an unflinching purpose. Before I can wonder why, he turns my head slowly around.

At first I can't see anything but then a breeze parts the smoky curtain to reveal what appears to be a deer frozen in its leap, struggling to free itself from a giant spider's web. It doesn't make sense until the wind carries more of the smoke away. More deer, birds and smaller animals appear in their frozen death throes, caught not in a spider's web but rather in something I've seen before: orange plastic construction netting. It's been strung across the horizon between steel poles rammed into the earth.

I hear the agonizingly high-pitched squeal of one of the deer and turn to see a man bashing the trapped creature across the head with a baseball bat. I cry out and my voice reaches the deer slayer's ears despite the Indian's attempt to stifle any sound. He takes me to the ground and lies on top of me, motionless in the sawgrass. With one hand over my mouth, he raises his other hand and, with a finger to his lips, cautions me to remain quiet.

"Dawson," a voice full of gravel shouts out piercing the smoke, "I think I heard something over here."

My eyes light up. I've heard that voice before.

"Like what?" This voice was a little further away.

"Like a voice."

"Check it out. Maybe it's that missing ranger's kid."

I struggle to get free but the Indian won't let me move.

"If it's her, you know what to do," the second voice shouts again.

"I know," the raspy voice replies, this time a little closer.

I hear the distinct sound of a pump action shotgun being loaded nearby. I freeze. I can hear the man getting closer. My frightened eyes lock with the Indian's. He moves his head steadily toward me and quickly replaces his hand across my mouth with his lips. I want to scream and try to shake my mouth away but he forces himself down even harder and follows my movements while moving one hand down to my wrist to pin me to the ground, and his other hand down to the knife on his hip. I stop trying to push him off when I realize what he is doing.

My god, is he going to try to kill this guy?

Before the Indian can bring his hand back with the knife to stop me, I use my free hand to push his head away. "Help!" I scream.

Before I know what's going on, he's gone: the Indian rolls with the force and direction of my shove and disappears in the smoke and sawgrass.

A shotgun blast tears through the smoke just inches above my head. I scream, roll onto my stomach and shout, "Please, don't shoot! I'm Stormy Jones!"

The shotgun is cocked again and another blast splits the parched earth just beside me, covering me with dirt and dust. Some of it gets in my eyes. Unable to see, I roll across the hot, dry Everglade bed and fall behind the stiff, dead stalks of a clump of sawgrass. My impact against the sawgrass reverberates up the grass and betrays my position. I hear the pumping action just before a third blast blows a hole through the sawgrass so close to the top of my head I can feel the air pushed aside by the pellets whizzing by. I roll onto my stomach and realize for the first time as the shredded sawgrass falls slowly over me that someone is trying to kill me. I hear footsteps approaching and try to bury myself in the earth. And although it may sound like a cliché about how fear can cause people to shit their pants, I'm suffering that same experience, but with a twist. My body wants to let loose another fart. Of course. So I squeeze my butt as tight as I can but it is to no avail as a stinky, stealthy one slips out and rises along the sawgrass.

"Whoe, man."

Talk about a "confessional." I could just die.

"Did you get her?"

"I think she got me," raspy voice replies.

I hold my breath; the man is standing next to my prone body.

"You killed her?" The second voice is closer.

"I think so." He pumps another shell into the shotgun.

"Dammit, man, we could have had some fun with her first."

When I hear that, I know it's worse than I could have ever imagined. My body is shaking and I try not to move. I feel the man's boot up against my shoulder. My heart is racing and is about to explode when he slips the boot's toe under my shoulder and unexpectedly kicks me over like some kind of fresh kill. I can't squeeze my eyes closed any more. They fly open and I see the smoking shotgun barrel only inches from my face. I look at the man holding the gun. I've seen him before but before I can remember where, the Indian has leaped out of the smoke, grabbed the shotgun and spun it and the man into the sawgrass. I jump at the sound of the shotgun blast.

"Kyle, are you all right?"

The second man is nearly upon me. I hear the first man and the Indian wrestling somewhere in the smoke and sawgrass until there is the dull sound of skull meeting the back end of the Indian's knife.

"Kyle! Answer me!"

The second man is standing right above me, his shotgun held at the ready. All he has to do is look down and I'm a goner. Instead of waiting for that to happen, I close my eyes, throw myself at the man's ankles and try to knock him over.

It doesn't work.

He aims his shotgun at me but never gets a chance to pull the trigger because the Indian is grabbing it and twisting it away. It discharges. I jump again thinking I've been hit but the blast has been directed safely away.

The Indian twists, falls to his back and kicks the man over his head. Neither will let go of the shotgun. Lying head to head on the ground, the Indian quickly rolls backwards and lands hard on the stunned man, straddling his chest. Before he knows what hit him, the Indian rips the shotgun away and back ends the butt of the gun across the side of the guy's head knocking him out in one neat motion.

I'm surprised to see the Indian stripping the man of his valuables. Within seconds, the Indian has taken the man's watch and a two-way pocket radiophone. He even takes the man's boots. Holding the shotgun and his booty, the Indian turns and vanishes in the smoke.

By the time I get to my feet, the Indian is stepping out of the smoke with both shotguns, another pair of boots and a second radiophone before disappearing just as quickly into another pocket of smoke.

I start after him thinking he's nothing more than a common thief when I run into him in the dense smoke. He's dragging the bithlo, his stolen treasures thrown into the center of the dugout. He motions for me to take the other side. I do without hesitation because I know who ever this guy is, he's probably my only chance at getting saved.

Man, look what he just did to those two guys who were out to kill me. He's just like Steven Seagal, only younger. And thinner. And cuter. Man, I can't believe I can't stop thinking about him like that. What the hell's wrong with me?

Before I can answer that question, the Indian lowers the bithlo to the ground, yanks out his knife and walks toward the orange plastic construction net and its collection of dead and nearly dead assortment of wildlife. The net has been strung up along the edge of another canal bank. This canal is much wider and the other side is untouched by the fire. We hear the soft bleating cry of a young fawn and he follows the sound to the net. The fawn is caught in the net just below its mother's dead body. It appears they have been trapped in the net for a few days. The fawn is too weak to struggle and the Indian knows it will soon die. I watch the Indian cover the small creature's eyes with his palm and before I can turn away, I see its short feeble struggle and its quick merciful death at his hands. I turn away and want to cry.

The Indian starts cutting down the net with his knife and the dead creatures, great and small, cascade like synchronized swimmers diving one by one into a pool. Where the net sticks, he runs alongside and cuts it free from the steel poles. One segment won't slip away because it's caught in overhanging branches and I can see that he's struggling to cut it away. I find myself moving towards his aid and within moments I'm by his side trying to free the net. He's surprised to see me there. So am I but I help him lift the section of the net off a branch that starts the final unzipping of the deadly veil. The weight of the dead animals pulls the net into the water with a resounding splash.

"What was that?"

The Indian and I look back at the bithlo. The radiophones are demanding an answer.

"Talk to me boys. What the hell is going on? I heard a big splash. I shouldn't be hearing a big splash. Over."

The response to the question is only static.

"Boys, I can't *hear* you." A moment passes before the radiophones bark to life again. "Okay, I'm coming in."

"Dammit! We better get out of here," I say and start to run toward the bithlo but stop when I realize the Indian isn't running with me.

"Didn't you hear? One of those crackers is coming back."

The Indian doesn't respond. He's thinking about something.

"C'mon! We gotta get outta here!"

He looks up, pauses, and then runs swiftly past me to the bithlo. He's already trying to drag it across the ground when I join him and take the other side. He wants to put it into the canal. The bow is already over the edge when we hear the high-pitched roar of an airboat. We drop to the ground and pull back the bithlo and try to blend in with the sawgrass.

I glance at the Indian for reassurance and I'm surprised to see him growing increasingly agitated as the airboat grows closer. I wonder if he's ever seen one before. Before I can come to any conclusion, he's strapped on his turtle shield, leaped over the bithlo and rolled to his feet behind the sawgrass. His knife is drawn. He looks back and motions for me to stay down and keep quiet.

I don't have to be told twice. I just hope he doesn't try to kill the guy. I look back through the sawgrass and see the airboat and know immediately who it is.

It's Bart Rader, a big nasty redneck who favors basic black for his clothes, his car, his dogs and his airboat, a color most in favor in the chic South Beach clubs but, alas, a place I know this guy would never get past the doorman. I remember dad saying "he and his family are third generation poachers on a mission to kill every last creature in the swamp for money and the fame it will bring the family name."

And then it dawns on me: those guys the Indian just took out are his brothers Kyle and Dawson. I've seen guys like that before. Most likely they're Hialeah born and raised and still living in that sprawling blue collar neighborhood on the edge of the glades and hating every minute of it because they're too poor to move and all of their neighbors, including the mayor and city council, have been replaced by a bunch of Cubans who don't speak English and don't care to try.

Rader's already stomping his boot and slapping his sweat-stained black Stetson against his black Levy's. I agree with dad's assessment of the man, "Yeah, pissed off and poor. Not a good combination."

Rader jams his hat back on, pulls up alongside the embankment, turns the engine off and glides to a stop. He reaches out cursing up a storm from his seat perched high over the flat-bottomed boat and grabs a tree branch to stop the airboat.

I see it getting closer and closer and try to bury myself deeper into the Everglade bottom. The flat black airboat, "better for night poachin'" dad told me, comes to rest just inches away. I can't see him but I can hear him jumping into the nightmare landscape that once was the Everglades. He only takes a couple of steps before pausing. I wonder if he's seen me or the bithlo. I hear him fumbling for something.

"Damn these walkie-talkies!" he growls in a harsh smoker's voice.

My God, he's going to call his brothers.

I look at the bithlo and hope the radiophones have been turned off.

"Where the hell are you guys?"

"WHERE THE HELL ARE YOU GUYS?" both radiophones squawk.

"What?"

"WHAT?"

I hear him pump a shell into a shotgun. I hear him walking slowly toward me. I pull up my legs and try to make myself invisible all the while thinking, *Where is the Indian?*

"What's this?"

Rader has found the bithlo. I know it's only a matter of time before—

"And what do we have here? Turn around little girl."

I try to play dead. Again.

"Okay, I'll just shoot you in the back."

"No, No, I'll turn around."

At that moment, the Indian is tapping Rader on the shoulder. Rader never heard him creep up from behind. When he turns on reflex, he's blindsided with the full weight of the turtle shield. He never knew what hit him. The Indian grabs the shotgun and takes it from Rader's unconscious hands before the huge man falls backward into the sawgrass landing with the weight of a giant.

I'd be lying if I didn't say I was *really* impressed. *Holy crap*, I think as I get to my feet, *this guy is the real thing for sure*.

The Indian puts the shotgun in the bithlo before stripping Rader of his radiophone, boots and watch. He puts the watch on his wrist and throws the rest into the bithlo. He looks at the black Stetson. The sweatband is decorated with a silver and turquoise amulet at the center with iridescent raven feathers branching from both sides. He tries it on. It's too big, but he decides to keep it anyway. He tightens the string pull under his chin and starts shouting and whooping and touching the unconscious man with a hard tap on the shoulder. He turns to me.

I try to smile. I'm pretty sure he's "counting coup," something I read about when I was trying to learn more about the Indians, a requirement the "Chiefs" demanded from me if I was going to become a member of their gang (although that was soon forgotten when Stanlo Osceola, the fifteen-year-old gang leader, discovered I would kiss him instead). It was a Plains Indians thing where warriors would tap the enemy with their hand or coup sticks and then run away without injury or anyone getting killed. It was a way to show their bravery and a way to humiliate their enemy at the same time without any bloodshed, a concept lost entirely on the white man.

The Indian extends his hand and raises his finger as if to say "Stay back" and "One moment, please" all at the same time.

I shrug "OK."

He turns to Rader and rips his shirt open, popping the buttons all the way down to his cowboy belt buckle which catches the Indian's eye. Within seconds, the turquoise and silver belt buckle is yanked out of Rader's pants and thrown into the bithlo with the rest of the booty. With a returning motion that I miss, the Indian pulls out his knife and starts carving something into the big man's chest.

"What are you doing? You don't have to do that! Please stop!"

The Indian doesn't stop or turn around.

"Please stop!" I shout and begin to cry. "He doesn't deserve that."

The Indian stops because he's done. He gets up, looks at his work and disappears behind the sawgrass.

I'm dumbstruck by what I see. The Indian has carved a ragged "N" across Rader's hairy chest and beer belly. The cut isn't deep, but the blood, combined with the man's sweat, is oozing down across his broad chest and backward from his big round hairy belly to collect in a puddle between the two.

I fall to my knees and, looking at Rader, cry helplessly. I wish I could help him, wish I could *want* to help him, but I can't make myself go to him.

You shouldn't have tried to kill me.

Suddenly I'm shaken by the sound of more booty being thrown into the bithlo. I turn and see a rifle, a box of shotgun shells and something wrapped up in a black plastic garbage bag. The Indian walks over to Rader, throws some flare cartridges around his body and stands a flare gun up between his legs at the crotch. I don't get a chance to question why.

"There they are!"

It's Rader's brothers coming out of the smoking sawgrass. They've come to and they're not too happy about it.

The Indian takes me by the wrist, throws me across the opposite side of the bithlo and motions for me to push it into the water. Just before its weight starts to turn the bow down over the canal's edge, the Indian again grabs me by the wrist, walks me back along the length of the rising bithlo and pushes me into it just as it starts to slide down into the water. I scream but the Indian is holding on and running right beside me. He leaps at the last moment and lands in a crouch behind me. As the bithlo glides into the center of the canal, he pushes me down, covers my body with his, and starts paddling with his hands.

"You bastards!"

I look back. The two men are standing at the edge of the canal bank. One of them shoots a flare at us. I see it coming like a red-hot meteor, zigzagging across the water and trailing smoke straight at us.

"Look out!"

The Indian stops paddling and folds his arms around me. The flare roars by just over our heads. He reaches over me, grabs his shield, shakes loose the pickings, turns quickly around and holds the shield up behind him just in time to ward off a second flare.

It glances off the shield and plunges into the water.

He whoops and yells and rises unsteadily in the back of the bithlo to look back at the men and to egg them on. I can't believe he's doing this.

"Man," I yell while grabbing the sides, "what are you doing? You could flip this thing!"

He turns back, yells something and points to his pole. I'm thinking he's going to push us out of there, so I grab it and slide it back to him. He picks it up and, to my astonishment, faces the men on the canal bank and begins wielding it around his body like some kind of martial arts expert.

The guys on the bank aren't impressed. Another flare is shot across the water and to my and their utter disbelief, the Indian slaps it aside with his pole.

This feat, worthy of the most outrageous Jackie Chan flick, gets the Indian to a whoopin' even more. He holds the pole above his head with both hands in a victory dance that turns him around and around in the bithlo.

I don't know what to think. All I know is that I want to get out of there as soon as possible. I get up on my knees and start paddling with my hands and the bithlo begins to move slowly through the water.

The men on the embankment begin to follow us with curses. Another flare is fired and the Indian bats it away with a slow, stylized sweep of his pole that shows both contempt and grace.

The men jump into the airboat and try to start it up. When it won't start, they look for the problem and find that the battery cables have been cut and the battery is missing. This *really* pisses them off. The cussing and stamping of their feet becomes almost comic until they hear the Indian whooping and stop to look back.

He's laughing and pumping the battery up and down over his head. I look back, see the battery in his hands and the empty garbage bag in the hull and make the connection.

One of the men drops another flare cartridge in the gun and starts to take aim when someone shouts: "Stop!"

It's Rader. He's holding his bloody chest and belly and staggering toward the airboat. The Indian stops his victory dance and all eyes are on the man. What strength he uses to call his brothers is all but lost when he continues to speak.

"He's got our radios. Without the flares, no one knows where we are."

His brothers take him by each arm and help him onto the airboat. Rader stumbles over to the wire cage surrounding the engine and propeller and calls out to the Indian in a weak, rasping voice.

"It ain't over yet, you little punk. I'm gonna get you if it's the last thing I do."

The Indian shouts something back, tosses the battery into the bithlo, picks up his pole and starts casually pushing us through the water.

"I mean it, kid," Rader coughs, "I'm gonna getcha!"

I'm surprised to see the Indian, not looking back, casually flick the men his middle finger. That little gesture brings on a chorus of curses. It's the last English I will hear for a while.

Chapter 4

Getting to know you

When I finish lacing up my semi-dry Docs and look at my watch I see it's almost two o'clock. It's been over an hour since the close encounter of the scary kind. The Indian has given me the black hat to wear and has draped the wet motorcycle jacket over my shoulders to protect me from the intense sunlight. He's been pushing us further along the canal without pause, without urgency, and without saying anything. In that time I've done nothing but think about everything that's happened.

I mean, what's with this guy anyway? He dresses like some kind of freakin' primitive but drinks Evian. He's with it enough to know what a battery does and the value of those 2-way radios. He's got body armor inside his sea turtle shield, his knife sure as hell isn't home made, he knows how to handle guns, and can kick ass better than Jackie Chan or Steven Seagal combined. It's like he's watched all their movies! But then he goes and acts like a freakin' wuss when he sees a helicopter or hears an airboat. This guy is giving me a headache.

I pause and look at the tediously flat panorama of ever-expansive sawgrass and hammock spotted landscape. The fires are now off in the distance, their gray smoking columns rising like an impenetrable wall on the horizon to prop up the impossibly bright sky.

But I'd be dead without him. He protected me in his arms, it was like he was folding his angel wings around me and he doesn't even know who I am.

That thought gives me the chills. I've made it a habit to avoid questions about death and God and angels. Those kinds of questions get in the way of the constant party I want my life to be.

We've only been together 24-hours and we've hardly spoken to each other.

I try to get something going, anything to break the tension and monotony. I touch the brim of the black cowboy hat and look back at him.

"Thanks, for the hat, pardner. We haven't been properly introduced. My name's Stormy Jones."

I offer my hand but he ignores it.

"Perhaps you've heard of me? I'm the missing park ranger's kid. My dad is the 'Great White Father' for all the Everglades."

Nothing.

"Hmm, not very impressed are you?" I turn toward the front with a shrug and add: "Neither am I. Trust me, I'd much rather be in New Jersey."

Despite my attempt at bravura by paraphrasing W.C. Fields, my voice cracks and I bite my lower lip and let slip a slight, almost untraceable-- I hope-- self-admonishing shake of my head.

Dammit. I can't let him know I'm scared. Or feeling sorry for myself.

I quickly turn around again and catch what I think is a slight smile on his face. As much as I may have caught him by surprise, I'd be lying if I didn't find that just a little creepy.

"Excuse me, but do you speak English?"

Nothing.

"My dad says all of you guys know how to speak English."

He looks past me as if I wasn't even in the bithlo.

"Okay, be that way," I say while turning away. "I've heard of the strong silent type but this is ridiculous." A moment passes before I add, "I just want you to know I appreciate everything you've done for me. You've saved my life more than once."

I'm embarrassed for saying all of that, especially when the last two sentences came out in a rush of words.

My god, I can't shut up!

I hope for some kind of response but the only thing I get is the bithlo falling out of its rhythm.

Maybe he's going to say something to me.

I turn around to look up at the Indian.

He's pulling something out from inside his sea turtle shield. It's a plastic pouch, one of those slide locking kind. He unzips it and pulls out a hand drawn map and compares it to something he's seen along the canal bank. I try to see what he's looking at. All I can see is the Everglades. When I look back at him, he's slipping the map back into the shield.

Man, he doesn't care what I see or know. I wonder if that's good or bad?

I turn away and look at the cluttered floor of the bithlo and remember the one thing I was trying to forget: the "N" carved in Bart's chest and stomach.

Is he going to let me go? Is he going to kill me? Stop it, you idiot. He could have killed you a long time ago? Then what is he going to do with me?

All good questions for sure but before I can come up with any answers, a bush slaps me across the face. He's turned the bithlo off the canal and is squeezing us through a tangle of underbrush into a narrow creek.

Within minutes, the creek has become a pond and the pond a wet sawgrass prairie scattered with mangrove islands. I know we've been traveling south because I've been watching the sun climb in the east and then descend in the sky. I figure we must be near Everglades National Park, or "the park" as my dad calls it, the southern most part of the Everglades and the least affected by the drought. So far.

Big deal. The damn park is only "4,000 square miles big." They oughta find me in no time.

Yeah, you'd be surprised how much I know about the Everglades. Thanks to my dad, I know just about everything. Thanks to my mom, I know I hate it with a passion. Too many bugs, too hot, and way too dangerous.

After a half hour of excruciatingly slow progress through the sawgrass and the mangroves, and after slapping dead hundreds of mosquitoes hoping to suck me dry, my faithful, but silent, Indian guide finally stops poling to look at his map.

Yeah, that's right, I think with a sad shake of my head and a hit off the last Evian, *you're just like mom said about dad. "He'd travel 500 miles in the wrong direction before he'd look at a map or ask for help."* A thought strikes me as I swallow the bottled water. *Now I'm worried; if this guy's lost, I'm in deep--*

I'm knocked back in the bithlo when he starts poling again but that thought doesn't leave me. It follows me as he weaves a convoluted path between a number of hammock islands before driving the bithlo toward one that is indistinguishable from the rest-- until the bithlo pops through the leafy overgrowth at the water's edge and glides toward its center.

I can't believe what I see. The hammock is covered with camouflage netting and the effect is like entering a circus tent; the shafts of light streaming through the dusty air, are diffused through the leafy canopy of trees and nets laced with foliage. Rising from the center of the hammock is a grouping of sable palms and beneath them, a single chickee, the Seminole's traditional dwelling. The open-air hut has a thatched roof of palm fronds and is built up off the ground on four *live* sable palm trunks. Camouflage netting hangs from the thatched roof and covers the chickee's four sides. With a final effort, he runs the bithlo up onto the sloping ground and gets out. I start to follow but he turns quickly around and motions for me to stay in the bithlo.

"Hey, no problemo, man," I say, trying to pretend I'm not the least bit concerned. "I'll just sip some of your mighty fine Evian." Trouble is, the bottle's empty.

As I lamely pretend to drink from the empty bottle, he unsheathes his knife and walks slowly up the rising path. He's looking at the ground and the trees and the shrubs surrounding the hammock. He pauses just before the chickee and falls to his knees. When he does, I see it for the first time: a trip line is surrounding the chickee at about ankle height, popping in and out of the tall grasses and shrubs growing around the chickee. When he touches it, it shimmers in the dappled light like a spider's web.

It's probably monofilament fishing line, something I know about thanks again to the teachings of my "Great White Father."

He loosens the line and allows it to rest on the ground before walking up to the chickee and running his hand down the edge of the camo netting which has been nailed to the posts holding the thatched roof. With a swift flourish, he throws back one side of the netting and jumps inside the chickee.

A minute later, he's outside and walking back to the bithlo. He motions for me to get out. I step into the water and then onto the beach but before I can take another step, he grabs my wrist and motions for me not to move. He turns back to the bithlo, picks up the sea turtle shield and makes me hold it like a pan so that he can load it up with some of the newfound booty-- including the heavy airboat battery.

"Whoe, man, what do I look like, some kind of squaw?"

I just don't know how to keep my mouth shut.

He pauses and takes a deep breath. I wonder even more if he speaks English. I don't trust him but I sure as heck don't want to piss him off. "That was a joke; my mom's one liner with dad since the divorce. I just substituted squaw for wife. Hope I didn't offend you."

If I did, I can't tell because he begins loading up the shield again as if nothing happened.

"Yeah, well I guess you had to be there."

My voice sounds strained as I struggle to hold the load in my arms. The Indian looks at me and sadly shakes his head.

"Hey, smart ass, let's see you do this." No one shakes their head like that at me, not even Tarzan.

He grabs my arm and yanks me back up to the chickee. When we get there, he takes the loot and throws it onto the raised chickee floor. That's when I see all the other stuff the Indian has been collecting. There are hundreds of water bottles, all brands; some are still in their plastic wrapped crates scattered across the rough-hewn log floor with a large

assortment of weapons and ammunition. I see assault rifles
and what could either be a crated bazooka or an over-the-
shoulder missile launcher, something my dad called a
"Stinger."

Before I can take it all in, the Indian swings his shield
over his shoulder, takes me by the hand and walks me down
the same path we took up to the chickee. Half way to the
bithlo, he stops and drops to his knees, bringing me with
him. He lets go of my hand, pulls out his knife and digs
around in the sand with the knifepoint. The knife strikes
something metallic. He puts the knife back in its sheathe and
starts digging with both hands into the sand. Within seconds
he has uncovered what I immediately know is a land mine--
not because my dad taught me about them too, but because
it's stenciled on the top.

I fall back in utter disbelief toward the sandy beach but
the Indian catches me. With his sweeping outstretched arm,
I get the idea real fast that the whole area has been mined.

"Man, are you freaking nuts?"

The Indian, of course, doesn't say anything but instead
gets up, walks over to the bithlo and begins to load his
shield with the remainder of that day's booty. When it's full,
he carries this load himself, steps over me and walks back up
to the chickee. He slides the shield across the floor and
jumps up behind it. Standing, he grabs the camo netting,
drags it across the entrance, and disappears behind it.

"Don't worry, buddy," I find myself shouting at the
chickee, "I could care less about what you got going on
behind curtain number three."

Inside I'm thinking, *Oh, man, I'm in the middle of
nowhere with a freaking lunatic! Why can't my life be
simple? Why does every guy I fall for gotta have some kinda
character flaw?*

"Fall for"? I know what you're thinking and so am I.

*What's the matter with me? Is that all I can think of? Sure
he's gorgeous; he could easily be the toughest kid in any
high school in the world and it would be cool to be his girl,
but so what. I mean, the guy doesn't think twice about*

cutting up a man and he must be paranoid as hell to lay land mines all around his chickee. If I just think about it for a minute, the guy is really scary. I must be nuts to even think that he and I could have a relationship. Hell, I don't even know his name.

That's when this thought hits me: *I can't believe he hasn't hit on me. I must look like crap. Dammit, I wish I had a mirror.*

You don't have to say it. I know I need help. Anyway, I start looking for something to see myself in and notice the reflection of the trees in the water. I make sure to follow the footprints in the sand so as not to blow myself up, crawl over to the water's edge and unintentionally put my hand in the water, disrupting its stillness. I can't find one Stormy Jones but instead find many, all of whom are undulating uncertainly on the surface.

Whoe, what a mirror. That's exactly who I am. I'm a scared mental case with multiple personalities in need of a makeover. Or so I've been told.

I touch my limp pink tipped blond spikes and can see, even in the water's far from perfect reflection, my gaping hair lost.

My God, I look terrible! No wonder he hasn't made a move on me.

I know, I need a good spanking or something. It's all about me, yada-yada-yada. Anyway, before I know it, my broken, jingle-jangled reflection on the water starts looking back at me with reptilian eyes. That's right, that crazy Indian's freaking Loony Tunes alligator has snuck up on me and is looking up at me through the water. I scream my head off and fall back against the sand and instantly remember the land mines. This sends a jolt of adrenaline coursing through my body which gets me up and turning toward the chickee. I know there are mines everywhere but I don't care. I just want to get away from the biggest, meanest alligator I've ever seen.

I'm screaming and waving my hands about and trying to tiptoe across the sand as fast as I can when that stupid, disgusting creature lunges out of the water, latches onto one of my Docs and starts dragging me back into the water.

Call me crazy, but if you ever wondered what you'd think about at a time like that, I'm sure you wouldn't have chosen this: I imagine I'm a wildebeest in some *Animal Planet* show getting dragged into the water by some giant crocodile. And then I see the fear in the big white eyeballs of that panther looking back at me just before he was dragged under the water by an alligator. I swear, I see all of this in less than a second.

I try to grab the bithlo and hold on but the damn gator starts pulling that too.

"Elichko, Haalpatee! Elichko!"

It's that equally crazy Indian and I'm thinking, *maybe we're made for each other*. I look around just in time to see him leaping over me and throwing himself between me and the gator. He grabs my leg, plants his feet in the mucky bottom, and falls backward against my thigh. I feel like I'm in some kind of nightmare tug-of-war when, in mid-scream, I look back and see the Indian hitting the gator over the head with a chicken roast.

That's right, a chicken roast.

Before I have time to wonder where he got it, the gator lets go of my boot and follows the bird's arc across the water. When it breaks for the floating chicken, the Indian turns quickly around, picks me up and carries me back to the chickee.

I know, it sounds romantic and all, being rescued by a long haired hunk in a loincloth and carried back to his love shack, but the only thing I'm thinking about is, of course, me as I look back at the gator through tears and watch it's big ugly mouth snap down once on the chicken roast making it disappear forever.

My God, that coulda been me.

I turn my head and bury it in the Indian's hair falling across his broad, naked shoulders. It smells of musty wild things.

Herbal shampoo?

I sniff again.

No way.

Way. He sits me down on the raised chickee deck and there, next to a sleeping bag and a folded towel is a bar of soap and shampoo. "Dove" and "Herbal Essences." Unopened, fresh from God-Knows-Where.

I'm shaking uncontrollably and try to stop crying. He jumps up and rummages for something in the chickee and returns within moments with a state-of-the-art solar blanket. Thanks to my dad, I know these highly sophisticated light weight blankets constructed of silver reflective Mylar are commonly known as survival blankets, "another spin-off," he liked to remind me, "of the space program. They'll keep you warm in winter and cool in summer." Of course I immediately wonder if I can use it as a mirror.

A sudden chill runs through my body. I fall against the Indian's chest and find myself saying through a quivering voice, "I don't think I'm going to make it."

What a wuss. Anyway, the Indian gently pushes me away and helps me lie down. I can feel him untying my bootlace and wish for the first time that the Docs weren't so fashionably long because, despite his gentleness, the pain is beginning to get to me. As the boot starts to come off, a sharp stinging sensation sets me upright and, instead of thinking about my foot, I see only the boots.

Oh, lord, look at my DM's!

This thought follows me back to the log floor where I slowly let myself fall. More than the pain, the sight of my prized $100.00 boots, now ripped, muddy, and wet, my most prized object of conspicuous consumption from a much more friendlier world and time, brings me to tears. I can feel him touching my foot in different places. I groan. He starts to remove my sock.

The skin and the sock were slowly becoming one in the mother-of-all science projects where you sacrificed a body part for an "A." I watch him pull out his knife and carefully cut through the sock and peel it away inch-by-inch from my foot until it is completely removed. I watch his probing fingers and feel a sharp pain. The foot is swelling up but I can't see any blood.

"Thank God," I whisper before falling slowly back onto the chickee log floor. The last thing I see before falling asleep, that will haunt my dreams, is the chickee ceiling. The pitched roof has been stuffed with more odds and ends of a modern civilization prone to war and survival.

My God, what have I gotten myself into?

##

I awaken the next morning to a cool salve gently applied to the wounds on my back. In my half sleep, I smile and moan with pleasure and turn toward the person I think will be my mom. When I open my eyes and see the Indian kneeling behind me, I recoil and gather the solar blanket and my knees up around me.

That's when I realize my foot is wrapped tightly in an Ace bandage. The Indian, for his part, doesn't say anything but looks at me as if he were looking at some kind of alien creature. I wonder if he's ever seen a white person before.

Maybe I'm the first white chick he's ever seen. God, where's some makeup when you need it?

I sit up on one elbow, turn my head away, and try to wipe away what I fear are mascara streaks down my face; but then, this is something I've always feared since spending my summers in humid South Florida. It has nothing to do with this guy. I surprise myself when I start talking to him.

"I'm sorry, I thought you were someone else."

Before I can say another thing, the Indian hands me a "Handy Wipe."

"You got to be kidding?" I grab it from his hand and quickly wipe my face. "Where do you get this stuff?"

Of course, he doesn't answer. He gives me a tin cup instead. I look inside the cup and sniff its steaming contents. It smells like some kind of vegetable soup. I drink it down as if I hadn't eaten in weeks. When there isn't anymore, I turn toward him with the cup in both hands and I swear I don't mean to act like this, but I put on a Cockney accent and pretend to be that cheeky little Dickens kid who had the audacity to ask for more.

"Please, sir, may I 'ave some more?"

He ignores me and takes the tin cup from my hands, puts it down and picks up a small brown vinyl wrapped package. He gives it to me. I look at it and read the label: MRE/Beef Stroganoff. I have to shake my head in amazement. MRE is explained on the side of the package as Meals Ready to Eat for the soldier in the field. The directions that are also printed there explain that all you have to do is open it and drop it into a pot of boiling water. It also says they are guaranteed to have a shelf life of ten years. When I look up, the Indian is pointing to a whole case of the MREs with entrees that range from a pedestrian chicken and fries offering to the more outrages delicacies of filet mignon and beef Wellington. But the thing that really lights up my eyes is the next package he has already grabbed up and is presenting to me: it's that big white towel with the soap and the shampoo but this time I see a conditioner too and best of all, a comb and a mirror. Suddenly I'm feeling I'm *in* a freaking Charles Dickens novel.

"You gotta be kidding!"

I sit up and take the package like a kid on a Christmas morning.

"Oh, I can't believe this. Thank you, thank you so much."

On closer inspection I see the shampoo and conditioner are H-E's "None of Your Frizzness."

Like he needs to worry about that problem.

Its essence is "Mandarin Balm and Pearls."

Whatever that is. Wait a minute, that must be what I smelled in his hair.

I turn to look at him but he's already up and walking over to a hose hanging from the thatched roof. Turns out the hose is attached to a jury-rigged shower. He shows me how to use it.

But he's not finished. He saves the biggest surprise for last. He walks over to a covered crate, reaches behind and pulls out a small TV set. My eyes blink and my mouth drops open. He shows me that it's plugged into an extension cord, which leads to a small box at the edge of the far end of the chickee. An old-school flat brown cable is plugged into the back of the TV and runs up one of the posts and disappears through the thatched roof. He turns it on. It's not the best picture in the world but despite the snowy black and white image, it sure seems like it. He throws me the remote. I can't take my eyes off the screen. When I look up, the Indian has jumped down and is standing by a portable propane fueled campfire on the ground. He shows me how to turn it off and shows me the propane matchstick to light it again. It's not until he points out the trip line has been reset that I see what's going on.

"You're not leaving me here, are you?"

He's stepping over the trip line and walking toward the bithlo.

"Can't you talk?"

Nothing.

I struggle to my feet and call out again.

"You can't leave me here all alone! Something could get me! What about those idiots you carved up? What if they find me?"

He turns and points at me and then the water. I look and see his freaking pet gator crawling out of the water. I fall against one of the posts holding up the thatched roof and shake my head in disbelief as the giant gator lumbers up onto the beach and plops down on the sand. The Indian pats it on the head, steps into the bithlo, and starts poling away.

"How am I supposed to cook anything with him there?" I shout after him.

"You'll figure it out."

At least that's what I think he said.

"Did you just speak to me?"

Of course, he doesn't answer me.

"This isn't funny! Are you trying to drive me crazy?"

He disappears within seconds behind the overhanging foliage.

"You bastard! If you can talk, why are you doing this to me? It's not fair! I wouldn't do this to you!"

I grab the post and try to ease myself onto the ground. I fail. I cry out and the pain in my foot takes me to the sand. I'm on all fours when I look up and see the gator.

My sudden movement has brought him to his feet and he's looking at me, his head cocked to the side to see me better with and to show off his big sharp teeth. My heart begins to race and my head starts to spin but I know if I faint it's all over. I catch my breath and slowly back away towards the chickee. Without taking my eyes off the gator, I feel for the post, grab it and pull myself back up onto my good leg. Holding on to the post, I throw my injured ankle over the edge and pull myself up onto the raised floor. I can hear my heart racing in my ears and can feel my body working overtime to pump perspiration out of every pore of my skin. I pause for a moment to look at the gator and to catch my breath.

The monster is eyeing me like I'm dinner.

I see the Indian through the overhanging branches. With each stroke of the pole he gets further away and smaller and my hope of surviving shrinks along with him. I muster up enough courage and strength to overcome any fear of the upcoming pain and pull myself up. My throbbing ankle nearly takes my breath away. I limp along the floor and yell out across the hammock.

"You're scaring me man! You're really starting to scare me!"

I hobble up to one of the posts and linger there for some time long after losing site of the Indian. Finally, resigning myself to my predicament, I slip gently to the floor and try my best not to cry because, as my dad has told me more than once, "crying won't solve anything."

Within moments my body unexpectedly becomes drained of its strength and it dawns on me, in one of those rare moments of clarity just before succumbing to an overwhelming urge to sleep, that the soup was drugged.

##

In my dreams, I argue with my father, wrestle with Eddie who wants me to put out, and give myself to the Indian, which brings my father back for an unwelcome encore. I also see a man's face staring at me from beneath the gaps in the log floor of the chickee. It's the same face I saw the night before looking at me from the dense hammock, a Seminole or a Miccosukee or whatever in war paint. The only thing that didn't come back to haunt my sleep this night were the bears.

##

I wake up hungry the next morning and am surprised to find myself wrapped in the solar blanket and the TV turned off.

He must have come back.

I crawl slowly out of my deep sleep.

I know I didn't drag myself into this blanket.

I look at the remote placed neatly on a folded bath towel.

And I know I didn't do that.

Neatness is not something I'm famous for. I see two small squeezable plastic containers lying next to the remote. One of them is a "Deep Woods" mosquito repellent. I can't tell what the other one is. When I stretch over to pick them up a sharp fiery pain reminds me of my wounds. When I stop clenching my teeth and squeezing my eyes, I look at the container. It's a can of spray "Bactine."

How thoughtful. This guy sure knows how to win a girl over.

I roll over onto my side and look out at the new day filtering in through shafts of sunlight in the dry, dusty air.

It's so quiet. So damn quiet. I think I could easily go stark raving mad here in a very short time.

I look for the remote, grab it and turn the TV on.

Mom and dad are on TV!

I sit up so quickly I get dizzy and have to force myself to focus on the small screen. Dad is looking straight at me and asking for volunteers to help search for his lost daughter.

Mom, just in from New Jersey, is standing stoically beside my dad in stylish dark sunglasses. I can't believe how bad my dad looks and how great mom looks. He's unshaven and has large dark circles under his eyes. He probably hasn't had any sleep since he lost me.

Serves you right. Serves you right.

On the other hand, I'm not surprised mom looks so good.

The woman comes alive every time a camera is on. She must be in her glory.

"Maybe I should disappear more often!" I shout at the TV. The station cuts to a commercial.

"Wait!"

I want to see more. I start flipping the channels but can't find my parents anywhere.

"Dammit! Dammit! Dammit!"

With each shout, I slam the remote against the log floor for emphasis. I feel the urge to cry but won't let myself. I wipe away a tear and try to focus on something positive.

"Well, at least they haven't given up looking for me."

The station cuts to a promo for an upcoming sitcom about young people my age facing one of life's big moments: high school graduation. I remember it was less than a week ago when I threw my mortarboard into the air and thought the rest of my life was going to be one long party. I couldn't wait to get out of the house, get a job and be on my own-- and never see the back end of a stinking, bug infested swamp again. Maybe somewhere down the road I might even go to college.

But my parents had other ideas. They wanted me to start college immediately after one final summer sojourn in the wilderness with dad. I thought, *you got to be kidding. What's in it for me?* "Negotiations" got pretty heated at times until they made me an offer I couldn't refuse. In exchange for one more summer in the woods with dad *and* going to college, they'd throw in something I always wanted: a motorcycle.

This, of course, was a no-brainer for me. I've loved bikes for as long as I can remember. Especially Harleys. Dad had one when we were one happy family. I loved riding in front of him when I was a kid. Dad had what they call a "full dresser." It had black leather saddlebags, a windscreen, and enough chrome to blind you. And that distinct, rumbling sound. "Potato-potato-potato." That's how he described it to me when I was just a little girl with ribbons and curls. I think it made me a tomboy. I know it made me a punk. Talk about attitude, Harley's got all those whiney Jap bikes beat by a mile. Anyway, even though my mother didn't really like the idea because motorcycles scare her-- I swear, I don't know how they ever got together-- the deal was made and I'd get a Harley Sportster, the lightest one they make, upon returning home from the jungle one final time. Although this wasn't something I planned-- I was ready to go back to work at the mall as a sales girl— with this deal I'll get an education and a shot at a better job *plus* a way cool Harley to boot.

At least until I turn eighteen.

That's what I thought back then. After that, the courts- and especially my parents- can't make me do anything I don't want to do. If it turns out college isn't a drag, I'll give it a shot. Otherwise, *arriba derchi, baby*-- Harley and all.

I know, it sounds calculating, but what can I tell you. I'm not perfect. And neither are my parents. Especially my dad. Up until a couple of days ago everything was going fine before he got this great idea. I mean, why couldn't he bond with me like other divorced fathers do? No, that would be too easy. God forbid we go see an R-rated teen flick or go shopping at a mall. No, the Great White Father's got to take me with him to fight a ragin', freakin' forest fire!

But I digress. I'm getting hungry and remember the MREs. I slowly get to my feet and hobble over to a case full of them. I start rummaging and find one that's perfect: scrambled eggs with hash browns. I find a couple of brands of coffee--

including Cafe Pilon, a strong local Cuban brew for espresso-- and some coffee pots. I choose the small camping version of an Italian made espresso machine.

One of the few things I came to like about South Florida aside from the Cuban boys and the way they danced was a strong delicacy called "café Cubano." Sold over the counter on every street corner *cafecito* in South Florida, the hot coffee is so potent it's traditionally sold only in a small plastic thimble-sized throw-away cup. And for good reason; a regular sized cup could easily send a big man to the moon and back. It's an acquired taste but when I realized this was one of the few ways my dad and I could actually do something that didn't involve sweating together in the wilderness, I made up my mind to get used to it and, in time, came to actually like it. When I found out the stuff was sold in the local mall's food court, I became a devotee because dad's "bonding drink" always led to an air-conditioned shopping spree.

After checking to see if that big freaking gator was around, I boiled up some water for the MRE and the café Cubano. The MRE was better than I expected, it even came with a tube of hot sauce for the eggs. The café Cubano was no different than those from the streets despite the fact that it was brewed by a small one-cup sized two-piece espresso pot.

"Um, boy, that's a good cup of coffee."

I find myself imitating dad, drawing out the first part for all it was worth. He did it each time we had a "shot"-- as he called it-- of the thick, dark brew. He told me some dead guy named Jackie Gleason who once had a TV show on Miami Beach use to say it at the end of every show when he drank his coffee. The joke was, dad explained, that the "Great One" as he was known, would imply by the tone of his voice and his body movements that there was something more than just coffee in the cup. Now it had become a phrase we always said together when we had our café Cubano; our own little secret joke because most people nowadays, according to dad, have never heard of the guy.

Thinking about my dad and me sharing our café Cubano makes me smile. I know it made his day when we could spend time together like that. He was a busy guy and always apologizing for not spending more time with me. I start feeling guilty about using those moments to get him to buy me "doodads"-- as he calls them-- and I quickly remind myself that it was he who should feel guilty.

After all, you're the one that insisted I join you in the middle of nowhere to fight another damn fire. I've spent my last five summers in a freakin' forest fire and I'm tired of it! Most kids get to go to a nice summer camp where, if they're lucky, they might get to see a wild raccoon or something. Not me, I'm sent off to a place that's always on fire and the critters are big and mean enough to eat you. Go figure.

I sigh and shake my head. I see the caked dirt on my hands and arms.

My God, I must be filthy.

I stand up and look at my legs; they're covered in blood and dirt. I lift an arm and sniff under my armpit.

"Oh, man! I'm skunk ape bait!"

I turn my head away its so bad.

Oh, no, maybe this is why he's given me soap and a towel. Oh, my God, I'm so embarrassed.

I spin around on my good foot and stop short. I see the rigged up shower inside the chickee, take one last swig from the coffee cup, and hobble across the sand. I place my hands on the edge of the raised floor, lift myself up far enough to throw my good leg over the edge, and roll into the chickee. There is a little discomfort with the swollen ankle, but it isn't as bad as I thought it would be and I hardly feel the pain in my back at all. I sit up and untie the Ace bandage. I can't believe how lucky I am, not a cut. I start to remove my bra and then pause to look around until I realize there isn't anyone to look around for.

Like, duh, you're in the middle of nowhere, stupid. Who's going to see you? The Indian? Don't worry 'bout him. That guy's probably gay. Unfortunately.

Then it hits me: *Skunk apes!*

I'm not superstitious, but if you smell as bad as I do and you're all alone stark naked in the middle of the freaking Everglades, miles and miles from civilization, skunk apes, Big Foots, Sasquatches, or whatever you want to call them suddenly become a lot more real. I can see them coming for me now, hundreds of them emerging from their jungle hideouts, sniffing the air, zeroing in on my stinky pheromones, all itching to get a piece of me.

I quickly remove my bra, lie back against the log floor and slide out of my dirty cut-offs and panties in record time.

I twist around, grab the post and struggle to my feet. I pick up my bath supplies and use the remote to turn on the TV, flipping channels to look for the news. The local Telemundo station is the only one I can get and, despite not knowing a lick of Spanish, leave it there and turn the TV around so that I can watch it while I shower. Who knows, maybe they'll have something about me in Spanish.

The shower is basically a garden hose nozzle attached to a long hose hanging from the thatched roof. A simple plastic shutoff valve controls the water between the nozzle and the hose. The Home Depot SKU tag is still stuck to the shutoff valve.

Mr. Handyman.

I reach up, step out of the way, and turn it on. I'm surprised the water is warm.

Not much pressure, but man, it's just right.

I step into the gentle shower and have to hold onto the hose to keep from falling. It is both a painful and pleasurable experience. The wounds on my back and forehead come alive like a forgotten sunburn but the water flowing across my body reminds me how great it is to be alive. I open my eyes and begin to shampoo my hair.

Oh what a wonderful thing a shower is.

I haven't felt this good in days and take my time washing my body. I watch the dirt and grime flow down my legs and away with the water through the openings in the log floor. I shiver when a rare summer breeze crosses my body. I see goose bumps magically appear on my arms, race across my breasts and down my legs. My nipples are standing erect and for the first time in a long time I feel young, healthy and free. This is the kind of exhilarating feeling you can only get when you're standing naked outdoors in a meadow and yes, even a swamp. For a second I almost believe I could live like this; until the water runs out.

Oh, please, don't.

I try working the valve back and forth to see if I can get the water flowing again, but there's nothing more than a trickle.

"I still have soap in my hair!"

It's not like you're at the Howard Johnson's or something. You shouldn't have taken so long. You idiot!

By this time you're probably thinking, this chicka sure does a lot of talking to herself. Trust me, I never did until I got lost in the freaking Everglades!

I yank on the hose in frustration and pull the whole contraption down on top of me right through the chickee roof. I'm knocked to the floor. My ankle is killing me. I grab it and roll over to look at the thing that hit me on the head.

The hose I yanked is attached to a clear plastic bag about as big as a large pillow with a silver vinyl backing that helps heat up the water inside. It's a portable solar water heater made for camping and I see the Indian bought it at Kmart.

Is everything off-the-shelf with this guy?

I moan and roll to the other side and see the crated weapons. I had forgotten about that part of the Indian and it makes me pause.

My God, what have I gotten myself into? Why would anybody need all these freakin' guns? In the middle-of-nowhere?

I remember the Stinger over-the-shoulder missile and quickly sit up.

Did I dream that?

I push up from the log floor and get to my feet, balancing on my good foot. I look around and find it.

Oh, please tell me I didn't see this. What kinda guy needs a Stinger missile?

Before I can answer myself, I interrupt my question with this thought: *I gotta get the hell out of here.*

Something easier said than done when you're stark naked, lame and in the middle-of-stinking-nowhere. The first thing I do is step on the soap, which sends me crashing back to the floor. The back of my head bounces off the logs and the last thing to enter my brain before slipping into unconsciousness is the word "klutz."

##

The sound of someone talking wakes me up to a pounding headache and a throbbing ankle. I start to turn and moan but catch myself when I realize why I'm so uncomfortable. I freeze when I realize I'm wrapped in the solar blanket again. I peel away a Velcro edge of the blanket to look at my watch and hope no one hears me. It's four-thirty. I peek out from under the blanket.

In the afternoon.

Pulling the blanket further away from my face reveals the Indian. I can't believe what I'm looking at. He's talking on a cell phone. In the middle-of-nowhere.

My God, his roaming charges must be--

I interrupt myself.

Are you nuts? The guy's wearing a loincloth, standing bare foot in the middle of the freaking swamp and talking on a cell phone like some kinda big shot and you don't think that's the least bit unusual? Instead you're thinking about cellular plans? My God, girl, you really don't have a clue, do you?

I happen to glance upward and see a huge old school TV antenna through the hole in the roof where the solar shower bag had once been. It's draped in camo netting. I can't digest this information because the Indian is getting louder. I look and see him yelling into the mouthpiece.

God, I wish I knew what he was saying. Whatever it is, it sure doesn't sound good.

He stops talking and looks at the phone, brings it back up to his ear, walks around a little bit, shouts again and then rears back and throws it through the hammock cover far out into the water.

Oh, my god, he just threw away a cell phone! This guy's got a temper. Oh, no, he's coming my way.

I pretend to be asleep when the Indian springs catlike onto the chickee floor. I didn't hear him land, but I know he's there. I'm scared and begin to tremble. I know it must be showing through the solar blanket. I try to act my way out of this situation by pretending to have a fever, which requires that I moan and turn at the same time. I feel his hands pulling the solar blanket down from around my face and realize that I'm still naked.

Oh my God, he's seen me naked!

Pretending to talk in my sleep, I pull the blanket up and try to roll to my side when the Indian reaches out and stops me.

What's he going to do?

He places his palm against my forehead and holds it there for a moment before taking it away. I moan some more. I don't hear anything.

Did he leave already? Darn it, I was trying to pay attention.

A moment passes and I still can't hear anything.

What if he's still there? He can't still be there. He must have gone by now. I gotta look. No don't, I advise myself but I've never been good at taking orders, especially from myself. I look.

His hand is in my face. It's holding a *Secret* "Clinical Strength" underarm deodorant stick. Up until that moment the trade marked double entendre "Because you're hot" use to bring a smile to my face. Now it just makes me blush. I'm so embarrassed.

"Hi, I'm Nokosee, a real human being. You *need* this."

I scream, grab up the blanket around me and back pedal across the floor. "You *do* speak English! I knew it! I knew you spoke English!"

"Eyelid flutter; gives you away every time. I was expecting more from you. For the Great White Father's daughter, that was some kinda lame acting."

"You ever heard of *REM* sleep?" I grab the human stink remover from his hand and pull my legs up close.

The Indian laughs. He has a nice laugh. Like his voice. It's boyish with just a tinge of manliness. And it has an accent, which I can't yet put my finger on.

"Why haven't you talked to me before?"

"I didn't have anything to say."

"Until now."

"Until now."

"So, who were you talking to? It looked like you were pretty pissed off."

"My father. He gives his regards."

"Funny."

A moment passes as we look at each other. I feel his eyes on my eyes and my hair and my heaving breasts. I squirm and try not to notice his loincloth and how it's hanging between his legs, touching the log floor as he squats. I look away and, try as hard as I can, can't help but cringe and sound like a spoiled valley girl when I ask, "Why do you dress like that?"

"I'm a freakin' Indian."

He says it just like I would. I could just die. I roll my eyes and turn away.

I must have been delirious. God, what else did I say? I'm so embarrassed!

I look at him and see he's still staring at me with a bemused smile.

"Think something's funny?"

He doesn't say anything but instead sits down, stretches out his legs next to me and relaxes back onto his locked elbows.

"I don't like being stared at. It gives me the creeps."

To him it was like I never said anything.

"What? Never seen a white girl before, Tarzan?"

"I like that one," he says with a smile. "And, no, I've never seen a white girl before."

I make a face. "You gotta be kidding."

"Nope. You're my first; at least the first one I've ever seen that wasn't on TV."

"Yeah, right." I turn away with a disgusted shake of my head.

"It's true, Stormy, you're my first."

It makes me uncomfortable the way he calls me by my name. I turn to him with a raised eyebrow. "What did you say your name was?"

"Nokosee. It means 'bear.'"

I exhale doubtfully and turn away. "Right."

Nokosee just smiles, shakes his head and looks at me. When I look back and see him looking at me with that same bemused smile I find myself talking over my fear.

"I'm tellin' you, man," I say while pulling out my hand from under the blanket and waving my index finger at him, "if you keep lookin' at me like that I'm takin' you down, right down to Chinatown."

Nokosee laughs out loud, sits up, claps his hands, and points at me. "DeNiro," he says, "'Meet The Parents.' Man, I loved that movie. Now DeNiro," he says while waving two fingers between his eyes and me, "you do well."

At this point I'm *really* beginning to hate this guy. I wish I hadn't done an impression. I remember my dad telling me that I seem to do them when I'm either nervous or want to please somebody.

Well, you're right, Mr. Can't-be-happy-your-daughter-wants-to-make-you-happy-but-must-always-analyze-everything-she-says-dad.

I look at the Indian, What's-His-Name.

God, I wonder if he's seen Elvis? Probably.

My eyes narrow on him.

He's a real smart-ass.

In frustration, I kick out my foot from under the blanket and shout, "So are you gonna take me home or what?"

"It depends," he says without skipping a beat.

"Depends on what?"

"It depends on you."

"Me?"

"Yeah. I've seen your dad on TV. I can tell he's really worried and he must feel guilty as hell but what's with your mother? I mean, every time I catch the news, she's got on some kinda new getup. It's like she's in a movie and has a different wardrobe for each scene."

I pause and coolly look him over. *Man, this guy sounds just like dad. He nailed mom right on the head first time out. What is he? Some kinda know all, all-seeing smart-ass Indian? He's too freakin' perfect. Give me stupid Eddie anytime. At least he knows how to dress.*

"Don't start dissin' my mom, man."

"Or what?" Nokosee waits for an answer staring down hard at me.

I blink first. I hadn't thought about my options.

"Are you gonna yell and scream and pitch a hissy fit? Go right ahead, be my guest but it isn't going to do you any good. No one's gonna hear you. Don't forget, you're," and this is where he actually does the quote thing with his fingers and lowers his voice to add import, "'in the middle-of-freaking-nowhere.'" He waits for a response but I can't argue with him. "I didn't think so."

But I can tell him off. "What, were you takin' notes when I was delirious? Get a life." I turn away as if I'm bored.

"I have a life and it's a good one too."

I look over the chickee. "You call this living?"

"Yeah, I do. But this isn't my whole life. I've got more goin' on than you can imagine."

"Yeah," I reply glancing-- so help me I wish I didn't-- at his loincloth, "I'm sure. Who are you trying to kid?"

"Stormy, let's just say, what you see is almost what you get."

"You know," I say unflinchingly while kicking myself for being such a smart ass, "I'm beginning to dislike you more and more."

"That's only because you haven't gotten to know me." Nokosee winks, reaches over and slaps me on the knee for emphasis.

I pull myself in sharply. "Don't touch me, Chief whatever your name is or I promise, you will pay."

Nokosee pauses. "I can't place that threat. It's not DeNiro. Is it Seagal?"

I look away and shake my head very slowly, cursing him under my breath.

"You know, Stormy, you gotta stop making these threats if you can't back them up."

I know, but I'm a chick with a chip on her shoulder and I can't help myself.

"Give me your hand."

I look up. He has his hand extended.

"What, are you nuts?" I gather myself into a tighter ball. "I'm not giving you anything except a good kick in the balls." I start to back away.

"Stormy, I promise I won't hurt you. Just give me your hand."

"No way, Jose."

Nokosee grabs my solar blanket and I try to hold on to it.

"You know I can rip this off of you if I want."

"No!"

Suddenly Nokosee removes his knife and rams it through the blanket. I let go of the blanket. Nokosee slides up and sits on the blanket. "Now give me your hand."

"Okay, you bastard, but you better not hurt me."

"Aw, geese, Stormy," Nokosee replies while pulling the knife out of the blanket, "there you go again."

I yank the solar blanket around me, find the edge and push my hand through until I see the knife in his hand.

"Wait a minute, you're not gonna try any of that Indian blood brother crap on me, are you?"

Nokosee sticks the knife back into its sheath. "Don't flatter yourself, Stormy. You're not worthy. Just give me your hand."

I don't trust him but then I don't have much of a choice either. Slowly, I extend my hand toward him. He scoots in closer and takes it with both of his hands.

"Stormy, I promise I will do my best to never hurt you."

He pauses to look steadily into my eyes. I *really* want to believe him.

"Oh, no, a real Boy Scout."

"Don't interrupt. I promise I will return you to your father unharmed..."

He pauses and looks at me with a sigh and raised eyebrows.

"As soon as he pays the ransom."

I yank my hand away. "You bastard!"

"Hey, it's not me. I want you outta here yesterday. It's my dad."

"That bastard!"

"You know him?"

"My dad doesn't have any money! He works for the Feds for crying out loud!"

"Oh, you mean the ones who can come up with a trillion dollars to fund the war machine? You don't think they can come up with a measly hundred thou?"

I stop short. A hundred thousand is nothing in the scheme of things, especially the way Nokosee presents it.

"What? You think you're worth more than that? I told dad we should have held out for more."

I'm so mad I'm seething. I yank the solar blanket around me and bury my head in it to hide the tears spilling out of my eyes. I'm thinking, *I can't win. You'd think lost in the middle of the freaking Everglades where there basically aren't any people would keep you from getting kidnapped and held for ransom. Not me. I mean, what are the odds of that happening?*

"Don't worry, Stormy. Dad's not greedy." I can tell Nokosee is bending near me by the sound of his voice, trying to see my face. "He'll take whatever he can get. I should get the go-ahead any minute now to take you back to the Outside. You just got to promise me one thing."

"What's that?" I ask like a big crybaby.

"You gotta promise to forget everything you saw."

I pause to think about it. It seems way too easy. I look up with a wipe of my tears.

"That's it?"

"That's it."

"And you'll let me go?"

"As soon as the money is delivered."

I pause again. "Assuming they get it, how are you going to collect it?"

"We have our ways."

"I don't believe you."

"Believe."

"No, I don't understand why you need a hundred 'thou,' as you put it, when you live like this."

"State-of-the-art weaponry doesn't come cheap. We couldn't figure out where to raise the cash for the stuff. And then you came along."

"Ever heard of Bingo?"

"Can't go there. They may look like us, but they're not us."

"Listen, man, I don't know what you're talking about. You're not going to be one of those cryptic, wisdom spouting Indian dudes, are you?"

"I'll try not to be. They bug me too. But you know, it's in the blood. What can I say?"

"You are one strange dude."

"Thank you. Coming from you, that's a real compliment."

"Did I tell you you're also a smart-ass?"

"Yes you did."

I shake my head sadly before pausing and wiping my eyes with the back of my hand. "Look, I'll do whatever it takes. I just want to get home. Okay?"

"I told you I would take you back."

Nokosee sees a tear rolling down my cheek and, without hesitation, whips out his knife and catches it less than an inch from my eye.

I jump back, checking to see if I've been cut. "Are you *crazy?*"

"Possibly." He runs the blade across his palm and blends the tear with his blood. I can't watch and turn away. "Until you're worthy, this tear will have to do."

"My god, man, you are freaking me out!"

"I know." Nokosee stops and looks away. "I freak myself out a lot too."

He turns, slips the knife back into its sheath and hops down from the deck.

"I'm sorry, Stormy," he says, walking alongside the chickee. "That was a pretty stupid thing to do with the knife and your face. Here," he stops, picks something up and throws it at me. "You might want these." It's my underwear, shorts and bra. They land in a heap in front of me. "I washed them out while you were sleeping."

I don't know what to think as I watch Nokosee walk away, his bulging back muscles rippling with each easy stride.

"What do you call this stuff again?" I ask.

I'm sitting on the deck with my back against a post and my legs outstretched. Nokosee is also stretched out on the deck, his back up against the opposite post. We have just started eating dinner, I've had a complete shower and, thanks to the fact that I'm starving, I'm not as mad anymore. Hunger has a way of making it easier to be civil to your kidnappers.

"Shepherd's pie."

"Not bad."

"Government approved."

"What's in it?"

"You don't really want to know, but I think some sort of meat-by-product."

"Oh, my God!" I throw the MRE onto the floor. "I'm a vegetarian!"

"Vegetarian: Indian word for lousy hunter."

"Funny. What, did you get that off some bumper sticker?"

"Actually, I got it off of AOL; some kind of Redneck promotion. I thought it was about us human beings but it was for some cracker standup comic."

"What's with this 'human beings' crap?"

"That's what we called ourselves before the white man discovered us. Most of us still do. I don't think many of us think of ourselves as Native Americans. We were here long before the white man called it America." Nokosee motions toward my MRE lying on the floor. "I don't think the Army's got anything for vegetarians. You better eat it, it's all we got."

I look at him with a disgusted shake of my head and slap at a mosquito. "Instead of buying more weapons," I say in frustration, "why don't you invest it in a real house?"

"What? You don't like the accommodations?"

"It's about a step up from a street person's."

"What's a street person?"

"You're kidding me, right? You never heard of a street person?"

Nokosee shakes his head as he chews a dinner roll.

"It's somebody who lives on the streets because he doesn't have a home. He's homeless."

"But I have a home."

"You call this a home? Bro, you *really* gotta wanna live in the woods."

"I do."

"Come on, are your trying to tell me you live in the swamp like this without air-conditioning on purpose?"

"What's air-conditioning?"

"Yeah, right. You're not a stupid as you pretend to be and I'm not as dumb as I may look. You know exactly what I'm talking about."

"Stormy, you know what's wrong with you?"

"If I want your opinion, I'll pound it out of you."

"What is that, some kinda punk thing? It's one thing to be pissed off at the world, but if you can't back it up, you better shut up. Know what I mean?"

I know I can't back it up, at least not with this guy. I shrug and look away.

"You don't have a clue how most people live." Nokosee extends his arms. "This is how most people live in the world. In fact, this is much better than how most people live in the world. Dad says more than a billion people around the world live on less than a dollar a day and without toilets."

I shake my head mockingly back and forth and whine, "I know; I'm spoiled. You sound just like my old man."

"The Great White Father speaks the truth."

I pause and look Nokosee over. "You know, you really are one strange dude."

"You're repeating yourself."

"Yeah, for emphasis. At least I'm not running around in a loincloth in some Godforsaken outback living like some kinda freakin' caveman."

"Chickeeman."

"Cute. I mean, it's like you can't make up your mind how you want to live. It's like you want it both ways."

"I only want it one way but I'm willing to use the other way to get it my way."

"You're getting cryptic on me."

"Sorry."

"You sound like some kinda Burger King commercial."

"Tell me, are those Whoppers as good as they say they are?"

"You never had a Whopper?"

"Pop won't let me. Thinks I'll get hooked on them and will want to defect."

I shake my head as slowly and as sadly as I can.

"Stormy, we borrow from the Outside to make our life easier."

"Don't you mean *steal*?"

"Well, technically, yeah, but I do plan to pay your world back someday."

"I'll bet. So why the hell do you need a Stinger missile?"

Nokosee pauses and studies my face before answering. "Now that's hard to explain, isn't it?"

"Hey, you're the one they'll be putting that question to after you get arrested. Maybe you ought to start working on an answer when you still have the time."

"Stormy, can you forget you ever saw it?"

"Well, according to my kidnappers, I better damn well forget I saw it if I ever want to get back to civilization. So, I guess I don't have much of a choice. I guess having one of them makes you the most powerful guy ever to wear a loincloth."

"Not to mention dangerous."

"For sure. So, what's the story?"

Nokosee stretches out and puts his hands behind his head. "Stormy, would you believe I've never been to the Outside?"

"Uh, you're getting cryptic on me again."

"The Outside; your world."

"Hey, just because I'm blond doesn't mean I'm stupid. I take AP classes. I want to know *why* you--"

"Whoop-tee-doo. Little good AP classes will do you out here."

"Do you even know what they are?"

"Little darlin,' I might be home schooled in the middle of the 'freakin' Everglades,' but that don't mean I'm a country bumpkin. Dad insists his kids learn as much as--"

"'Kids.' You mean there's more of your kind roamin' around out here?"

"I've got a sister."

"Poor kid. How old is she?"

"Fourteen."

"What's her name?"

"Do you want her Seminole name or the English translation?"

"Both."

"Gerryragni, which means 'Hair' in English."

"Your sister's name is *Hair*?" I ask incredulously.

"Yeah. My dad loves the musical. Named her after one of the writers. We call her 'Gerrycurl' because she's got mom's curls. 'Gerry' for shorter. Stormy, aside from knowing every song from 'Hair'-- You know it's the *tribal* rock musical, don't you?-- my sister and I are trilingual. Your dad was right about us Injuns. We all know English but because of my Cuban mom, us chickee dwellin' cavemen also know Spanish."

"Whoop-tee-doo." I am more impressed than I sound. "So, what was the reason you need a Stinger missile for again?"

"If I told you, you wouldn't believe me."

"Oh, I don't know. If someone had told me there was a tribe of crazy Indians running around the Everglades with Stinger missiles over their shoulders a few days ago, maybe. But after what I've been through, I don't think anything you say will surprise me."

Nokosee pauses and then sits up with his legs crossed underneath. "Being the Great White Father's daughter, I know you've met other Seminoles and Miccosukees before. Can you tell me what makes me different from them?"

"No problem." I sit up, eager to let it all out. "First of all," I begin, counting out a finger on one hand with a slap of the other hand's index finger, "you're the only Indian I know who walks around in a loincloth."

"Excuse me," Nokosee interrupts with a raised hand, "if I sound a little PC here, but I think the correct term is 'Native American' although we prefer *human being*."

"Well, excuse me, Mr. Trilingual Know-it-all, but you did ask me a question. May I finish?"

Nokosee raises a cautioning finger. "And the correct term for what I'm wearing is *gee-string*."

"Pul-*leeze*.."

"I kid you not. It's another Native American term that has found its way into the English lexicon."

I have to pause and look him over. "Like I said, you are one freaking weirdo."

"Thank you. Again, coming from you, that's a real compliment. As you were saying?"

I eye him steadily before slowly beginning to count off again on my fingers. "Right. Aside from knowing way too much for a guy in a *gee-string*, you don't think twice about carving your initials into somebody, you aren't afraid to wrestle wild gators instead of the dwarf and drugged kind your bros wrestle for the tourists, you can kick butt better than any Indi-- Native American—C'mon, Nokosee, I'm a human being, too."

"Ugh," Nokosee interrupts with his best clichéd movie Indian impersonation, "and a mighty fine human being, too."

I wonder if he finds me attractive or if he's just playing with me. I narrow my eyes on him. "As I was saying, you can kick butt better than any *human being* I ever met, it looks like you travel the glades by foot and bithlo instead of airboat, you live in a camouflaged chickee in the middle-of-nowhere that *almost* has all the conveniences of home—I'm still looking for your toilet-- and you basically are trying to live with one foot in your world and one foot in my world, or as you call it," and this is where I slash the air with punctuation marks, "the '*outside*.'"

"Not bad, but I've been told by my father and mother that we live like our brothers on the reservation-- but with more class, whatever that means."

"Wrong. At least they have toilets."

Nokosee puts up a finger again, gets up and walks over to some boxes, reaches behind and pulls up a gray plastic cube shaped object and brings it over to me. He brushes the dust off and sets it down in front of me.

"Voilà! Your toilet, my lady."

I know exactly what it is having used one like it many times on camping trips with my dad. It's a portable, waterless toilet that treats its waste chemically; an off-the-shelf item found in every Sears store in America.

"My God, man, why didn't you tell me about this earlier?"

"I never thought about it. Sorry."

"You 'never thought about it'? How do you—Never mind, I don't want to know. Look, as much as I'd like to continue this discussion with you, I gotta use it."

I start to get up and Nokosee grabs me under the arm.

"Thanks, Nooksy, but I'd like some privacy."

"It's *No-ko-shee* and I'm only helping you to get over behind the boxes."

"Sorry. So why don't you build me some crutches or something, Mr. Handyman?"

"Why do that when I can just give you a pair that are lying around here somewhere?"

"My God, is there anything you don't have around here?"

"Yeah," Nokosee says as he helps me around the boxes, "there's one thing I don't have."

"Yeah?"

"A mate."

I push his hand away and laugh out loud. "A *'mate?'* You really are a caveman aren't you?" I put the portable toilet down and turn to Nokosee. "Do you *mind?*"

Nokosee raises his hands for the universal sign of *"Excuse me!"* and backs away.

"Keep going."

He backs further away.

"Keep going."

I wait for him to jump down onto the sand before dropping my shorts and sinking below the boxes. "The way you're going," I tell him from behind the boxes, "you'll be lucky if you meet any girls at all."

"I met one," he shouts back.

"Who? She'd have to be lost out here--" I cut myself short. "Oh, no, Tarzan boy," I shout, "don't start getting any ideas. I'm not *your* Jane."

"I'm not saying you are. I'm just saying I met a girl out here in the middle-of-nowhere. Besides, you aren't what I'm looking for. You don't have what it takes."

"Damn right. Who'd want to live like this?"

"That's not what I meant."

"Trust me. I have what it takes. I just don't want to live like this. Where's the TP?"

"Sorry. That's a plains Indian thing."

"You idiot. I mean where's the toilet paper?"

"Oh, I ran out."

"Are you kidding me?"

"Sorry."

"You gotta be kidding me!"

"Me no kid."

"Aw, geese, I can't believe this."

"Just do what I do and stop your whining."

"What? Jump off the pot and rub my ass on the floor?"

"Make note," Nokosee says, "Cute but crude. Fine, figure it out yourself. I'm outta here."

"No! No, please, you can't leave me like this! What *do* you do?"

"I use the biggest leaf I can find."

"But there aren't any around!"

"That's why I always check first to see if I have toilet paper."

"But I didn't know!"

"Now you know."

"But that's not fair!"

"Hey, welcome to my world, kid."

"You bastard!"

"That's Nokosee to you."

"Screw you! If I ever get home I'm gonna make you pay for this! For kidnapping me and everything!" I start to cry.

"Stormy?"

I scream and nearly jump off the pot. He's right behind me, not looking, but right behind me just the same.

"What are you doing sneaking up on me like that?"

"I can't help it, I'm an Indian. It's in my blood. Here, use this with my compliments."

He's holding up the front page of The Miami Herald. I see my face on it; a photo dad took of me when I was in full punk regalia, a photo he said he would later use to blackmail me when I was a mother. As it turned out, it was the only picture he ever took of me. It's not the most flattering picture but what are you going to do? It shows me leaning against a brick wall with a cigarette in one hand. The other hand is raised toward the camera, its middle finger upright but hidden by a censored Photoshopped blur because the

Miami Herald is, after all, a family newspaper. My face is frozen forever with my best Billy Idol-all-the-way-from-Elvis curled upper lip. I'm wearing a t-shirt I made using a stencil. Despite not approving of the "theme," Dad helped me make it— he cut the acetate with his trusty X-acto Knife. And then he started pushing my buttons when he was taking my picture so mom could see what we were up to. He called me a "poseur." I flipped him the finger and said, "Pose this." That's when he took the picture.

"Where'd you get that?" I ask.

"Home delivery."

"Give it to me!" I yank it from his hands and start to read it.

"You're welcome." He turns and walks away. "Just remember, your reading material is also your TP. Read it or lose it."

"I must be famous." I know, what a Paris.

##

It's night now. I'm lying on my side, one arm holding up my head as I read the paper by the light of a battery powered Coleman lantern. Nokosee settles behind me.

"Have you memorized it yet?"

"Ha-ha, real funny. Is this how you know so much about me?"

"Yeah." He's rubbing something in his hand. "This might sting a little." He rubs it over my deer wound and I cry out.

"What is that stuff?"

"It's an ancient Seminole healing ointment."

"It smells familiar."

"Maybe it's the aloe."

"No, aloe doesn't smell like that."

"Oh, then it must be the Bactine."

"Bactine?"

"Yeah."

"I thought you said it was an ancient Seminole healing ointment?"

"It depends on what you mean by 'ancient.' I mean my mother was using it on me for as long as I can remember. It works, you know. Except for your choice in hair color, you're going to look all right."

"Don't start."

"Hey, for a little kidnapped girl, you sure don't show much respect to your kidnappers."

"Like you're a kidnapper. Your Loony Tunes dad put you up to this. Right?"

"I hate to take you away from your reading," he says, ignoring my question, "but I want you to roll over. I want to look at your ankle."

I groan like it's a big inconvenience but do as I'm told. I rest on my elbows as Nokosee begins to unwrap the Ace bandage. "So Nooksy, you—"

"No-*ko*-shee."

"I don't know, I kinda like Nooksy better."

"I don't." He gives the bandage a yank.

"Ow! Okay, whatever you want just don't take it out on my foot." Nokosee doesn't say anything. "Man, you sure can get bent out of shape quickly. Lighten up, you'll live longer."

Nokosee pauses and sighs. "You know, I think you're right. I must be doing something wrong. I've never heard of kidnappers getting dissed the way I am. Maybe I should find a new line of work."

"Maybe you should."

He laughs and starts applying a new ointment to my ankle.

"So, No-*ko*-shee, you aren't the kind of kidnapper that would actually hurt somebody, are you?"

"What do you think?"

"I don't know what to think. I know you've got a bad temper. I mean, I can't believe you tossed that cell phone just because the batteries were dead."

"The batteries weren't dead. I was talking to my dad. Anyway, it was no big deal. Those cell phones are easily replaced." He turns to me to say "I can get them for a *steal*."

"So, what, do you steal everything you need?"

"Pretty much so if isn't provided by Mother Earth."

Hearing him talk like that makes me laugh.

"I'm sorry, but what are you, some kinda pagan too?"

"A little bit of both. Mom's a Catholic and dad leans toward our traditional gods but basically, I think he's an atheist."

"Ou, man, that feels so good." Nokosee is massaging my foot and ankle.

"Not bad for a pagan caveman, hunh?"

"Not bad at all." I settle onto my back.

"Stormy, I hope this doesn't sound like bragging, but my father has raised me to be something bigger and better than most men."

"Is that why you haven't tried to hit on me?"

"Man, talk about an ego. You know, it's not always all about you."

"It isn't?"

Yeah," he laughs, "well, maybe if you hadn't been wearing those boots."

"Maybe what?"

"Maybe I'd have made a move on you."

"I don't have them on now." I wiggle my big toe against his hand. He playfully slaps it away.

"And maybe if you didn't stink so much."

Now I slap him. Playfully, of course. He starts wrapping up my foot and ankle with the Ace bandage.

"As I was saying," he continues, "he's got big plans for me and my sister. He's trying to mold us into something he calls the 'New Seminole.' Right now I'm on a 'walkabout.' It's something he came up with that would mark my passage to manhood. It's a new tradition based on a movie he saw years ago about an aborigine doing the same thing I'm doing except that guy did it in the Australian outback. He played the movie for us a few nights ago on 'movie night.'"

"'Movie night'?"

"Yeah, it's a family tradition. Once a month dad disappears for a few days and returns with a bunch of

videos. We watch one a week. This week he made it into a
big ceremony and, after seeing it, sent me on my way."

"In the middle of the night?"

"Under a full moon, it's the best time to travel. Much
cooler."

"But how do you know where you're going?"

"Hey, I know the Everglades like the back of my hand."

"So, why did you need a map to find this place?"

Nokosee pauses and looks up. "You don't miss much, do
you?"

"I try not to, especially when I'm being kidnapped. So
why the map?"

"Remember, I'm on a walkabout. I've never been this far
east. Dad made me a map. Okay, hows that?"

I sit up on my elbows. "Not bad...for a pagan caveman."

Nokosee smiles and looks at me. I'm smiling too.

"You're welcome."

"So tell me Big Chief Medicine Man, is that all it takes to
become a man, just walk around in the Everglades for
awhile?"

"Let's see you try it in a gee-string."

"Trust me, I don't need to prove anything to anybody and
I'm sure as hell not gonna be traipsing around this God
forsaken place in a gee-string. I've got way too many
mosquito bites on my butt as it is."

Nokosee holds out his gee-string and does a dead on
impersonation of a fast-talking TV infomercial spokesperson.
"Something that wouldn't have happened had you been
wearing Tonto's new handy dandy multi-purpose all-natural
G-2000 gee-string. Hey, are mosquitoes biting your ass?
Cover it up with a G-2000! Can't find a dishtowel when you
need one? Look no further!" Nokosee picks up the front and
wipes his hands. "And when you can't find the toilet
paper..." He whips around and acts as if he is about to drop
his drawers.

"Stop! Stop! I get the point." I'm laughing when Nokosee
turns around smiling.

"Anyway, it's about more than running around in the glades in a gee-string. It's about surviving. That's the key. But in this case, dad wants me to go into the Outside, to see, to learn and to make up my own mind about what it has to offer. If I return to my father, I will get to wear the Coat of Honor."

"The what?"

"The Coat of Honor. Oh, it's very beautiful. My mother and sister have been working on it for months. It has many bright colors, all hand sewn into different patterns. It will mark my passage to manhood."

"Hmm, sounds like a plan, I guess." I'm thinking, how naive you are. I can't tell him that, in the Outside, his mark of manhood can be bought at any souvenir shop on the res and that they'll sell it to anyone, even children.

"Plus," he adds as an afterthought, "I'm supposed to bring back Osceola's spear. You wouldn't by any chance know where it is, would ya?"

"'Osceola's spear?' I never heard of it. It's probably in some museum somewhere."

"Probably. Anyway, I'm taking you back to civilization no matter what."

"What?"

"If pop gets the ransom, fine. If he doesn't, that's okay too. It don't matter to me. There is no way I'm going to let anything happen to you."

"Oh, my God, you are so cool!" I'm so excited I throw myself at Nokosee to give him a big hug, but he reacts to my sudden movement by turning away and my momentum sends us both to the floor with me landing on top of him. "Thank you! Thank you, Nokosee!"

"So does this mean you want to mate?"

My eyes blink. I didn't see that one coming. I have to laugh and start to push away. "Oh, you are so bad." But he won't let me go. We're so close I can see the irises in his beautiful eyes moving to focus on mine.

"But that's what you like about me, right?"

"You want the truth?"

Nokosee holds up his right hand, which looks pretty silly since he's lying flat on his back. "Only but."

"You scare the crap out of me."

"Well, that's a start."

He lets go of my hand. "Stop it. I'm serious." I push away and sit up. "How could you cut up a guy like that?"

Nokosee sighs, puts his hands behind his head and stares at the thatched roof. "Good question. I wish I had an answer for you. Sometimes I scare myself. At least I didn't kill him."

"Oh, and that's supposed to be a good sign?"

"Considering how I was raised, yeah."

"Meaning?"

He turns to me. "I think my father is basically insane."

"So join the club."

"No, really. Does your dad wear the ears of the men he's killed around his neck?"

"What?"

He sits up. "I didn't think so. The ears are vintage VC. He served three tours in country and when he came back he just wasn't the same."

"I'm sure."

"He hates the Outside. With a passion. I guess that's why I do things like that. I think he passed on more to me than just his good looks."

He smiles at me before turning away. An awkward moment passes between us because I don't know what to say. This is like way too much serious stuff and it's hard to be my typical smart ass self about it. Since he's not looking at me, I find I can't take my eyes off of him. For the first time, my big gorgeous Tarzan hero looks more and more like any other boy. "How old are you Nooksy?"

"That's No-_ko_-shee." He turns back to me. "Seventeen summers."

"Nice touch. Very authentic Indian."

"How old are you?"

"Seventeen winters."

"Nice touch. Very authentic Smart Ass."

I have to admit it, I like it when I get Nokosee riled. Or any guy for that matter. It's a talent I discovered when boys discovered me. As you already know, I'm not one to keep my mouth shut especially around guys with big mouths. Once I saw I could make boys stammer and stumble over themselves just by speaking up, I was never ever going to keep my mouth shut again. As I grew older, I became more sarcastic, something I think I picked up from my dad. Too bad for Nokosee, he doesn't have a chance. Maybe that's another reason I'm attracted to him because it's something I can do and he can't. I need to know something, so I fall into my manipulative mode where I pretend to be shy. "When we get to the Outside, are you going to hang out for a little while?"

"You forget. I'm a ruthless freaking kidnapper. Hanging around wouldn't be the smartest thing to do."

"Okay, so if you *weren't* a ruthless freaking kidnapper, would you wanna hang out a little while?"

"The less the Outside knows about me the better."

I shake my head and sigh. *This guy is making me nuts.* A moment passes before he says something.

"Why do you want to know?"

"Oh, just wonderin'?"

"Would you like me to?"

"Maybe."

I steal a glance and break out in a smile; a genuine smile because he knows I'm playing him, because he's wearing the cutest grin I ever saw. I blush. He could have me right then and there if he wanted to but he's shy, or nice, or something but he won't make a move. To be honest with you, he could have had me long ago—and it has nothing to do with that Stockholm Syndrome stuff where hostages fall in love with their kidnappers. I forget how many times he saved me from getting killed by man and beast over the last couple of days, but that probably has a lot to do with it. And the fact that he's drop dead gorgeous. And the fact that he scares the living daylights out of me and fills my head day and night with his name and images of his fearless strength. And he's

only seventeen. Where or where will I ever find a guy like
this in the Outside? As far as I'm concerned, he's a keeper
and I'm going to keep him as long as I can by any means
necessary. I turn to him. "How 'bout you?"

"Maybe."

He smiles at me giving me hope before adding this: "But
I'm on a walkabout. My father will be expecting me to return
within a few days."

I just stare at him thinking I've just been bested in my
own game, suckered in with a cute grin. I don't know what
to say which might explain why I say this: "Don't you find
me the *least* bit attractive?"

Nokosee turns away and I swear, blushes under the
fluorescent light from the lantern. "Too attractive." He picks
up a rolled sleeping bag still rapped up in its plastic pack
and throws it at me.

"Hey!" I'm a little ticked off and confused by his response.

Nokosee ignores me, turns off the lantern and crawls
inside another sleeping bag before saying without looking at
me, "Sweet dreams, sweetheart."

"Humphrey Bogart?"

"'The Maltese Falcon.'"

Okay, so maybe he's going to be a tough nut to crack, but
I'm game. After all, how many kids our age know who Bogey
was? And who can impersonate him? I look at the sleeping
bag I'm holding. It's from Sears. I open it up, snuggle in and,
thanks to our nutcase dads, spend the rest of the night
talking about our favorite old movies they exposed us to
before falling asleep.

Chapter 5
Inside Outside

Morning finds me waiting in the bithlo with happy expectations like a child going to Disney World. Lying beside me in the dugout is a pair of brand new still-in-their-plastic-wrapper aluminum crutches. I'm barefoot. My injured foot, wrapped in the Ace bandage, is stretched out in front of me. When Nokosee pushes the bithlo into the water and jumps in behind me, I actually clap my hands joyfully and say, "Yes!" Nokosee smiles and shakes his head.

Within an hour, Nokosee is pausing to check the map and his hand held Global Positioning System. I'm not too surprised he has one. The sophisticated tracking device uses a satellite link to accurately find your position anywhere on earth within a few feet. Nokosee checks the latitude and longitude numbers on the liquid crystal viewing screen and matches them with numbers on the map. I'm watching him and see from Nokosee's reaction that the numbers match. But how we got to this position in the first place is the thing that perplexes me the most. I can't figure out how he distinguishes one hammock from the other on the Everglades landscape since they all look the same.

However he does it, only Nokosee can decipher which way to go. He turns off the GPS, folds up the map, and puts them back in the plastic Zip Lock pouch. He stuffs that into his sea turtle shield and shifts it onto his back. He turns to me in a playfully funny monotone.

"Paleface, how's your back?"

"Me beginning to burn, gee-string man."

"Let me put some more lotion on you."

He kneels down behind me, opens a pink "My Little Pony" backpack (I can only hope it's "Hair's"), grabs some Coppertone 45 and begins applying it to my back and arms.

"The cuts are healing."

"I know, thanks to your ancient family formula."

"Here, put some more on your legs."

When I turn around to take the lotion I stop short and laugh. "Oh, man, you never stop surprising me."

"What?"

"Like you don't know."

He shrugs.

"Wayfarers?"

"You know them?"

"It's the only kind my dad will wear."

"Same here."

"Where'd you get them?"

"You heard of 'off-the-shelf?'" Nokosee asks while rummaging around in the backpack.

"Yeah?"

He brings up another pair; the tag is still hanging from the sunglasses. "This is 'off-the-truck.' Here you go."

I take them and put them on. "Cool."

"That's what my father says."

"What's his name?"

"Seminole or English?"

"Both."

"Busimmanolotome. It means 'Panther.'"

"'Barry Manolow told me?'" I ask.

"Told you what?"

"What?"

"Nothing."

"You know Barry Manolow?"

"*You* know Barry Manolow?" I ask incredulously.

"I got most of his records."

"Oh...my...God." I say it slowly and shake my head sadly.

"What, you don't like his music?"

"You gotta be kidding me, right? You're putting me on."

"No, he's one of my dad's favorites."

"Well, if that's true, your Wayfarers have their work cut out for them." I have to laugh as Nokosee stands back up and starts poling again.

"What?"

"I wish you could see what you look like."

"Cool, right?"

"Right. Way cool." I smile and turn around.

"It's a Gestalt kinda thing, I guess."

"It's a what?" I ask while applying lotion to my legs.

"It's how you look at things. It's something my father's been trying to teach me for as long as I can remember. I must be one confusing sum of my parts, eh, pale face girl."

"That's for sure."

"I keep you on your toes, right?"

"You said it, Jack."

"That's No-*ko*-shee to you."

"Right."

"At least I'm not boring."

"Not yet." I smile. *This guy's not even near boring. That's for sure.* "Say, Nooksee-

"It's No-*ko*-shee with a long 'O', Girl-With-Name-Of-Bad-Weather. Where'd you ever get a name like that?"

"It's my nickname."

"I know. Did you earn it during a hurricane or something?"

"No, it's not an Indian thing. We don't get named because someone happened to see a moose or something when you're born. I got it because of my personality. When I was a little kid, I guess I was mad about everything. I kinda made it a lifestyle."

"For sure."

"Anyway, you wouldn't happen to have some cigarettes in that magic backpack of yours, would you?"

"Sorry. Except for the peace pipe, I don't smoke."

"Bummer. I could use a smoke right now."

"Did you know tobacco is a subversive plot by our people to get back at you for stealing our land?"

"It's not working very well."

"Yes, I know. It's taking longer than we thought. We'll have to work on something faster."

"Too bad you guys didn't discover booze. It might have worked."

"Yeah, but we aren't giving up."

"I know. Casino gambling, right?"

"Right."

A whole day passes under the hot summer sun. When I mention how hot it is, Nokosee says, "It's hotter than a goat's butt in a pepper patch." I laugh, and before you know it, we're exchanging redneck sayings. Dad would frown on this because, as you may recall, he doesn't want me sounding like I don't have "no edumacation." But I don't care. It helps kill time. The one's I share mostly come from "The Chiefs;" Nokosee's mostly from his dad.

Nokosee often refers to the map to find his way through the hammock maze. I am by this time utterly confused and lost; after a while all the hammocks begin to look the same no matter how hard I try to practice the Gestalt thing Nokosee has been teaching me as we ply our way ever so slowly through the wet prairie. By the time we pull up under another camouflaged hammock I'm sure of only one thing, Gestalt is not a Seminole word.

This hammock also has all the conveniences of home and, with the possible exception of the Stinger missiles, the local armory. By the second hammock, I'm more at ease and, I hate to think, more at home.

My God, I think while showering, *just because I know how to operate the shower without pulling it down on my head doesn't mean I could live here! I don't care how good looking this guy is, how he makes me laugh or how safe he makes me feel, I ain't ever gonna live in a snake pit like this.* I pause to catch my thoughts. *Why do I keep fantasizing about this? I must be crazy! The guy's got land mines all around the perimeter of his chickees. God, he's even got me talking like some kinda soldier. When was the last time I ever said 'perimeter'?* I look around to see if I can see him. *I can't believe he doesn't want to see me naked?*

Wait, he's already seen me naked. I know, I know. But I was unconscious. I wasn't really there. It's not the same. Most guys I know would be all over me. I'd be fighting them off at every turn. Not this guy, he doesn't seem to be the least bit interested. I don't get it. He must be gay.

I decide to take action by taking advantage of an opportunity that presents itself the next morning to see if he really is gay. Nokosee is swimming in the water under the spreading branches of the hammock. I decide to join him. I drop my crutches at the water's edge and take his extended hand. I pretend to lose my balance and fall into his arms. I look up at him with my big sad blue eyes and the next thing I know, he's picking me up and carrying me out into the deeper water. He gently sets me down, turns and dives into the water. While he's underwater, I quickly unsnap my bra, slip it off and throw it onto the hammock shoreline. By the time he pops up about 10 yards away, I've settled into the water and removed my shorts and undies. I wave to him. When he dives and starts swimming underwater towards me I squeeze my clothes into a wet ball and throw them toward the shoreline. When he pops up next to me, I rise slowly out of the water while pulling my wet hair back as casually as possible. I let a moment pass before looking at him. I'm surprised he isn't looking at my boobs. Instead, he's looking me straight in the eyes.

"Feeling a little chilly, are you?" he asks with an arched eyebrow and cocked head.

"A little," I reply with a sly smile. I take a breath and dive under the water and make it a point to show off my stark white and impossibly firm butt. I guess it was too much for him because he grabs my foot and starts hauling me back through the water. I'm scared, I guess I finally went too far and pressed too many buttons because, despite who I think I am, I'm not ready to lose my virginity in the middle of the freaking Everglades to a guy I hardly know.

I emerge coughing up water and puking snot out of my nose. He grabs me around my waist and pulls me toward him. I try to push away but it's like pushing against a granite wall. Despite my efforts, I can't free myself from his grip.

And then I feel it. Big, long, and hard.

"Stop!" I scream. I start slapping his chest with my fists. "Let me go!"

Nokosee pushes me away and I fall backward into the dark, tannic water. When I come up coughing and spitting, I push my hair away from my eyes and see him standing there breathing hard with his hands on his hips and looking away.

"I'm sorry," he says. "I didn't mean it."

"No, Nokosee, I'm sorry. I shouldn't have been teasing you."

He looks at me. "Is that what you were doing?"

"Yes. I was trying to find out if you were gay and--"

"—And now you know. Are you satisfied?"

While I'm trying to wipe away the snot from under my nose I stop short when I look at him. "Nokosee, am I making you blush?"

"How can you tell? I'm a freakin' Indian."

"You *are* turning red!"

He turns back. "It's all I can do to keep my hands off of you."

I gotta tell you, I didn't expect to hear him say that. I didn't know guys like that existed. In that one sentence, he made me feel special. And less than worthy. It was my Adam and Eve moment. For the first time I saw what it really was all about, you know, sex and all of that commitment and love stuff. Whoe, talk about heavy. I suddenly didn't like myself very much anymore. I turned around and started looking for my clothes but I couldn't find them anywhere.

"Where are my clothes?"

"Dammit!" Nokosee sees King Roar swimming away. "Haalpatee! Haalpatee!" He starts running in the water toward the gator but it begins swimming faster. "Haalpatee!"

"Are you telling me that gator just ate my clothes?"

I'm crouching and trying to cover myself as much as possible in the shallow water near the shore when Nokosee stops, turns around, and looks at me.

"Aw geese." Nokosee sighs and shakes his head. "Give it a rest."

"What? You think I'm still trying to seduce you? Your stupid gator just ran off with all of my clothes!"

"I can't believe this is happening to me." He starts walking through the water toward me.

"*You* can't believe this is happening? How do you think *I* feel?"

"Why are you botherin' to cover yourself up now after what you just did?"

"I'm sorry, Nokosee. Please forgive me."

As Nokosee strides by I lose my balance-- *really*-- and unintentionally, instinctively-- I *swear*-- grab the back of his loincloth for support and end up dragging it down with me into the water.

Man, I wish you could have been there. It was one of the funniest things I ever saw. Here's this big macho guy who could probably kick all those Ultimate Fighter jocks with their cauliflower ears with one hand tied behind his back acting like a little prissy prude screaming his head off. I've never seen anybody work so hard to keep his pants on, or in this case, his gee-string up. I start laughing and have to let go. That only makes him crazier. He yanks up his gee-string, turns around and yells at me in a voice register approaching falsetto.

"Grow up!"

I *really* want to tell him I'm sorry but I can't stop laughing.

##

The price I pay for yanking on Superman's cape keeps me naked in the water another hour. Nokosee is making me wait there where it's "safe" while he sits in the chickee eating an MRE and watching me. I don't know what to do. Either the gators will get me in the water or some kind of explosive device will kill me on the beach. I'm not in any hurry to find out-- or getting naked for Nokosee again. So I just stay in the water hoping that he won't let anything happen to me. Maybe if I begged it would help, but I refuse to beg. I don't know what finally made him throw me a solar blanket. Maybe he saw me shivering. Maybe he just finally got over being mad. Who knows? In any event, he can't break camp fast enough.

I fashion a short mini dress out of the solar blanket and know I look like some kind of lost space alien sitting in the bithlo. Because of the reflective nature of the item, it can be seen for miles, perhaps even on Venus.

I don't know where we're going. Nokosee won't speak to me. I turn around to try to break the tension.

"Penny for your thoughts?" I ask with an innocent smile.

"Man, do I feel sorry for your old man. I can't wait to give you back to him."

I turn away and pout. "Oh, you're no fun."

"I didn't come here to do the Great White Father's daughter. I'm on a bigger mission."

I laugh out loud. "Oh, please! You're killing me! You're so out of it, it's scary! Anyway, there was no way I was going to let you *do* me."

"I could have if I wanted to and you couldn't have stopped me."

That makes me stop and think. He's right, of course, and I'm glad it turned out the way it did. I don't want the rest of the trip to go on like this so I try to add a little levity. "Yeah, but you're a pagan caveman *gentleman;* you'd never do anything like that. Right?"

My voice shakes and gives me away because, as I'm talking, I can see in my mind how it could have turned out. Nokosee doesn't say anything—unlike me; I just can't seem to keep my mouth shut.

"Anyway, aren't you saving yourself for some Indian princess? That's it, isn't it?" I say as I turn around to face him. "You're scoutin' for a chickee chick! You've gotta go inside the Outside to find-- What was it you called her?" I pause for effect. "A *mate*? What, aren't I good enough for you? Not pure enough for the New Seminole line?"

Nada from Nokosee.

"Oh, that's right, get stoic on me. Typical New Seminole." I turn away and shake my head disappointedly. I feel like I'm in a bad marriage. And I'm trembling.

##

For the next four hours, no one speaks to each other; the silence is more deafening than the dry hot stillness of the Everglades. Even the ever-present buzzing insects are hushed by the oppressing sunlight and heat. That all changes when I happen to look up and see a few turkey vultures circling overhead. I wonder if they know something I don't. When I turn to call Nokosee's attention to it, I see what the buzzards are really circling over: a wrecked, smoking helicopter. I point and yell, "Nokosee! Look! It's one of the park helicopters!"

Of course, he's seen it long before I have, probably been closing in on the circling vultures for God-Knows-How-Long. I watch him exhale and collapse upon himself.

"Let's see if anyone's alive," I say.

"Let's not," Nokosee replies. He drives his pole hard through the water.

"What, are you crazy? Maybe someone's still alive!"

"Trust me, no one's alive."

"But you just can't go by without checking. What if you're wrong?" I'm ignored. No one ignores me. "Screw you!"

I turn around, throw my legs over the side of the bithlo and jump into the water; it comes just over my knees. Before Nokosee can react, I've already made a few awkward strides toward the wreckage.

"Get back here!"

I look back and see his intense, almost frightened look. "Up yours!"

He throws the pole into the bithlo and jumps into the water. I see him coming toward me, splashing through the water as if he were possessed. I turn and try to out run him through the shallow water but my injured ankle is slowing me down. I can hear him closing in and try to concentrate on the wreckage and as my eyes tighten on my goal, I begin to see the outlines of two bloated bodies hanging out of the crumpled cabin; two men being picked apart by a pair of buzzards. I stop running.

Is one of them my dad?

I see the rotting flesh and their naked bones; and the evenly spaced bullet holes marching across the broken fuselage toward the shattered glass and the bodies before Nokosee grabs me and spins me around. The buzzards flutter upward for a moment before returning to their afternoon snack.

"Is that my father?"

"No," Nokosee says while struggling to hold me back.

"How do you know?"

"Let's get out of here."

"It's the same helicopter isn't it?"

"What are you talking about?"

"It's the same one that spotted us a few nights ago! I know it is!"

"No it isn't. Let's go."

"No!" I scream, pounding my hands against Nokosee's chest. "It's the same helicopter and you know it! Someone shot it down!"

"You're crazy!"

I start kicking and Nokosee twists me around in his arms and, with my back to him, puts his finger on a spot on my neck. With just a little pressure, he cuts off the blood flow to my brain and within seconds, I'm dead weight in his arms. When I wake up a few minutes later, I'm back on the bithlo and moving swiftly through the still water. I grab my stiff neck and moan, "You bastard."

He doesn't say anything. I turn my head to the side, cover my eyes and begin to cry softly. Within minutes, my soft crying has turned into *real* body wrenching sobs.

"Stormy," Nokosee finally says, "you're going to have to trust me on this one. Your father wasn't in that wreckage."

Holding my neck, I try to stop crying and turn to look up at him. "How do you know?"

"I checked it out when you were out. It wasn't him."

I pause and look at him closely. "You're lying," I cry, wiping away my tears with the back of my hand. "I can tell. You never checked it out."

"Fine, don't believe me but think about this: if it was him, we would have heard about it by now on TV."

"I want to believe you, but I don't trust you anymore."

He doesn't say anything. I roll over onto my side, rest my head on my arm and try to stop crying. I know that if my father were alive he would be very disappointed in me for crying. Like going all the way, it's not something Sam Jones' little girl does.

I'm sorry I can't be everything you want me to be, dad. But then, I don't know anybody who could.

I can't shake loose the thought that my dad was in the wreckage; that it was the same helicopter that had swooped low over the hammock the first night of the fire.

Now it all makes sense. I know the chopper was loud, but I swear I heard machine gun fire. That's why it pulled away so quickly. Someone was shooting at it. But who? Nokosee was with me. Is there someone else out there? Who'd shoot down an unarmed helicopter?

His dad.

That guy sounds crazy enough to do anything. Sane people don't need to stockpile Stinger missiles. He was the one Nokosee was arguing with on the stolen cell phone. Yeah, his dad is probably telling him to get rid of me. I know too much. Thank God his son has a mind of his own.

I pause to sort through a number of reasons why Nokosee wants me to live, but I only need one reason that negates all of the above.

He's not taking me to my father; he's taking me someplace to kill me!

Chapter 6

Death on the Water

I decide to fight back. Somehow.

My God, the guy's a freakin' killin' machine.

We enter another canal and Nokosee is hugging the right bank to conceal his presence in the tall sawgrass that has grown up on its sides.

I can't overpower him. He's the strongest person I ever met. He uses that knife like those samurai do in those '60's Japanese movies my dad has made me watch since I was a kid. Tifuro Mifune. I'm probably the only girl my age who knows who starred in those movies. Directed by Kurosawa. Dad says that name so reverently it scares me. God, he even had me learning karate.

I look at the water passing ever so slowly by.

Wish I hadn't given it up.

I see Nokosee's reflection in the water.

I don't like sitting in front of him like this. He could slip up behind me and cut my throat. I wouldn't know what hit me. The first opportunity I get I'm gonna shake this guy before he does me in. And if I can't do that...If I have to, I'm gonna kill him. If that's what it takes, I'm gonna kill him.

Like I could kill him. Anyway, no sooner do I make that decision, fate hands me the opportunity to find out if I could. My outer space mini dress has attracted the attention of a small private plane. The sun reflecting off the material has caught the pilot's eye and he's tilting his wing toward us.

Nokosee hears the plane's engine and turns quickly to it. He sees it swooping low over the canal and coming our way.

I dive into the water, swim toward the center of the canal and start shouting and waving my hands for all I'm worth. I look back and Nokosee is already swimming towards me. I use my crawl stroke to swim away and swim right out of my mini.

Nokosee sees the reflective blanket floating on the water, grabs it and takes it down with him, diving below the surface just as the plane roars by. I keep waving and watching the plane and when it flies by just over my head, I know exactly what it is. It's a Micco. The Seminoles make them and I swear Nokosee's dad is flying it! I mean there was an Indian inside wearing a Seminole jacket and war paint and the plane is all black except for its tail which has four stripes painted across it—white, black, red, and yellow; the colors of the Seminole flag—and a red fist holding a tomahawk. I look back. Nokosee is swimming after me. I turn to swim and stop short. I can't believe what I'm seeing. I scream.

Hundreds of dead fish are floating toward me. The smell is overwhelming. The idea of swimming through them repulses me and I can't hold my breath long enough to swim under them because there's way too many.

Nokosee chooses for me. Before I'm aware of his presence, he swims up behind me, slips his arm around me and drags me back to the bithlo. I scream louder this time and start kicking and flaying my arms because I am *so* frustrated and angry and try to shake loose but I cannot. When we reach the bithlo, Nokosee orders me to get in and get dressed.

"No!" I yell while hanging onto the side of the bithlo. "You're trying to kill me!"

"What?"

"So I won't tell anyone about what I saw!"

"Oh, please," Nokosee replies angrily. "If I wanted to kill you, I could have drowned you just now!"

I don't have time to consider that because the dead fish are floating in on the conversation.

"Oh, God!" I cry out. Before Nokosee knows what has happened, I'm out of the water and in the bithlo. He throws me the space dress and follows after me. While I'm wrapping it around me and Velcroing up the sides, Nokosee drives the pole through the floating carcasses.

"What's happening?" I ask.

"I don't know."

An undulating carpet of death soon replaces the water's surface. When we look down the length of the canal all we see is more dead fish and a dark, swirling cloud just over the water that obliterates the horizon. As we push on, we hear a low humming that comes and goes with the swarming of a hundred thousand flying insects. Many are giant horseflies and, in their feeding frenzy, begin attacking us. The bites are painful and plentiful, with the rapidity of machine gun fire.

"Jump in the water!" Nokosee yells.

"No way!"

"It's either that or get eaten alive." Nokosee drops his pole into the bithlo and dives in.

I see the pole and think about escaping but the intensity of the aerial onslaught quickly quells that idea. The insects are biting me all over. Slapping at them does no good.

Nokosee reaches up out of the rotting, stinking, bloated fish bodies, grabs my arm and yanks me out of the bithlo. When I come up I know the putrid mess is all around me and I don't want to breathe or open my eyes-- until I bang my head against the bithlo and all of the horrible sights and smells come rushing in. Gasping, reeling, I grab the dugout and find Nokosee next to me.

"Get behind me." He swims around me through the dead fish and flies and grabs the bithlo. "Hold on and start kicking."

As we start kicking and pushing the bithlo through the water, a horse fly bites me on the temple. I cry out, slap at it and miss. Another one takes a bite out of one of my hands holding onto the bithlo. I yell, slap, and miss again. "I can't take this anymore," I yell.

"Here," Nokosee shouts over the din, "hold on to me. Put your head in the water and only come up to take a breath."

Again, I don't have to be told twice. I lock my hands around Nokosee's broad chest and bury my face in the water. His body is pushing aside most of the dead fish but when I hear him cry out, I realize that he is still getting bitten.

I start kicking harder and try to concentrate on my kicking so I don't have to hear him, or think about him. I can *feel* his bites. His arms and shoulders are trembling. I know he's trying to keep from crying out, just like my dad.

You remind me so much of my father. Macho men. No wussies here. So gallant. Eddie you're not. That jerk. I can't believe I'm even thinking about him.

I try to focus. *Lord, please help me help Nokosee.*

I can't believe I prayed. It's so unusual. You know what they say, there are no atheists in fox holes. Not that I am one. I'm officially a Lutheran like dear ol' dad. I don't know how he can sit there and listen to that stuff. The music sucks big time. Hasn't anyone in the Lutheran church discovered rock n' roll yet? My God, we're still singing hymns that are 500 years old and they wonder why no one's going to church? At least when I get back home mom doesn't force me to go to church. Hell, she doesn't go either so it makes it pretty easy.

I pause again to offer up another prayer. *I'm sorry, Lord, for everything I just thought. Please forgive me and help me focus. Help us get out of here. Amen.*

"Stormy?"

I raise my head out of the water.

"You been prayin'?"

"Why?"

"They're gone."

"What?" I look around. "Where'd they go?"

"They just disappeared. They're all behind us now." He turns to me. "C'mon, get back up in the bithlo."

"Oh, my God, Nokosee!"

Nokosee's face and arms are covered by hundreds of red welts from the insect bites. His eyes are nearly swollen shut. I extend my hand to touch his face but he grabs it and, looking down and to the side like a blind man, tells me once more in a shaking voice to get into the bithlo.

"Nokosee, please, let me help you."

"Just get into the bithlo." His arm begins to shake and he lets go of my hand and grips the bithlo.

"You're having some kind of reaction!"

"No," Nokosee replies, his voice quivering, "I'm not having any kind of reaction. Just get back into the bithlo. Please."

I can't take my eyes off of him but I do as he says. I lean over, grab his arm and struggle to pull him into the bithlo. Nokosee groans and falls onto his back.

"Stormy, get the magic backpack."

I pick it up.

"Open it. See the small Tupperware container? It's got papa's miracle salve in it. Throw it to me."

I pop the lid and sniff. "This is the stuff you used on me." He nods weakly. "It works." He nods again. "Let me put it on you." I kneel and apply the salve over his face and arms.

"Thanks."

"You know, you could probably make some money off this stuff."

"Yeah," Nokosee says weakly, "Papa Big Chief's Miracle Salve."

"Yeah, but with your face on it."

"Before or after the miracle cure?"

"After," I say warmly. "Always after."

Nokosee doesn't hear me. He's trying to focus on anything but the pain. I continue to massage in the lotion and am surprised to find myself smiling at him.

"You are my hero," I say softly because I don't want him to hear it. And because I mean it. "I'm not going to let anything happen to you either." I turn away and look at the canal bank.

I can't see the horizon because of the tall sawgrass and shrubs that are growing along the bank. I start to stand but stop to catch myself, to steady the bithlo. I rise slowly to an almost erect posture and, getting my footing, stand as tall as I can.

To the west lies the endless Everglades; to the east, the endless Everglades. The smoke and fire are far off in the distance behind us. I look down at my suffering Adonis.

I can't believe this is happening to me. I can't believe I found someone like you in the middle-of-nowhere. There is no way I'm going to let anything happen to you. There is no way I'm going to let you get away.

I see his body tremble and quickly drop to my knees to ask if he's okay. He doesn't hear me. I look for something to cover him but can't find anything. Except for my space dress. I rip it off to cover his body. Once I've tucked it around him, I carefully lean back and grab the sea turtle shield and start to put it on my back to keep from getting sunburned but stop short. The words he crudely painted on the sea turtle shield, the ones I never really looked at because I thought they were written in Seminole suddenly leap out at me. It's English and he's written them backwards! I start following them across the shield and break out smiling when I come to the end: If you can read this, you're too damn close!

What a kidder. Yeah, a kidder-killer. Or a dyslexic kidder-killer.

I remember the map and look inside. The body armor reminds me again of my many unanswered questions but I try to dismiss them. I open the Zip Lock pouch, pull out the map and unfold it.

Nothing too unusual about it; its your basic U.S. Geologic Survey map. Very business like in its approach to telling you where you are; no cute pictures or color, just lots of dots scattered across the line map of a vast collection of white space filling the area between Naples and Ft. Lauderdale. This vast white space is the Everglades and the Big Cypress National Preserve. It shows where the canals have been dug and the roads have been laid but it can't show you where the hammocks are because there are just too many of them and they're always changing and, let's face it, if you've seen one, you've seen them all.

Except on this map. Nokosee's father has put an "X" and the longitude and latitude of every hammock he's stockpiled with contraband and weapons. I see another "X" marking a spot with "R.P" written above it. Believe it or not, I've been there. It's the Raccoon Point oil well site. That's right, they're pumping oil out there. Been doing it since the 1970's. Dad wants to see it shut down; fears if anything should go wrong it will destroy the Everglades. I see the words "New Seminole" written in a curve between the Everglades and the east coast of south Florida. It's been underlined twice. I see a list of phone numbers on one side of the map. They have all been crossed out except the last one.

These must be phone numbers from the stolen cell phones. I wonder if he's got another one around?

I look in the shield behind the body armor. I can't see anything. I slip my hand down between the body armor and the sea turtle shell. It touches something; I bring it up. It's a medicine vial. The name on the prescription has been inked out. In its place the word "cyanide" has been written. Immediately I think of the Nazis. My dad made me watch the History Channel with him so I "might learn something." I did. I learned that the top SS boys and Hitler himself committed suicide by biting cyanide capsules.

My God, is this what his father wants him to do if he's caught? What the hell is going on here? Screw that.

I toss the vial into the water and dig into the shield again. This time I come up with another cell phone. I quickly flip it open.

"Ou, Motorola, the best."

At least it is according to my dad because it was made in the U.S. of A and, I can hear him now, "you should always buy American first." I turn it on and check the battery level. It's low; real low. I look at Nokosee. He's still shivering but it doesn't look like he's going to be able to stop me either. I punch in my dad's cell phone number. The phone is ringing.

"Oh, my God," I shout out loud. I can't believe it. It keeps ringing. "Please, please, somebody answer it!"

And someone does.

"Hello?" It's my dad.

"Daddy!" I scream.

"Stormy?"

I can hardly hear him. The signal is fading in and out. "Daddy! I'm alive! I'm still alive!"

"Where are you?"

I look around. "I don't know! Wait a minute!" I look at the map but can't figure out where I am. I look up. "I'm in a canal in the middle of the freakin' Everglades!"

"What?"

I can hardly hear him. I look at the phone. It's dead. "No!" I put the phone back to my ear. "Daddy! Daddy!"

Nothing.

I scream and throw the cell phone far out into the water. I ball up my fists and hit my sunburned thighs and curse the God I prayed to only minutes before.

"Why are you doing this to me?"

No answer.

I shrug and try to get a grip. I concentrate on bringing my breathing down and look up. Nokosee is still out of it, still shivering. I pause and wipe away tears that are welling up in my eyes. I take a long deep breath and then let it out. I put the map back into its pouch, slip it in behind the body armor, and slip the shield over my back. When I pick up the pole and rise tentatively to my feet and find myself standing stark naked in the bithlo with a shield on my back and a fallen warrior hero at my feet I am immediately reminded of the ancient Mediterranean culture of the Amazon warrior. All armies feared these women because they fought with such fierceness.

And they fought stark naked. If I'm not the closest thing to an Amazon warrior in 3,000 years, I'll be surprised.

I take the spear-- because that's what it is to me now, because that's how Nokosee used it-- raise it over my head with both hands and yell as loud as I can to any living thing that might hear me.

"I will not die! Do you hear me, you bastards? I will not die!"

Chapter 7

Further

If I hadn't applied Nokosee's purloined sun tan lotion, I wouldn't be thinking, an hour later, that it's pretty cool being the only stark naked Amazon warrior in the world. Despite my mother's repeated warnings about the dangers of too much sun, I'm poling through the water confidently knowing I'm getting an all-over tan and some exercise to boot. Considering what I've just been through, I'm proud of my positive outlook, it's something I've been working on, to, as mom says, "turn lemons into lemonade." I know I'm a whiner; my dad never fails to remind me of that and for the last year I've been making a dedicated effort to change my approach to the world.

He'd be proud of me today.

I pause and correct myself.

No, he'd have a problem with the nudity.

I turn and scan the seemingly endless Everglades. There is nothing I can see that tells me I'm living in today's modern world and there is no mother or father to admonish me for my wanton ways. I find my nakedness in the wilderness to be exhilarating; it empowers me and puts a surreal edge on the moment. If there ever was, to paraphrase Tom Wolfe, "a girl in full," it's me. I start singing out loud and a little off key-- I don't care, who's going to hear me? Nokosee? He's dead to the world-- the Alice Cooper hit my dad introduced me to and later regretted: "I'm seventeen, and I'll do what I want! Seventeen, I just don't know what I want! Seventeen, I gotta get away!"

I lift the pole and, in a crouch, play it like a StratoCaster low on my leg, head bopping to the chords I'm humming. My head is full of songs and the breeze across my body calls up another one with the goose pimples and my nipples that I rise to sing, shaking my breasts like some kind of bar top stripper: "I'm too sexy for my body, too sexy for my clothes."

Sure, they're old, written before I was born, but like my dad has said more than once, "they still rock," and after enough summers, I've come to agree.

While shaking my boobs, I have to laugh. "If I'm as bad as you think I am, then daddy, you made me that way. It's all your fault, daddy, I'm a bad, bad girl. It's all that rock and roll you made me listen to. 'No! No! You can't listen to rap! It's the music of a bankrupt culture! Listen to this stuff instead.' Well I did, daddy, and now I'm dancing the hootchie-kootch stark naked in the middle of the Everglades with a pagan caveman."

I pause to look at Nokosee.

"Well, he's not actually dancing at the moment. He's just kinda lyin' there looking too good for words, but this guy can do anything and I'll bet he could dance the pants off anybody too. Look at me! Yahoo!"

I lift the pole above my head with both hands and dance in a circle in the back of the bithlo, rocking it back and forth.

"Talk about a vision."

I scream. It's Nokosee. His voice is weak and shaky and he's peering up at me, squinting at the sun over my shoulder. I catch myself in mid-turn, drop quickly to one knee in the bithlo, fold my arms across my boobs and come eye-to-eye with his gee-string. He's got a hard on.

"Nokosee!"

"Whatever I drank in the smoke hut," he says, pausing to catch his breath, "I want more of it."

"I thought you were sleeping."

"I was until I heard you singing. You should stick to dancing."

"And you should mind your own business."

He's in no hurry to turn from my eyes. Or put it down. He's smiling when he says this: "You really are something else."

I look away, embarrassed. "Is that good or bad?"

"It's good."

"Thanks, I think."

"I like your spirit."

"Well, that's a first. No guy ever told me he liked my spirit before." I try to be mature and look back.

"Yeah, well, that and the other things that go with it." An eyebrow starts dancing. "If you know what I mean."

I do. "My God, Nokosee! You're supposed to be sick!"

"There are no secrets in a gee-string. Know what I mean?"

"Who's teasing now? Give me back my space dress," I say firmly.

"Remind me to keep my mouth shut." He sits up and struggles to free himself of the blanket.

I grab my space dress. "Nokosee, it's not your mouth that got you into trouble. Do you mind?" I motion for him to turn around so that I can put it on.

Nokosee turns slowly onto his side and looks toward the bow. "Yeah, guys in gee-strings don't stand much of a chance in singles bars."

"Trust me, in your case, Nokosee, that isn't necessarily so."

"You mean I might get lucky?"

"Again, in your case, my pagan caveman, luck would have nothing to do with it."

"Can I turn around now? It's kinda uncomfortable laying like this."

"I'll bet." Thank God for Velcro. "Yeah, you can turn around."

"Think you and I might go dancin' someday?"

"It depends."

"Depends on what?"

"It depends on whether or not you pick me up in a loincloth."

"And if I did?"

"That's a good question. What kinda car are you drivin'?"

Nokosee laughs, shakes his head and looks away. "Too much."

"What's so funny?"

Before he can answer, a deep rumbling roar begins to rise out of the sawgrass. We turn to it. It's racing toward us but we can't see it because of the tall sawgrass. As it quickly closes in, the sound becomes a high-pitched whine and the surface of the water begins to vibrate. Nokosee looks from one side of the bithlo to the other and for a third time, it looks like Nokosee is afraid.

Suddenly, the biggest passenger jet I've ever seen explodes out over the tops of the sawgrass. The huge shadow casting wings of the A380 AirBus race over us-- close, low, and so loud I have to cover my ears.

Nokosee jumps back and falls out of the bithlo into the water. I grab the sides and, crouching, try to steady the bithlo to keep it from flipping over. But the noise is so loud, I let go to cover my ears again. I can feel the heat from the four mammoth jet engines. I look up to see four blinding suns spouting flame and black smoke as the jet rising majestically into the air. And for the first time, I know exactly where I am; I'm almost home.

"Welcome to my world, kiddo," I scream over the impossibly loud jet engines. I look down at Nokosee cowering against the side of the bithlo. "Heap big medicine," I shout while pointing at the receding mechanical marvel. "Heap big medicine!" I look down at him, laughing. "Nokosee, you should see yourself." I try not to laugh because it's so embarrassing.

Nokosee blushes again and turns away as if ashamed. He sees something on the water and tries to pick it up but whatever it is, slips from his hand. I look closer as he tries again and it turns out he's trying to pick up a rainbow. But it's not a rainbow, it's an oil slick and it's all around us. And there's something else. We can smell it. He sees them first: hundreds of rotting fish are floating toward us. Again. He struggles to pull himself back into the bithlo and falls into it shivering. He looks up and sees me kneeling over him.

"Are you okay?" I ask.

"The...The rainbow is killing the fish," he stammers.

"That's no rainbow, you idiot! It's an oil slick." I look around. "But you're right about one thing, it's killing the fish." I turn back to him. "Nokosee, welcome to the Outside. I guess it begins here. It ain't Oz; our Yellow Brick Road is paved with dead fish. How appropriate. The rainbow, however, is a nice touch. All I have to do is follow it and it'll take me home. It's on the other side of the sawgrass, not that far away. Thirty years ago Miami wanted to build a new airport in the Everglades to handle the new bigger, faster supersonic transports that were coming. They got as far as one runway when Congress deep-sixed it. They use it now for pilot training, touch-and-goes, that sort of thing. And you know what? I bet there's a control tower there for somebody to tell these pilots when they can land and I'm going to find it." I get up and start to pole toward the other side of the canal bank.

"No!" Nokosee tries to get up.

"Don't try to stop me, Nokosee!" I hold the pole in front of me, ready to bring it down across his head. "I swear I'll clobber you aside the head with this thing."

Nokosee settles back but when I relax for a second, he springs toward me and tries to grab the pole. On a better day it would have been no contest but on this day, Nokosee is a little weaker and a little slower. And a little less lucky. I crack him hard across the top of his head with the pole and he falls in a lump at my feet.

Holy crap! I hope I didn't kill him!

I cautiously squat before him and look to see if he's breathing. He is but his head is bleeding and a nasty white knot is growing on his temple.

Oh, man, I can't believe this! I didn't mean to hit him that hard.

I start to move toward him to see if I can stop the bleeding when King Roar rises slowly up out of the water beside the bithlo. The damn thing scares me silly anyway, but seeing it rising like a submarine so close to me, so big and black and as long as the bithlo, makes me forget where I am and I lose my footing and stumble onto Nokosee knocking the wind out of him.

Nokosee's moan excites the crazy gator. I guess it thinks I'm trying to hurt his little buddy or something because it opens its big tooth infested mouth and bites the bithlo. I jump back and would have flipped the whole thing over if the gator hadn't been trying to eat the other side. He lifts himself out of the water and tries to crawl into the bithlo.

Oh my God, he's trying to capsize us!

The bithlo rolls down toward the gator and water rushes over the side. I try to hold on and throw my leg over the opposite side but the giant gator wiggles itself off and dives beneath the surface.

The bithlo rocks backward and I'm thrown out. I feel the gator's rough, jagged skin brush my legs underwater just before the tail slams against them.

I'm in the air, trailing a stream of water as I arc across the sky. And I'm screaming too. And, all of a sudden, it's in slow motion: I look down and see Nokosee on his side, his face in the water coming over the edge.

I reach down and grab the bithlo and fall onto Nokosee. Again. The impact makes him cough up bubbles.

"Nokosee!"

As I struggle to lift his head out of the water, I see the huge dark shape of the alligator swimming swiftly and silently beneath the bithlo.

Oh my God, he must have been following us all along.

I turn and shout over Nokosee's bleeding head.

"Look you crazy gator, he's still alive!"

Nokosee coughs up more water and falls back into the bithlo.

"Now leave us alone!"

King Roar surfaces next to the bithlo. I see the gator eyeing me with its one good devilish eye and then Nokosee who is trying to sit up. I help him and hold him in my arms as he spits out something in a hoarse voice that makes the gator slap its tail against the water, splattering us with the remnants of the broken rainbow before disappearing beneath the surface.

"He's always been out there, hasn't he?"

"Forever," Nokosee answers weakly.

I turn to Nokosee and see the blood running down the side of his face and suddenly don't feel like the Queen of the World anymore. "I'm so sorry."

"Man," Nokosee says while tentatively touching his head wound, "that was one hell of a wallop you gave me."

"I'm so sorry, Nokosee. I didn't mean to hit you that hard."

"Tell my lawyer."

"You got a lawyer?"

He gives me a look and sadly shakes his head.

"Well, I don't know," I stammer, all flustered and nervous. "I figure you might have one on retainer or something what with all the kidnapping and gun running you're doing."

He looks at me again and rolls his eyes.

"Nice move," he says while feeling the bump on his head. "I'm impressed. Man, do I need an aspirin. Could you get me the 'magic backpack?'" As he struggles to sit up, I reach behind him and pull out the pink "My Little Pony" backpack. "Look inside. I'm sure I've got some in there."

"Are you kidding me?" I ask as I start rummaging around. "What don't you have in here?" I stop short. "Whoe, what's this?" I pull out a pack of Trojans and show them to Nokosee.

"In case I get lucky." He turns away with a shy smile and looks at the water.

"Well, the way you're going, buddy, living out here like some kinda swamp rat, you're gonna need something like Lottery luck for you to score."

"Stormy," he says, still looking at the water, "I think I have scored. I just need to collect the check."

"Are you trying to tell me something?"

Nokosee pauses before turning from the water to look at me. "No. I'm just talkin'; dreamin' out loud. Hell, I've just been knocked on the head. I don't know what I'm saying. I'm delirious. That's why I need those aspirins?"

"Forget the aspirins." I'm curious about what he's implying. "Are you still attracted to me? After all this?"

"Call me a Neanderthal," Nokosee says slowly, "but I still am."

"What, was it the way I brained you?" I ask with a nervous smile. "Is that what it takes to win the pagan caveman's heart?"

Nokosee just smiles.

"Is it my eyes?"

"Sky eyes," he says with a tender smile.

"What's that in Seminole?"

"I can't tell you."

"Why not?"

"Tradition. We like to keep some things secret from the white man."

"C'mon, Nokosee."

"Sorry."

"So this is how you plan on scoring points with me? Let me tell you, it isn't working."

Nokosee pauses and then says: *Holatte-Sutv Turwv.*"

"Sounds like a Starbuck's coffee." I repeat it as best as I can. "Could that be my Indian name?"

"You mean your human bein' name?"

"Yeah, my human bein' name?"

If you want it to be."

I try the name out loud again. "I like it. Do you have a last name?"

"Sure. Why wouldn't I?"

"I don't know. I don't want to assume anything about the," I pause to add quote marks in the air with my fingers, 'New Seminoles.' Maybe it's some kinda white man thing."

"It is but my father says we're descendants of Osceola so I guess that's my last name. I've never really thought about it. Does it matter?"

"Not really." I start playing with the sound of my new Seminole name and the Osceola surname together in my head. "Just curious."

"So, Stormy Jones," Nokosee says slowly, measuring his words, "are you still attracted to me?"

I pause and the first words that rush into my mind are, *Oh my God, yes!* But I don't say them. Instead I say this: "A little."

"What would it take to make it 'a lot'?"

I don't know what to say because, despite having never met a guy like him before I can't see anything ever coming of it. I'm a city girl, he's a pagan caveman and there's just no way this is ever going to happen. Before I get a chance to respond, Nokosee asks me a question.

"Would it take a Corvette?"

I turn to him. "You must think I'm pretty shallow."

"Would it take air-conditioning?"

I take a deep breath and try to stop the tears welling up in my eyes. "Yeah, it would take air-conditioning. Here!" I throw the backpack at him. "Look for your own damn aspirins. And as for these," I hold up the Trojans, "you just ran out of luck." I rear back and throw them over his head into the water.

King Roar breaks the surface, swallows the condom pack with a smack of its giant mouth, arches its back and dives silently beneath the water, dragging down its long prehistoric tail, one supple dragon vertebrae after another.

I turn away to wipe my eyes.

"I'm sorry, Stormy. You didn't deserve that. I didn't mean to hurt you. I think I'm just mad I can't have you."

"My God, Nokosee," I shout, turning swiftly on him, tears rolling from my eyes, "do you always have to say everything you feel?"

Nokosee is caught off guard. He's surprised by my reaction. "I'll try not to in the future," he says. "I guess I'm just not use to talkin' to people. I only have my family and--"

"Shut up! For Pete's sake will you please just shut up?"

Nokosee sees how angry I am and turns away. The bithlo drifts into the foliage along the canal bank. He grabs a tree trunk and pushes the bithlo back towards the center of the canal. With a painful effort, he turns and calls out to King Roar. The gator breaks the surface next to the bithlo. I sit up and try to squeeze myself into a smaller space as Nokosee stretches out across the bithlo, grabs a rope attached to the bow and throws it into the water.

"Haalpatee, elichko!" he yells at the gator.

The animal takes the end of the rope in its mouth and, with a powerful stroke of its tail, moves quickly ahead. When the rope is drawn tight, the bithlo is yanked forward, jarring us. Nokosee watches for a moment and then turns around. He digs into the backpack, finds the aspirins and pops two into his mouth. He grabs a bottle of Evian rolling about in the bithlo, unscrews the cap and takes a long swallow. He sees me looking at him.

"My father said you used to be able to swallow your aspirins by leaning over the side of your bithlo and grabbing up a handful of water. I guess those days are gone, hunh?"

I don't say anything but I want to reach back into that time where you could lean over your dugout canoe and grab a handful of water to swallow your aspirins with. I want to do it now for Nokosee but I don't. I'm still hurt and I look past him at the gator.

"Don't worry, Stormy. He promised to take you home."

"Nokosee," I say looking him straight in the eye, "just because I'm not everything you want me to be doesn't give you the right to start dissin' me."

"I wasn't. I guess you've forgotten. I really can talk to the animals."

He smiles, picks up his shades from the bottom of the bithlo, adjusts them on his face and reclines in the dugout, hands behind his head.

"Dr. Doolittle, my ass."

"Speaking of which," Nokosee says in a shaking voice, "would you like to know your Seminole name for that part of your body?"

"Smart ass."

"I was thinking," Nokosee says with a pause, his teeth chattering, "'tight ass.'" He smiles, lets go of his hands and lowers himself slowly into the bithlo.

"You smug bastard!" I look around for something to throw at him. "If I had something to throw at you, I'd throw it!"

Nokosee just smiles and lies back in the bithlo. I look at him for a moment and then turn away in frustration.

He makes me so angry! How can he even think I'd be willing to live out here in this God forsaken hellhole? He's got to be kidding. He is one self-absorbed conceited pagan caveman jerk. He really doesn't have a clue. He's so friggin' naive. And judgmental. That kind of crap won't even get you to first base with me. Of course, I was thinking about hitting a home run with him. Until he started getting crazy. Why is it I'm always attracted to the lunatic fringe? Why can't I find a normal guy mom and dad would love to see me with? Some guy in polo shirts and pleated pants?

I hear my dad's voice from its command post in the brain terrain I lost to him from our many battles. It's shrill this time: *"Not another guy with a chip on his shoulder and a pierced tongue!"* I pause to look at Nokosee and add in my dad's voice echoing out of its bunker, *"And a loincloth!"*

Yeah, that would really freak him out.

##

Hours drag by. The languid passing of the changeless world around us lulls us to sleep. I fall asleep in the back of the bithlo with my parents' voices ringing in my dreams. I'm curled up and using the sea turtle shield as a pillow. Nokosee's voice awakens me. I'm surprised to see that it is night and that we are still moving under the light of a full moon. We are no longer in the canal.

Where is that crazy gator taking us?

Nokosee's moaning draws my attention away from King Roar. I see Nokosee shivering and can hear him talking in his sleep. I call out his name but Nokosee can't hear me. I get on my knees and edge closer to him. I stretch across his prone body and put my hand on his forehead and can feel his fever. He needs something to cool him down. I squeeze between him and the hull, remove his sunglasses and, lying face to face, reach across his body, scoop up some water and let it flow onto his heated brow. He says something that sounds a little like Spanish and acts as if he were trying to drink some water. I look around for a water bottle, grab an Evian from behind his head, pop the cap and bring it to his lips. He can't get enough. I pull it away a little so he won't choke and give him more when he can drink it safely. The bithlo stops moving and I look up.

King Roar has left us alone in a secluded marsh, the water a shimmering plain reflecting the moonlight. The only thing I can hear is the occasional hum of a mosquito and the croaking of a few frogs somewhere in the distance. I reach over him, scoop up some more water and wet his brow and face, smoothing the water across his handsome bronze features. I unfasten the Velcro tabs, slip out of the solar blanket and throw it across both of our bodies. I hear Nokosee call my name and see a smile appear on his face. I smile too and lean over to kiss him tenderly on the forehead. I grab his shaking hand and settle in next to him. Looking up, I'm startled by the millions of stars I can see. Back in Milltown, where the lights of the city mask the celestial show, I never bothered to look up into the night sky because there wasn't anything to see. But here, out in the middle of the Everglades, I'm reminded I'm floating in a timeless universe of beauty and mystery.

I don't know where we are, but I've never felt this peaceful. I look at Nokosee. *Maybe you've got something to do with it.* I lift his calloused hand from under the blanket and kiss the back of it before yawning. *Or maybe I'm just tired.*

I shift onto my side and with his hand in mine, I close my eyes and take his smile and my name on his lips to sleep with me.

##

Later that night I dream his father Barry Manolow-or-something stops by to see how his son is doing. He looks like the face staring up at me from under the chickee floor a few nights ago and the one staring down at me from the little black airplane. His face is wearing war paint and I see he's got his Purple Heart pinned to his headdress. Seeing Nokosee wrapped in the arms of an Outsider makes him draw his knife. He could kill me so easily. Nokosee would awake and never know what happened to me. He'd never suspect his old man had murdered me because it's so easy to die in the Everglades. I could have rolled out of the bithlo in the middle of the night and drowned. Or been eaten by King Roar.

Standing in the water, he looks around for the old gator. Although he gave the disfigured monster to Nokosee when it was still a hatchling, he knows you can never assume they have been tamed. He sees its head gliding silently toward him through the broken panes of shimmering astral light on the water like a malevolent shadow. He turns back to me.

Oh, if he could only make himself do it. Then he would be worthy of this last mission he has set out for himself and his son. Perhaps another time.

Nokosee's father slips the knife into its sheath and backs silently away. When he feels his camo painted bithlo against his back, he turns and, with one smooth motion, pulls himself back into the dugout. There is no splash or sound of dripping water to betray his presence. He rises with the driving pole in his hand and looks one more time across the water at his son before pushing himself away with a heavy heart and mind.

This was not supposed to happen. Nokosee was destined for greatness. He was the Human Beings' Messiah, what the Ghost Dancers had prayed over a hundred and twenty years ago for. He regretted not killing me when he had the many opportunities and worried that he would later pay for this lapse in will. Or so I dreamed.

##

This was Nokosee's dream as I lay sleeping next to him. He tells me about it later, when we're in the Outside. He sees trees and sawgrass drifting by. His eyelids want to draw down the curtains and he struggles to keep them open. He sees a Seminole warrior wearing the world-renowned patchwork coat. He's straddling a giant alligator and pulling its fierce mouth open. Nokosee's eyelids begin to flutter. He's still superstitious enough to believe in omens and fears what this image might portend. He gasps and struggles to sit up, to find consciousness. He's still not sure he's awake when he sees the huge image again. It's looking down at him and falling away. Nokosee suffers vertigo and grabs the sides of the bithlo.

And then he sees these words: NEXT LEFT. J.T. OSCEOLA'S AUTHENTIC SEMINOLE INDIAN VILLAGE, HOTEL, CASINO, AND CONVENTION CENTER.

He sits up and sees his vision is nothing more than a billboard.

"Stormy, I don't think we're in Kansas anymore."

"What?" Nokosee's voice is dragging me out of my fitful sleep.

"Wake up." He's already getting up, taking the solar blanket with him.

I wake up but don't see the billboard; it's behind me now. I do see an African American family. They're holding cane poles and fishing from the side of the canal bank. They're standing and pointing at me and shouting about something.

The alligator!

I remember now and turn away in what seems like slow motion in this surreal world I've wakened into. I see the gator's thick black tail carving a v-shaped undulating, rippling path through the water.

Nokosee comes into view. He's standing with his back to me and looking at what I realize for the first time is my home. I see people, all colors, shapes and sizes rushing to the canal bank. Some are taking pictures. Some are running along the canal bank shouting at me.

"It's that girl! The one lost in the swamp!"

"Look, mommy! She's naked!"

I look at myself and quickly grab the solar blanket Nokosee had casually discarded. I wrap it around my body and turn to the voices rising from the canal bank. I see a fat, very white woman waving a camera at me.

Tourist. Too pink for someone who lives here.

"You're Stormy Jones, aren't you!" the fat, pink tourist shouts.

"Yes," I find myself shouting back, "Yes I am!"

"Who's the Indian?" someone shouts, a man's voice.

"He's," I turn and start to speak but I'm interrupted by another voice from the bank.

"Why's he dressed like that?"

It's another kid's voice. I find the voice and the kid it belongs to. The little boy, about five years old, is pointing at Nokosee. The kid's mother pulls him away and tries to shield him from seeing what she believes was a carnal moment between two people.

This is not at all like Disney World. Walt would never allow someone to run around his property half naked and enjoying sex.

"Space girl!" Another voice.

I turn to it: two teenage boys with Holocaust haircuts and baggy urban clown pants. They're pointing at me and laughing.

"Nice legs, space girl. Why don't you dump the freak and his ride and trade up to me and my Lexus?"

My eyes blink. Nokosee. I turn to him and see him glaring at the boys.

"Nokosee, don't do anything stupid."

I'm surprised to find my hand on his arm.

"Do you remember the promise you made to me?" he asks without turning away from the crowd gathering on the canal bank.

"To love and cherish you forever?"

He turns to me. I'm still looking at the people but I can feel him looking at me. I smile and turn to him. I got him going. He doesn't know if I'm being serious or not. Funny thing is, neither do I. "Don't worry. Your little secret is safe with me."

"I want you to make me another one," he says, looking me hard in the eyes. "Promise me you won't tell anyone I speak English and Spanish."

"Why?"

"Just promise," he says urgently.

"I promise."

He turns away and glances at the boys on the canal bank in such a way it makes them wince before putting on his Wayfarers. I can't help it, but I slip my arm around his waist and pull him closer to me. He looks down, I look up and I don't want this moment to end. He lifts his arm and puts it around me and squeezes tight. I'm in love. When we turn and look across the bithlo at the new day looming ahead of us, I can only hope it will only get better.

Chapter 8

Family Reunion

King Roar walks up the boat ramp like he owns the joint. The huge old gator heralds our arrival by bringing chaos to the waterfront and pretty much shuts down the airboat and swamp buggy rides for the day. Women and children (and a few men) are screaming, pushing and shoving others out of the way so that they can get as far away as possible from the enormous and frightening memento of their mortality, a closeted and terrible thing not to be reminded of when on vacation.

The more rational and experienced linger to watch the spectacle, albeit from a safe distance, like the cracker and Seminole airboat operators flanking both sides of the bithlo.

When I see the TV station trucks with their telescoping dish antennas towering over the heads of everyone in the background, all pointing to Miami some thirty miles away, I find myself nuzzling up close to Nokosee and holding on tight.

"I'm scared," I whisper.

He turns slightly to me, his eyes still on the people gathering around the boat ramp and barely moves his mouth when he replies. "You're scared? Isn't this what you wanted? Before this day is over, everyone in the world will know that Stormy Jones is back in town."

"But I look like crap."

He catches me peering over his shoulder at the frenetic crowd and laughs. "You break me up."

I grip what little flesh I can find on his zero percent body fat body and give it a playful twist.

"Like, ouch," he deadpans.

I slap him and hug him tighter. "Thanks for saving me, Nokosee."

"That's Nooksy to you."

I rub my temple on his magnificent rock hard chest and just smile.

When the bithlo is halfway up the concrete ramp, Nokosee yells out over the length of the rope to the gator and it stops and settles its huge bulk down with a sudden finality.

Nokosee takes my hand and leads me across the flotsam lying about the floor of the bithlo. He steps out and picks me up as if I was no heavier than a cloud in the sky, and brings me to him, face to face. Nothing is said as we look deeply into each other's eyes.

"Hoo-we," a girl's voice teases, "look what Little Miss Punk Rocker brought home."

"Chickee bitch," I inform Nokosee.

"Is she Indian princess material?" he asks without moving his mouth or taking his eyes off of me. He sets me on the ramp.

"I think I better keep an eye on you."

"Is he tamed?" This is Stanlo Osceola, the longhaired leader of my Seminole gang the Chiefs. He has his gang with him, two more boys his age but with stubble heads and more MTV generated urban attitude. All of them are wearing their gang jackets: Technicolor Seminole patchwork zip-up shirt-jacs with the word *Chiefs* embroidered on the back.

Without looking, I raise my middle finger and point it in Stanlo's general direction as I say this to Nokosee: "C'mon, let's get famous."

"Whoe," he whispers, "this is where we part company. I'm not here to get discovered. I'm on a mission, remember?"

"Hey, that's right. Where's the drop-off?"

"The what?"

"The place you pick up the ransom."

"Oh, that. There's been a change in plans. Dad's dropped the ransom demands. He just wants me back pronto."

Nokosee turns to leave.

"What, are you crazy?" I ask with a nervous smile, "I'm not letting you go anywhere."

I grab his wrist and start pulling at him but he twists his arm and slips out of my hands.

"Nokosee, c'mon, please. Don't do this to me." I reattach myself.

"Stormy!"

It's my dad. I turn around and look. He's running through the crowd at the edge of the boat ramp. He's wearing his Smokey-the-Bear hat and his olive green park ranger uniform, the one with the shorts cut so unfashionably high on the thighs they reveal a tan line that makes me cringe every time I see it.

Except today. Today I only see the father who loves me and whom I love back despite everything I may have said about him. I run up the ramp, pulling Nokosee with me.

But Nokosee yanks me back. I forgot about the giant alligator and dad tells me later he didn't see it-- only me-- but when it stood up on its feet and roared, you can bet everybody saw it. Poor dad tries to stop but he loses his footing on the slippery boat ramp and slides with a knee-jerking, elbow-stabbing palsy toward the creature before falling onto the algae covered concrete.

The crowd screams.

Pop's sunglasses go flying as he slides down the ramp on his ass. You can see his Paul Newman eyes-- despite thirty years of faithfully wearing sunglasses-- are deeply creased with crow's feet. He reaches for his holster and yanks out a decidedly non-issue Glock 9 but he's shaking so bad he can't find the trigger. Maybe if his shorts were a little longer he could develop some friction to slow down, but nothing can stop him from sliding directly into King Roar's open mouth.

Not even Nokosee.

"Haalpatee!"

The giant gator stops in mid chomp as if it had been caught doing something naughty.

"Elichko! Elichko!"

Nokosee grabs King Roar's snout and pulls my dad out of its mouth. Dad rolls across the boat ramp and before he gets a chance to shoot the gator, Nokosee yanks the gun from his hand and stuffs it into the waistband of his gee-string.

I can't believe what I'm seeing. I look around and happen to catch the Chiefs. They can't believe it either.

"Haalpatee, ahmachamee!"

King Roar's response is so loud that it silences the crowd.

Nokosee, waving his arms about to get the gator's attention, runs past me toward the water and the gator follows. I back up and give the gator plenty of room to pass before running over to my dad.

"Haalpatee! Haalpatee! Elichko!"

Nokosee stops at the water's edge and waves the gator toward the canal. King Roar lumbers up to Nokosee's feet and-- the crowd will vouch for this-- looks up at him like a dog looking up at its owner with beseeching eyes, begging to stay.

"Get out of the way, kid!"

It's Harold Cypress, a big-bellied tribal cop with a shotgun coming at him through the crowd.

Nokosee backs into the water and yells at King Roar to follow but the gator doesn't want to leave him.

I can't let the cop shoot the gator. Or Nokosee. I throw myself up against the guy. There's a shotgun blast.

Nokosee looks back and sees me wrestling with the shotgun. When he turns back to King Roar, this time millions of years of evolving life preserving instincts gets the gator scrambling down the ramp and into the water. Within seconds King Roar has become nothing more than a good story to take back home from a vacation as he dives and disappears beneath the dark, tannic-clouded water.

The tribal cop pushes me aside. I slip and fall on the ramp and slide toward my dad, legs spread akimbo giving him a picture of his daughter I'm sure he won't be able to shake from his mind until the day he dies. When I spread eagle him, a nervous communal laugh ricochets through the crowd. Dad, cursing and blushing a deep crimson, slaps at my legs, pushes off and tries to get to his feet but he can't find his footing. Meanwhile, the cop has pumped another shotgun shell into the chamber and is walking toward the water. Nokosee is walking with no-nonsense strides toward him and when the cop raises the shotgun again to shoot at the fleeing gator's wake, Nokosee neatly and with a modicum of effort slaps it from the cop's hands. By the time the cop realizes what's happened, he's looking down the twin over-and-under barrels of his own shotgun.

"Don't!" I cry from my prone position on the boat ramp.

Nokosee looks at me. The cop moves for the shotgun. Nokosee hits him across the face with it and knocks him out. He collapses in a heap on the boat ramp as only as only a fat man can.

Dad has found his footing and is helping me up when he turns to look at Nokosee. I can see by the look on his face he already distrusts Nokosee and finds him dangerous. This is not what I was hoping for when I introduced Nokosee to him. I knew getting past the loincloth would be tough enough for dad, but seeing the guy of my dreams taking out one of the tribe's deputies will pretty much make getting dad to accept Nokosee damn near impossible.

"Kid," dad says to Nokosee, "you better drop those weapons right now."

Oh, right, I forgot that part. The fact that Nokosee has disarmed dad and the deputy isn't helping matters either.

"Dad," I say, pulling on his arm to get his attention, "this guy saved my life. Don't hurt him."

"'Hurt him,' he just assaulted a cop."

I pull my dad around to look at me. "Dad, that was his pet gator. He was only trying to protect it. He *saved* you!"

Dad finally looks at me. "Are you alright?"

I have to shout over the swarming, shoving media surge and the people yelling and screaming all around us. "I'm fine, dad, thanks to him." I turn to Nokosee as the press runs toward him, slipping and sliding and stopping a safe distance away to form a pushing and shoving cacophonic wall of flesh, microphones, and television cameras.

"Who is he?" dad asks.

"I...I don't know."

"What's his name?"

I lead my dad and the reporters attached like remora down the ramp.

"No--" I stop short. "No tellin'. I don't think he speaks English." The last thing I need is my dad thinking Nokosee and I are on a first name basis-- or that he's got secrets, big secrets. I push through the shouting and surging media wall. "Excuse me. Let us by."

"That's crazy," my dad adds, "They all know English."

"Not this one," I lie knowing it won't be the last. I stop and look up at him. "Dad, I think I'm the first white person he's ever seen." Well, at least that's true. At least in the flesh.

"Poor guy."

"Dad!" See, I wasn't lying about my attitude. I get it from him. He can't help himself and neither can I.

He squeezes me tightly while looking at Nokosee. "I'm kidding." And then he finally gives me that big hug I've been looking for. "Oh, God, Stormy, you don't know how much I missed you."

"Same here, dad, same here." And that's the truth.

"So where'd you find this guy?"

I look up at dad. He's looking over my shoulder at Nokosee.

"Dad, he found me. He's dumber than dirt but he's got brass balls bigger than Big Foot."

Dad looks down at me with a quizzical smile. "Where'd you learn to talk like that?"

I'm trying *way* too hard to keep Nokosee's cover. I wish we hadn't spent that one day exchanging redneck quips because now I can't get them out of my head.

"From you dad," I stammer. "You're turning me into a real redneck."

I give him a fleeting glance. He's looking down at me with that same look of mistrust I've seen ever since I started showing interest in boys. I never could lie convincingly to him and knowing that makes me even more nervous. I feel my face redden and my armpits start working overtime.

I turn back to look at Nokosee. Looking lost and confused under the media stampede, he's backing into the water, a place members of the 4th Estate fear to tread, especially when it might harbor things that can eat them. Or maybe their caution had something to do with the loaded shotgun in Nokosee's hands and the dazed deputy at his feet.

Dad starts leading us toward him. He looks at the bithlo and the Evian water bottles scattered about in the hull and then shouts over the rat-a-tat-tat questions being fired at Nokosee and us by the media, "Ontee! Ontee!"

"Dad? What are you doing?"

"Just being friendly," he replies without looking at me. "Echee shakalishchee!" he shouts.

Oh, my God, I'm so mortified! I know exactly what's going on here. Do you always have to make them feel like criminals?

I push away from my father and elbow my way through the rabid journalists and emerge stumbling into the water. Nokosee catches me. I grab his hand and try to bring him out of the water but he won't budge. I turn back to my dad further up the boat ramp and shout, "He saved my life! Isn't that good enough?"

"Yeah, isn't that good enough?"

It's John Soto, head muckraker on the city's first free weekly tabloid, THE TIMES ARE A CHANGIN', and prime pain in my dad's side since the fires began-- seasonally now for the last five summers. His weight and his short legs kept him from getting there quicker. It's Soto's-- and much of the three million people living in south Florida's opinion- that the fires are a direct result of Sam Jones' mismanagement. And Soto has made it his personal goal to prove it.

The last thing dad needs is for Soto and his minions to pick up on what he will be the first to admit is one dysfunctional family. He ignores the crack, puts on a smile and motions for Nokosee to come closer. "Ontee! Ontee! Give me the guns."

I'm simmering in place when I look back at the water and whisper, "Be cool. He treats all my boyfriends like this."

Nokosee is taken back. I'm sure he's surprised to find he's been elevated to boyfriend status. I'm not. That's all I've been thinking about. Maybe he'll want to hang around now. He lets me lead him up the boat ramp.

Dad, head of the Inquisition, is waiting there, doing his best impersonation of Columbus meeting the Indians with an outstretched hand. Nokosee pauses, looks around like Billy Jack-- his dad made sure he saw that movie too-- with his eyes all tight and all before flipping the shotgun around, cocking it open and emptying the shells onto the boat ramp where they bounce off Harold's head waking him up before rolling into the water. He snaps it shut and thrusts it at my dad like some Marine might do towards his drill instructor.

Dad takes it and holds it in one hand while extending the other. "Now my gun," dad says all equally Billy Jack steely-eyed.

Nokosee doesn't flinch. In fact, it looks like we have the makings of a Mexican standoff until I reach for dad's gun in Nokosee's loincloth. He grabs my hand, but won't take his eyes off of my dad.

"Please, Indian dude," I say, "you gotta give up the gun."

Indian dude. I don't know where that one came from. Just know I'm nervous. Not only is my dad meeting my new boyfriend for the first time, he's also trying to disarm him. In any event, I nearly blow it for Nokosee because it almost makes him crack a smile. But he doesn't hand over the gun.

"Dad, I'm telling you, he doesn't know English."

"Ec ca ef ce," dad says.

Nokosee keeps staring at my dad for a moment longer before pulling the Glock from his gee string. He flips it around, and hands it over, butt-end first. Dad grabs it, but Nokosee won't let go.

"Mvto," dad says.

Nokosee lets go of the gun and dad points it at him.

"Harold," dad asks the prone deputy, "are you okay?"

Harold moans and rolls over onto his side.

"Can you get up?"

Harold grunts and staggers to his feet. Dad catches him and holds him up. "You alright, buddy?"

"Why wouldn't I be?"

"Right. Here, take your shotgun back."

"How'd you get that?"

"Point it at him."

"Dad!"

Dad turns to Nokosee. "Turn around."

"Dad! What are you doing?"

"What's it look like I'm doing? Get away from him."

"No! He saved my life! He saved *your* life!"

Nokosee doesn't move. Dad says it in Muskogee. Nokosee sighs and turns slowly around. Dad says something again to him. Nokosee puts his hands behind his back. Dad sticks his gun back in its holster and pulls out some plastic wire handcuffs. When I see what he's up to, I throw myself between them.

"You can't arrest my boyfriend! He saved my life!"

"Symona!"

It's mom. I cringe and I swear everyone cringes with me, their voices rising in unison with one word on their lips, "Symona?" My given name has a way of doing that to people especially when it's shouted through the nose. My mom's harsh New Jersey accent deserves a black belt it's that lethal. I'm so mortified I want to die. Now the whole world knows I'm something called a "Symona." I turn to "the voice," a.k.a my mom.

Mom, Lisa Jones, pressing fifty and winning the good fight to look young for her age, is pushing through the crowd in an outfit that surprises even me. It's as if she has adopted a new character straight out of some safari adventure series, this from a woman who abhors the outdoors. She's covered in khaki; big pocketed shorts, epaulets on her shirt, knee-length khaki socks which is, as far as I'm concerned, a major fashion infraction and grounds for a legal separation of child from parent and, God forbid, a pith helmet. But not just any old pith helmet. This one has a built-in solar powered fan. I can't believe this is happening to me. Now I've got my parents standing around in front of all these TV cameras in these really stupid clothes they insist on wearing with my dad arresting my boyfriend to boot.

I look at my dad. Our eyes connect. He looks down at Nokosee's wrists. I look too. The tricky old guy handcuffed my boyfriend while I was reeling from mom's visual and aural assault.

"Dad!"

Dad whips Nokosee around and removes the knife from its sheath. He looks at if for a second before sticking it in his pocket and, turning, pushes Nokosee up the boat ramp and through the crowd. I can't believe this is happening. I grab dad's arm and try to stop him. He tries to shake me loose but I won't let go.

Dad looks up and searches the crowd. "Lisa!"

Mom pops through the media phalanx and stops short.

"Lisa, take Stormy!"

"Mom, tell dad to let him go!"

Mom doesn't know what's going on or what to do.

"Lisa, get her off of me, goddammit!"

"Mom, he's trying to arrest my boyfriend!"

Mom's eyes blink a couple of times and her mouth drops open when she gets a load of Nokosee in his loincloth. She can't move and for a moment, it looks like she might even faint.

"Dammit, Lisa, get her off of me!"

Mom makes a move for me but I stick my leg out to keep her away.

"Symona!" she yells.

I guess she didn't like what was looking back at her from under the space dress because she grabs my leg and tries to force my leg down.

"Mom, this boy saved my life and dad's trying to arrest him!"

"Sam?"

"He assaulted Harold!"

"Mom, he's only arresting him 'cause he's my boyfriend and he wears a loincloth!"

"Lisa, she doesn't even know his name!"

That's when I sink my teeth into dad's wrist and discover he screams like a girly-man.

"Symona!" Mom tries to pull me off of dad.

"Harold," dad says in mid scream, "take this kid!"

Harold looks at me and makes a face.

"Not her!" dad screams while trying to keep his balance, "Him!"

Dad throws Nokosee toward Harold who grabs him from behind and points the empty shotgun at the back of his head. And then dad turns to me.

"No!" I scream.

Dad picks me up and throws me over his shoulder.

"Put me down!"

He spanks my bare ass. I scream like a stuck pig. Cameras flash.

"Sam," mom yells, "her ass is showing!"

"Goddammit!" dad yells. He rips off his Smokey-the-Bear hat and slaps it across my bare behind.

I rear up and scream again I'm so angry and frustrated. This isn't the kind of family reunion I had in mind. I start kicking and screaming and throwing the biggest hissy fit the Everglades has ever seen as dad tries to carry me up the boat ramp. From my perch high above his shoulders I can see over the heads of everybody. The media is having a field day at my expense, but I can't stop. I look for Nokosee. He's looking up at me in a way I'll never forget, like I'm some kind of crazy lady. And I am, and I can't stop it.

My knees are pounding like pistons against dad's chest when he makes it up the boat ramp to the gravel road and loses his hat. Thanks to YouTube, I moon the world. The next day, my bare ass rockets to the top as the most downloaded picture on the Internet and will stay at number one for almost a year where it becomes the Most Viewed,

Most Discussed (Ugh!), Most Linked, and the top of the Top Favorites.

"Goddammit! Lisa, get my hat!"

Mom runs around us, grabs up the hat and slams it against my bare behind. Mom and dad can't get out of there fast enough and begin speed walking down the dusty road with mom holding dad's hat against my soon to become famous buttocks with one hand while holding onto her pith helmet with the other.

"Have you seen the missing helicopter?"

It's a Soto question, breathless and fearless. The fat little reporter is racing right alongside us with a microphone held up toward me. I see it and start crying. It all comes back and I basically lose it in great convulsive heaves I have no control over. I fall against my dad's shoulders and cry like a baby.

"Get away from us, you fat little bastard!" Dad yells. "Can't you see she's been traumatized?"

"Why is he handcuffed?" The "fat little bastard" just won't give up. This gets me hyperventilating.

"I guess you missed the part where he cold cocked a deputy," dad says, panting heavily and looking steadfastly ahead.

"The same one that's got the empty shotgun pointed at the back of his head?"

"It's empty, Nokosee! Run!" I yell.

Dad looks up at me. "I thought you didn't know his name?"

I don't know what to say so I just start crying and screaming and hitting dad with my fists and knees. Nokosee tells me later he didn't run because the timing wasn't right. When I asked him if I was ever a factor, he said, "That too." *To know him is to love him.*

"You're right," Soto continues not missing a beat and struggling mightily to stay up with us. "I missed that one,"

"And for carrying a concealed weapon," dad wheezes.

"That ain't no concealed weapon!" I shout.

The world pans from my ass to my sobbing, heaving face.

"Look at the guy," I cry, "where's he gonna conceal it?"

The cameras tilt down to Nokosee.

"Good point," Soto says. "So why is he handcuffed again?"

"Because he's my boyfriend!" I cry.

"Because he's a kidnapper!" dad shouts.

"Kidnapper?" Soto asks.

"No he's not!" I shout.

Dad, desperately seeking a way out, sees somebody up ahead who might help him shake these reporters loose. "J.T.!" he shouts, his voice cracking under the stress. "J.T.! Over here!"

Chapter 9

Osceola's Spear

James Tiger Osceola is kicking out the kickstand on his customized black Indian motorcycle, the one with the Seminole patchwork paint job on the fenders and the airbrushed spear arcing across the sides of the gas tank, when he hears my dad's voice. I see him look up. He freezes when he sees the noisy throng headed his way. J.T., as he is known to the world via the resort's multi-million dollar advertising campaigns and the tribe's cable access TV show which he fronts as their charismatic spokesperson, is sporting a silk and satin patchwork zippered jacket and a matching patchwork bandanna that covers his graying ponytail. As the Tribal Council Chairman, he single-handedly brought the tribe prosperity even beyond the wildest dreams of the white man. A handsome and nearly fit 250 pound six-feet-four-inch ex-Viet Nam Vet and winner of a Purple Heart, J.T. can trace his lineage all the way back to his namesake. In the 1970's he took advantage of the fact that the tribe, like other Native American tribes, is looked upon by the federal government as a sovereign nation, and is therefore exempt from most federal laws. Reaching back to Nokosee's take on history, J.T. encouraged the tribe to begin selling discount tax-free cigarettes to the public from tribal land. Back in 1977, these "smoke shops" made a killing, excuse the pun, and gave the Seminoles an enterprise that didn't rise or fall with the economy (tourism) or the weather (ranching and farming). He later opened the *first* Native American high-stakes bingo hall in the U.S. and successfully fought off government legal challenges. Encouraged by the Seminole tribe's successes, more and more Native American tribes began offering gambling on their lands. Today gambling is the biggest income producer for the Native American nation. Always on top of things, he runs his tribe like a business and encourages and rewards each member for ideas and information—good or bad-- that will make it more money or run better. I found out later he got a call on his cell phone from a tribal member of my arrival and the TV news crews that had descended upon the boat ramp. That was more than enough to get him out of his swank air-conditioned office at the resort and convention center less than a mile away. Still, he hadn't been prepared to see all three of the Joneses together in one place at one time. Looking straight ahead at a possible public relations catastrophe, I can see J.T., still straddling the black Indian, whip out his Blackberry and bark into it just like Captain Kirk of *Star Trek* fame. Growing up around him, I'm pretty sure this is what he said: "Memo. I must be notified ASAP of all future sightings of a Jones family reunion."

J.T. clicks off, slips the device into his pocket, dismounts, and takes a deep breath before walking toward the poster family for dysfunctional kin.

Dad is actually running now-- albeit awkwardly and with great effort accompanied by audible wheezing-- towards J.T., trailing a line of ever-growing reporters from television, radio and print. I'm bouncing out of what the media will later call my "space dress" and have to cover my boobs with my arms. Mom, still holding the hat over my bare bottom with one hand and holding her pith helmet with the other, is smiling nervously and looking furtively from side to side for the cameras while trying to keep pace with dad. Seeing all of this coming at him must have dredged up a Viet Cong banzai attack in J.T. and I'm thankful he didn't suffer some sort of post traumatic stress syndrome that would have called for him to pull out his trusty military issue .45 from his shoulder holster and blow us all away starting with me (we have issues; I think he's a pompous fat ass and he thinks I'm a smart ass). I can just hear him grumbling something about "stupid tourists" under his breath. In J.T.'s mind, anyone who isn't a Native American is just visiting.

"J.T.!" dad yells again, "Get them off me!"

That's something J.T. doesn't need to be told to do. The last thing he wants are members of the press talking to anyone about anything he doesn't know the answer to in advance. He looks to his right and sees the new village restaurant and souvenir store. He sees the Seminole manager holding the glass door open and standing in the threshold looking at the surging crowd. With a shout, J.T. gets the man's attention and tells him to keep the door open. He turns back and directs us with an outstretched arm toward the safety of the restaurant.

"What's going on?" he asks, trailing us on the run.

Dad, sounding like he is about to die as he climbs the three steps up to the building, says in measured breaths, "I'll tell you later." He turns to Harold. "Bring him, too."

Harold has to push Nokosee into the restaurant not because my hero is putting up resistance, but because he's seen the black Indian and can't take his eyes off it.

That's Osceola's Spear! I think just before the glass door closes on us.

J.T. stays outside and faces down the crowd with the best PR smile he can muster. "Folks, this is as far as it goes."

"C'mon, J.T.," a reporter shouts back. "What's going on here?"

"I haven't a clue," he says with a shake of his head. "When the head honcho for the Everglades asks for help, I'm only too happy to oblige. But I'll tell you this, as soon as I find out what's going on, I'll call a press conference and you'll all find out together."

"What about Tarzan?" someone asks.

"Tarzan? What're you talking about?"

"The kid in the loincloth!"

"Where?"

"Inside the store!" someone shouts impatiently.

J.T. turns quickly around and looks inside the restaurant. Sure enough, there's a Native in a loincloth in his store. He can't believe he didn't see him but then, he couldn't see anything except my family. We have a way of doing that to people whenever we're together.

J.T.'s never seen the kid before and that makes him uncomfortable and he doesn't like being uncomfortable. Now, twice in less than a minute he has been caught off guard by questions he has no answer for. He turns back to the crowd and, smiling gamely, says, "Like I said, once I figure out what's going on here, I'll call a press conference."

"Have you ever seen that kid before?"

J.T. looks down. It's Soto again. He's the last to arrive. Breathing hard and sweating profusely, the little fat guy starts J.T.'s adrenaline pumping and the chief begins to sweat right along with him.

"Of course I have," J.T. says not at all convincingly.

"What's his name?"

J.T. pauses. "That's for me to know and for you to find out."

"You don't know, do you? In fact, I'll wager this is the first time you've ever seen that kid."

"Well, I'm sorry to disappoint you, Mr. Soto, but I know everyone in the tribe on every reservation in Florida."

"But not this kid."

"And why wouldn't I?"

"Because he doesn't live on a reservation or even in a city. He's one of the renegades we've been hearing about, the ones living in the Everglades hijacking trucks and robbing tourists at gunpoint."

J.T. pauses to study the fat little reporter. "You know, until you have proof like a photo or an actual 'renegade' in custody, those rumors are right up there with Big Foot. As for the kid in the loincloth, I know exactly who he is and why he's dressed that way."

"Why's he dressed that way?"

"Because he's one of our actors rehearsing a new show for the casino. There, does that make you happy?"

"Chief, I've been around you long enough to know when you're speaking with forked tongue."

That little quip gets a few laughs from the crowd and, although J.T. is smiling right along with the rest of them, I'm sure he wishes he were alone with the little ball of blubber someplace far out in the Everglades where he could kill him, dispose of his body and return to his role as a pillar of the Seminole and Chamber of Commerce communities-- despite the innuendos spread by the little guy's rag.

J.T., looking down from the top step at the reporter, with a straight, sympathetic face, begins by calling him the Seminole name he has bestowed upon him in the same manner George W. Bush hands out nicknames, a word which roughly translated means, "Shit-for-Brains."

"Na ro ipl Ekvlpe, it just so happens—"

"Whoe, wait up," Soto interrupts. He's wondering why some of the Seminoles standing around him are laughing, "What'd you just call me?"

J.T. slowly repeats it knowing no Seminole would ever tell the reporter the truth.

"What's that mean?"

"Seeker of the Truth," J.T., responds with a kindly smile.

"You better hope that's what it means."

"What?" J.T. asks with a cocked head and a daring voice, "Are you planning on suing me if it isn't?"

"Damn right."

"Na ro ipl Ekvlpe, you must have forgotten. As a member of a sovereign nation without courts, you cannot sue me. But I, on the other hand, can sue you-- as I'm currently doing right now your sorry excuse of a newspaper for the lies it printed about me and my people."

"Yay, Chief!" a Seminole shouts.

Suddenly a chorus of "Chief!" "Chief!" "Chief!" rings out around Soto from a cadre of Seminoles pumping their fists into the air.

"So sayeth the Great Chief," Soto replies seemingly unfazed while writing in his notebook.

J.T. sighs, shakes his head and smiles at the other journalists. "Like I said, once I talk to Sam Jones and find out what's going on, I'll call a press conference." He turns and signals to the manager on the other side to unlock the door.

"Chief Osceola, how long will that be?" a TV reporter asks. "Can you give us something for our five o'clock news?"

"Jenny, would it be live?"

"Unless you get it to us earlier."

"Let's shoot for live. I'll see what I can do. I'll have my people get in touch with your people."

"How 'bout my people?" Soto asks.

J.T. shakes his head. "All people," he replies with the sincerest smile he can muster while spreading his arms inclusively to the throng of reporters below. "Okay?"

"I can hardly wait," Soto replies.

J.T. turns, steps through the doorway and tells the manager to lock it behind him. With his back to the windows where the media is jockeying for position to point their cameras, I see J.T. take a breath and roll his eyes. He sees me and nods. I'm holding onto my mom now, crying and watching J.T. work the crowd. J.T. turns and tells the manager to close the Venetian blinds so no one can see in and then turns back to us. He sees Nokosee staring at row after row of the patchwork jackets for sale on racks near the cash register. To shut me up, dad agreed to unhandcuff Nokosee, which affords him the opportunity to absent-mindedly feel his erect nipples while looking at the merchandise. I'm hoping he's doing that because it's so unexpectedly cold inside and that he really wasn't lying to me when he said he didn't know what air-conditioning was. Otherwise, it would just be creepy.

When J.T. sees Nokosee feeling himself up in front of the customers, he runs up and slaps his hands. Nokosee, engrossed with the patchwork jackets, is caught off guard. He looks up at J.T. and J.T. stops short. He only stares at Nokosee for a second or two but I'm sure he's thinking he's never seen this kid before and he should have because he's supposed to know every freaking Indian on the res. Again, J.T. finds himself in unfamiliar territory and he doesn't like it. Talk about a control freak. Three surprises within five minutes is making him a very uncomfortable CEO. He backs away and stumbles into us.

"J.T.," dad says while absently trying to shake the pain from the bite I put on his wrist, "Can Lisa take Stormy through the back entrance?"

"Through the kitchen?"

"Yeah. I don't want her talking to the press just yet. I want to get her home and washed up first."

J.T. looks us over for a moment and then probably thinks that's the best idea he's heard all day, anything to get us out of the probing eye of the media. "No problem."

"Great."

"Just one thing," J.T., adds, "we need to confer first before she meets the press. Okay?"

Dad turns to mom and me. "Stormy, go with your mom and don't give her any trouble. I'll catch up with you guys in a second."

"What are you going to do with my boyfriend?"

Dad sighs. "Look, I'll bring him by a little later. Just go home with your mom."

"You're not going to throw him in jail are you?"

"No, now just go home with your mother. I'll be there shortly."

"With my boyfriend?"

"For crying out loud!" Dad stops and catches himself. "Yes, with your boyfriend. Now please go!"

I really want to believe him as my mom starts leading me away. "Nokosee!" I shout out.

He turns around.

"I love you!" I shout and wave. He waves back and smiles uneasily. I'm sure he's embarrassed. I know I am. I can't believe I shouted the "L-word" much less said it. Talk about acting out. I'm hoping I didn't scare him away.

Later I learn from Nokosee that my dad asked J.T. to dig around to see what he can find out about him. I guess he thought Nokosee wasn't listening in but when you start whispering around somebody Nokosee told me it's only natural to want to listen in, especially if you've been trained

by a whacked out father to be on the alert for just this kind
of behavior. He pretended to be watching a tourist mom
picking out a patchwork jacket for her five year old
daughter. He couldn't understand how this was possible
because he had been taught by his nutcase dad that the
patchwork jackets were symbolic of a boy's rite of passage to
manhood, especially marking Nokosee's place on that
warrior path as the first of the "New Seminole." As much as
he found it perplexing, my dad caught Nokosee's ear when
he told J.T. to be careful with him, that he's a kidnapper.
When J.T., asked how much did he pay them, dad had to
admit that he later got a call from somebody who told him
they changed their mind, that it was all a misunderstanding,
and that I would be delivered unharmed. J.T. laughed and
said Nokosee wasn't really a kidnapper after all. Dad said
"technically," but he wanted to use it as an excuse to "put
him behind bars" until he can figure out what's going on.
That's when he told J.T. about his conspiracy theory, that
Nokosee was part of a band of "renegades" out in the
Everglades who were basically "up to no good." This would
help explain the truck hijackings on Alligator Alley and the
Tamiami Trail over the years and the reports by hunters and
birdwatchers of seeing Indians and other people roaming
the outer reaches of the Everglades. To J.T.'s benefit,
according to Nokosee, he told dad he was full of it, that he
should stop reading Soto's rag, that if there were any Natives
living in the glades outside of the tribe he'd know about it
because he was, after all, the "freakin' Chief of the
Seminoles."

I think J.T.'s denial of the renegade rumor was a business
decision. The last thing he needs is for the world to think it
could be dangerous visiting any of his enterprises. I also
think he knows he's got a real problem on his hands because
he knows the renegades exist. The last thing he wants to do
is to confirm it with a white man. No, this is an internal
thing, and he'll deal with the renegade situation himself.

To make a long story short, the thing that really pissed me
off though is that dad tried to stick Nokosee in jail on a

bogus kidnapping charge. Again, to J.T.'s credit, he told dad to "fagedabouit," that he wasn't going to allow him to arrest one of his own—something he had no right to do anyway. He told dad he would see him later with "the kid" after he figured out what to do with him.

Of course, daddy will pay for that little lie to me somewhere down the road I can promise you that.

I know, I'm not very nice. Blame it on my raging hormones. Everyone else does. Including me. How else can I explain my behavior, my uncontrollable desire to make love to Nokosee? But you know what? It's deeper than that. I know my dad and my mom. The last thing they want is for me to have a boyfriend like Nokosee. Trying to have him arrested for kidnapping me is about as low as you can go. Trust me, if that had happened, it would have made me totally bonkers and I would have become their worst nightmare—if I'm not already.

Chapter 10

Home Sweet Home

J.T., with a cigarette hanging from his mouth, yanks back the shower curtain in the Park Ranger compound bathroom, leans into the shower and turns off the water. He says something to Nokosee in Muskogee and throws him a towel. He turns Nokosee around and I close the crack in my bedroom door a little so that he doesn't see me. I'm leaning against the door frame across the hallway from the bathroom with a towel wrapped around my hair after taking a shower and thanking God that Nokosee is standing naked only a few feet away from me. I would never have even thought about hoping for something like that because it would have seemed too impossible only an hour ago. To say I'm excited would be an understatement. Thinking that I might actually get to hang out with Nokosee tonight, I'm getting dressed to impress. I already have my black denim Brazilian-cut jeans on. They look good on my hips and hide the cuts on my legs from the sawgrass. I picked a black bare midriff tank top to go with them. It has Iggy Pop's face on it. It's hard to believe he's the same age as my dad. He's sticking out his tongue and giving the world the finger. My kind of guy even if he is an old dude. While I'm listening in, I'm typing in things I want to do with Nokosee on the memo program on my cell phone. I've got so much I want to show and do with Nokosee that I don't want to waste one second. Especially when I know Nokosee's got this mission thing going where he has to get back to the swamp. Trust me, I will do *all* I can to make him reconsider.

When J.T. brought Nokosee over to the compound ostensibly for a shower, I could hear dad, mom, and J.T. going at it about the options he was giving them regarding Nokosee. There were only two in J.T.'s opinion: either leave him be or send him packin' to Oklahoma to be picked and probed by a Bureau of Indian Affairs cultural anthropologist. But, as long as he was Chief, there would be no arrests.

I guess Nokosee was listening in because that's when the bathroom door starts rattling. J.T. excuses himself, walks over and opens the door. It appears Nokosee has a problem with doorknobs. He says something to him, points to the clothes he brought over from the store, shuts the door behind him and walks back into the living room.

After J.T. passes, I open my door a crack so I can hear what's going on in the living room next to my bedroom and start typing my "to do list" again in my cell phone.

"Folks," J.T. says, "whatever you decide, know this: we've got ourselves National Enquirer stuff going on here."

"What do you mean?" dad asks.

"If the Ed Sullivan Show were still on, that kid who just used your shower would be the top act."

"You're dating yourself, big guy," dad says.

"Get to the point, J.T.," mom interrupts.

"Stormy was right. Nokosee's never seen a white person before and he's on a 'walkabout,' something his ol' man dreamed up that's supposed to make him a man. When he returns, he gets to wear the 'Coat of Honor'-- our trademark Technicolor jackets. His ol' man has taken one of these things you can buy in any of our stores on the res and made it into some sorta sign of manhood. I mean, he's even got the kid believin' that each one of these colors and stripes are like some kinda symbol that tells who you are, what you're famous for, who you love and," he pauses for effect, "who you've killed."

"What?" mom shouts.

I stop typing in my cell phone and wish my mom would keep her mouth shut.

"Lisa, I was kidding about that last one. Listen, it's really no big deal. It's just one family living out there. They're harmless. Just tryin' to recapture their roots. Happens all the time. Once it gets too hot for them or they start freezing their asses off during the next cold spell, I can guarantee they'll throw in their Indian blankets just like all the others faster than you can say, 'What were we thinking?'"

"Sam," mom says in measured tones, "you gotta do something about him."

"Like what?"

"I don't want Symona hanging around any more boys. Especially killers!"

Oh, great! Now Nokosee's a killer! Way to go, J.T.!

"Lisa," J.T. tries to interject, "I said--"

"Sam, that's why she's out here with you," mom continues, "in the middle-of-nowhere! Away from her friends and their backseats! I thought she'd be safe here!"

"Safe?" dad shouts back, "Who needs backseats when you got the whole goddamn Everglades!"

I pound in a final message into the cell phone memory banks before tossing it on the bed and yanking the towel from my head. My blond hair still has its pink highlights but, instead of sticking up at the center, it's now circling my head like some kind of punk angel's halo. I pick up a pair of beat-up black high top tennis shoes and put them on as the argument on the other side of the wall becomes more heated because J.T. made the mistake of laughing at dad's remark.

"Yeah, sure, J.T.," mom says, "go ahead and laugh. You're just like him; two more adult American men who never grew up; it's becoming a defining characteristic of the American male, he just never grows up and becomes responsible, everything is a joke. But you don't have any girls, either, J.T."

"Thank God."

"Yeah, you better thank God. With guys like you out there and your predatory ways, it ain't easy staying young and innocent."

"Darlin'," J.T. replies in a slow southern drawl, "I haven't stalked any females since I got married over thirty years ago, so I think you better back off."

"Calm down, Lisa," dad says.

"You calm down! You'd think a mother could trust her daughter would be safe with her father. But what happens? Her father-- 'The Great White Park Ranger'-- do you know she calls you that behind your back?"

"Hell, she calls me that to my face."

"He takes this city kid," mom continues, not missing a beat, "who won't even go into her own backyard because it's hot and it's got bugs-- takes her into the Everglades with him to fight one of the worst fires ever recorded—"

"Yeah," J.T. interrupts, "that was pretty dumb."

"Stay out of this, J.T.!-- and then promptly loses her there only to be found by some kinda throwback to the past who's been raised in the swamp by...by *renegades!*"

"Well," J.T. drawls, "I wouldn't actually call them 'renegades.' Maybe 'renegade wannabes' might be more accurate."

"Shut up, J.T.! Just shut the hell up!" mom shouts. She is almost crying. "My baby has been lost in the goddamn Everglades with a wild, half-naked boy! A man! Did you see how he looks?"

"It could have been worse," dad interjects. "She coulda spent the night in the backseat of a Chevy in New Jersey."

J.T. laughs.

Mom screams in frustration. "This isn't some kinda joke!"

"You're right, Lisa," dad says. "I'm sorry. Just calm down."

"Don't tell me to calm down! You were supposed to protect her. Being out here was supposed to be good for her. It was going to expose her to new ideas, new---"

Mom stops short and turns to the sound of a body crashing against the hallway wall.

It's my body. I'm hopping on one foot while leaning against the wall for support as I lace up my shoe.

"Did someone say 'exposed?'" I ask. "You should have seen the size of that pagan caveman's schlong."

"Symona!" mom shouts.

I yank the knot tight and stand. "I mean," I continue, using my hands to illustrate my point, "this guy had to be at least a foot long for crying out loud."

"Oh, my God!" mom cries before covering her mouth.

"Okay, that's it, Stormy!" dad shouts. He starts for me but mom holds him back. Suddenly, the bathroom door begins to rattle violently.

"Hey," I say, "that must be him now."

I walk over to the door and throw it open and step back. I don't know whether to laugh or cry when Nokosee steps into the hallway. His white cowboy shirt is unbuttoned revealing his exquisite bronze body. He's wearing a pair of China-made moccasins and, as everyone can see, he's also wearing boxer underwear: the Fruit of the Looms are sticking out of the zipper.

I start laughing as I walk over to him. "He might not know how to open a door or pull up a zipper," I say in my best southern hick accent, "but ma and pa, he's all mine." I step behind him and give him a hug. "Hey, big boy, let me show you how to do it." I reach around, push his boxers back through the zipper hole, and yank the zipper up. I turn to mom. "I mean, c'mon, *Mother*, this dude is even safer than Rafael or whomever you're humpin' this week."

Dad shakes loose from mom, grabs my wrist, yanks me away from Nokosee, and slaps me across the face.

No one, not even dad, saw that one coming.

I deserve it. I crossed the line and pushed way too many buttons. My face is stinging and tears burst from my eyes. I'm more embarrassed and angry than hurt. At least I know I can take a punch because that slap is a real dilly. I can tell dad wished he hadn't done it. I can see it in his face and the way he tries to come to me with open arms but I'm not ready to kiss and make up. I duck his outstretched arms and he makes an effort to stop me but Nokosee grabs his wrist and applies some kind of Steven Seagal move that drops him screaming in pain instantly to the floor.

The side of my face feels like it's on fire as I pause in the hallway to watch Nokosee take dad's gun and throw it into my room. When dad tries to get to his feet, Nokosee adds a little more pressure on the wrist, which sends him back to the floor with a cry.

Mom screams and J.T. makes a move. Nokosee, without looking and without letting go of my dad's wrist, kicks out and catches J.T. in the chest, which sends his 250 pounds reeling backward into the living room up and over a chair.

The quick, violent power on display sends mom over the edge and into a higher octave, an ear piercing mega scream from hell.

I grab Nokosee's wrist. "No! No! Don't hurt him, Nokosee! Please let him go!"

Nokosee pauses, gives a quick, cutting glance at me and then mom-- which immediately shuts her up-- and then lets dad go when he realizes he's gotten carried away. Again.

Dad falls against the wall and grabs his wrist. "I'm sorry, Stormy. I didn't--"

I won't let him finish. With tears rolling down my face I bolt for the front door. Mom tries to stop me but I shove past and run out of the house. I stop outside for a moment and look back. I see J.T. has gotten to his feet and is scrambling to block the door. Nokosee feints a move and J.T. can't fall backward fast enough to get out of the way. Nokosee kicks the screen door off its hinges, hops down from the wooden porch and meets me on the front lawn. We grab hands and run.

Chapter 11

Showtime

King Roar's distinctive bellow brings Nokosee and me to a sudden stop. We hear it again. I look at Nokosee and can tell something is wrong. He turns and runs toward the boat ramp.

"Nokosee! Wait for me!"

##

Although Billy Joe Cypress is billed as the village's official alligator wrestler, J.T. sees him as the village idiot. The once famous pro wrestler "Chief In-Your-Face" is standing in the middle of the gator wrestling pit reaching out toward King Roar with a gator snare, a long steel pole with a looped piece of braided steel cable on the end wrapped inside a heavy-duty water hose.

Billy Joe had forgotten how big they can get. As far as he was concerned, King Roar was the mother of all alligators.

A long time ago when he first started gator wrestling, before he had lost J.T.'s respect, Billy Joe Cypress had been embarrassed by his opponents' diminutive size. That changed one day when one of the frisky little bastards got lucky and bit Billy Joe's right pinky off and the media, having a slow news day, swarmed down on him like a pack of locust on wheat. He was the lead story on two local stations and got a passing mention by Tom Brokaw at the end of his prime time newscast. Most of the stories portrayed him as a lone eccentric figure at an equally odd job. All of them made a point of emphasizing his Native American heritage and his stint with the WWF.

He was a national joke for about a week. Amazingly, the incident boosted tourist revenues and J.T., following a meeting with his PR firm, suggested over a few beers that maybe Billy Joe might want to consider "losing another finger or something say six months down the road." The PR firm figured the Seminoles could continue to reap the benefits of added media exposure so long as Billy was willing to lose a body part for the tribe.

Billy Joe, at first, wasn't too keen about the idea, but when J.T. said he would introduce profit sharing into the mix, Billy Joe agreed.

Three fingers and two toes later, the tribe was becoming prosperous with each loss of a body part and Billy Joe Cypress was becoming something of a national celebrity all over again for all the wrong reasons.

But it didn't bother him; he was getting rich, especially after the ad agencies discovered he could sell their products. Band-Aid sales went through the roof. The one where he was inside a gator's mouth in the middle of the Everglades making an emergency phone call on his cell phone sold more long distance service plans for AT&T than anything to this day. What finally killed it for him was when he realized he was getting to a point where he had to either sacrifice something significant or lose the world's interest. Not in a hurry to rush into making such a choice despite the pressure from the front office, he procrastinated to the point that tribal sales plummeted. Advertising contracts were broken because he wasn't losing his body parts fast enough to keep people interested.

Because he couldn't, excuse the pun, pull it off, Billy Joe developed a really stupid backup idea that went from bad to worse the minute he tried it, an idea that forever changed U.S. labor laws concerning safety in the work place. Secretly, on his own, he had prepared a gator by shaving down and removing some of its teeth for what he thought would be the ultimate comeback. That day came when, performing in front of a handful of tourists, he pretended to let his hands slip from a gator's jaws while his head was still in its mouth. Instead of rocketing him to newfound fame, his desperate little act had the opposite effect; it horrified everyone who saw it (which was basically everyone on the planet thanks to five different home video angles that found their way onto television news and the Internet). It made them question just what they needed for entertainment. Not liking the answer, Billy Joe's career as an infamously inept gator wrestler finally came to a thankful conclusion when the Feds stepped in to clean up the workplace by making it illegal for anyone in the U.S. to endanger their lives or anyone else's life for money, something the ALCU vowed to fight in court.

Had Billy Joe known that J.T., desperate for tribal revenue because he had overextended the tribe's investments based on projections based on Billy Joe's continued loss of body parts, was planning to open the nation's first gaming casino on Native American land only a few days later, he wouldn't have attempted such a risky trick. On the other hand, Billy Joe's squeamishness jump-started a new golden era for Native American tribes everywhere.

Now, facing down King Roar, Billy Joe Cypress is thinking about his second comeback; this is the biggest crowd he's had in years. He just hopes no one can see how scared he is.

"Hey, Billy-boy!" It's Bart Rader. If you look hard enough, you can see the scab that formed around Nokosee's carving job just above his tank top. "Watch out! That one sure ain't like the other sorry ass jokes you've been rasslin'!"

King Roar has also brought Bart's skinny, alcoholic father Charlie, and his brothers, Kyle, Clint, and Dawson, and everyone in the village including what seems like the ever-present media on fire watch to the gator wrestling pit.

The men have been drinking all day. Watching Billy Joe Cypress make a fool of himself would be a pleasant distraction from what was becoming a very difficult time in the plotting process against Nokosee and me; none of the men could keep track of their plans. What with all the alcohol consumption, it was becoming too confusing.

"This ain't one of J.T.'s!" Billy Joe shouts back. "Get these people outta here!"

The guys just laugh at each other until Nokosee pushes through the crowd. Seeing him shuts them up real fast. I arrive seconds later and see them but pretend I don't. Believe it or not, I had forgotten about them. So much had happened in between. Like falling in love. I step back a couple of steps into the crowd hoping they won't see me. In any event I'm sure seeing Nokosee brings back memories of pain and fear. And silence.

Nokosee doesn't see them, his eyes are on King Roar and is startled to find the gator is facing down the once famous Billy Joe Cypress. He tells me later he is even more taken back when he sees the puncture wounds running across Billy Joe's face and neck. The last time he saw Billy Joe Cypress was about five years ago on a videotape called "When Animals Attack!," a collection of the most outrageous animal attacks on humans ever caught on home video. Billy Joe's segment was featured on the video box cover and helped sell millions. I learned later that Nokosee's father would bring it out periodically to remind his children what "stupid Indians do to entertain the Outside," and how the Outside will exploit you if it gets half the chance, reminding them that "the Seminole"-- Billy Joe Cypress-- never made a dime off the video. What Nokosee's father failed to tell his kids was that the tribe's lawyers later stepped in and negotiated a settlement that managed to get more money into Billy Joe's nearly fingerless hands and the Seminole's coffers.

Yes, Nokosee had pretty much forgotten about him until today. Seeing the teeth marks reminded him how his father reacted when they watched it on TV. He laughed his butt off and said the "greedy bastard deserved it for acting like such a damn fool." When Billy Joe holds up his hand and motions him to stay back, Nokosee doesn't take notice and rushes right past. Maybe it has something to do with the fact Billy Joe only has two fingers left on that hand and, perhaps because of this, the gesture lost its impact. In any event, it would take more than a two-fingered man to stop my man.

"Haalpatee, elichko! Elichko!" Nokosee yells.

When the half-blind gator whips its head around toward the familiar voice, Nokosee starts walking toward it. Bart and the others, smelling blood I guess, exchange glances. A TV news team pushes through the crowd and stops beside the men.

Nokosee approaches the gator like a gladiator in the center of the circle of people. When King Roar cocks its head to look at Nokosee, a nervous hush rolls like a wave through the crowd. Nokosee, talking softly, inches closer and finally settles gently onto his knees beside the nearly twenty-foot, one thousand pound beast. Parents pull their children away to keep them from seeing the carnage they're sure will soon follow. When Nokosee pats its deadly snout, the crowd sucks in its collective breath. When he inches along on his knees, leans over and hugs the thing of nightmares, the crowd shouts and applauds in a communal release of nervous tension.

Unfortunately, that only scares King Roar. He lunges toward the vague figures in the distance and Nokosee jumps onto its back to keep it from attacking and to whisper something into its ear. The gator stops immediately.

"Will you look at that?" Bart says in a loud voice so everyone can hear, "The little Injun has gone done tamed the wild beast."

"Hell, son," Charlie says in a drunken slur, "it's just 'nother one of J.T.'s scams to pump up the cash register. That gator's drugged I tell ya. It's gotta be. Anybody could do that."

"Anybody?" Kyle asks while winking at Bart.

"Anybody."

"Ten bucks, old man, says you can't pet it like that kid."

Charlie has to think this one over. Bart isn't so sure about this idea either. "Dad, I don't think so."

But Kyle won't give up. "C'mon, daddy, put your money where your mouth is or shut up. Hell, you've killed bigger ones than that."

Kyle catches himself and covers his mouth and pretends to have blurted out some big secret. He looks around the crowd and explains in a louder voice, "But only during gator season."

The crowd joins him in the shared joke and laughs along with him. Sensing they are on his side, Kyle turns to the crowd and urges them on with a chant. "Pet it! Pet it! Pet it!" When some people begin to chant along, Kyle pushes his dad toward the gator.

"Okay, Okay, don't push me!" Charlie pauses and takes a long swig from his beer can. When he tries walking a straight line toward the mother of all gators, which he fails miserably, I start getting nervous.

Kyle thinks it's a real hoot but the crowd and Bart, seeing the old man can barely walk straight, are beginning to have second thoughts about what is transpiring.

Charlie isn't too impressed with a two-fingered man either so when Billy Joe Cypress tries to stop him from getting any closer to the gator, he pushes him aside with a drunken curse that disses Billy Joe and his ancestors. Billy Joe could probably have stopped him with his three-fingered hand, but that remark about his ancestors pretty much stopped that from happening so Billy Joe lets him go with a shrug and a dismissing wave of one of his digitally challenged hands, hoping, I'm sure, the gator makes him pay for the slur.

Charlie stumbles onward and stops less than a prudent distance from the gator. King Roar lurches and Nokosee has to shout at it and dig into the dirt to corral its movement, which, even for Nokosee, can't be done.

Charlie falls backward a few steps, his body waving unsteadily as it tries to find vertical. He takes another swig from the beer can and studies the animal for a moment before hoisting the can over his head as if he had accomplished something worth applauding. But no one applauds. In fact, the crowd is getting a little uneasy and quiet.

Charlie bows toward them, loses his balance and stumbles toward the gator. King Roar lurches and Nokosee holds on again, yelling now at both the gator and the drunken redneck less than ten feet away.

"What'd you say, boy?" Charlie asks loudly. "I don't know no Seminole." He turns to Nokosee in a near whisper. "Here you go, boy. I hear you carved up my son. This Bud's on you," and he begins to pour it over Nokosee's head.

King Roar lunges at Charlie. Nokosee plants his feet into the soft sand and tries to stop it but he can't—until he yells at King Roar and the gator stops on command, dropping to the blazingly white sand of the gator wrestling pit like a half-ton of bricks.

Charlie, backpedaling, catches himself and, trying to steady his gaze on the gator says, "Damn, maybe I shoulda got somethin' for the gator, too."

J.T. is out of breath when he pushes through the crowd. He can't remember seeing this many people watch somebody wrestle a gator and for a moment he finds himself doing what he usually does, making mental notes on how to tap into and market a crowd pleaser for the tribe before it dawns on him that something is wrong, that no one is smiling or talking among themselves. He sees very quickly that he has a possible lawsuit on the horizon, maybe even a class action suit if this thing gets out of hand and there is enough media here now to make sure every angle is covered for the plaintiffs. He yells across the open space at Charlie.

"Charlie, whatever you're doin,' stop. It's not one of my gators!"

Charlie tries to focus on J.T. He takes another sip from the can and discovers there isn't any beer left. He looks at the can and says, "Screw it. I need a drink." He throws the can at the gator and starts to walk away.

Unfortunately for Charlie, he misses the gator and hits Nokosee.

That's enough to set King Roar off again. Dragging Nokosee with him and, one-and-a-half drunken steps later, Charlie's leg is in the gator's mouth.

Charlie didn't know what hit him. King Roar strikes before the first scream from a child in the crowd could reach Charlie through his alcohol-deadened senses. The tremendous pressure of the gator's jaws on the leg breaks it below the knee in the first microsecond of the attack. A second later, Charlie is beginning to feel the pain and, although it would demand a sober man's full attention, Charlie is experiencing a sensory overload of the highest magnitude because the gator is thrashing him from side-to-side as if he were nothing more than one of my old Barbie dolls.

The crowd is horrified. People are screaming and crying and pleading for help because this is not what they were expecting to see on their vacations and are unprepared for Nature's way of dealing with stupidity and reminding them that when they least expect it, the world, despite the insulation their creature comforts bring them, is really a very cruel and unforgiving place. It's too much for most of them to watch and, with the first panicked family running for safety, chaos follows as the crowd starts running over each other to get away from Nature's latest nasty surprise.

Bart turns and screams at Kyle to "Get the shotgun!"

Charlie is thrown into the air. His back hits the dirt first followed by his nearly severed leg. Although the pain is there, it's the odd angle his leg has taken that reaches up through the alcohol fog first. It scares the bejesus out of him. When he looks up at the onrushing shape, he instinctively raises his arm to protect himself. Half a second later, King Roar has bitten down on his arm and wrenched it from its socket, tearing both arm and sleeve away from Charlie's body.

Nokosee jabs his thumb into King Roar's good eye and the gator throws the arm away, spinning it in a slow arc across the dirt road toward the retreating tourists, splashing them with blood and enough bad memories to last a lifetime.

Charlie is screaming now and rolling across the dirt, shooting staccato arcs of blood in the opposite direction each time his gushing socket rotates up from the earth creating a disjointed, Morris Code trail of dark crimson dots in the sand.

Charlie's arm rolls to a stop at Billy Joe Cypress' feet and I see him blink at it uncomprehendingly. He's probably thinking what I'm thinking: Fingers! And they're *moving!*

Billy Joe, fixating possibly on the fingers, grabs the hand with his hand that still has an opposable thumb as if he was shaking hands and feels it tighten around his own. The feeling is so unexpected that Billy Joe screams and tries to shake the hand loose but it won't let go.

Billy Joe is screaming and dancing around, trying to shake loose the dismembered appendage and spraying a circle of blood on everyone foolish enough to remain around the gator pit-- including me. When I turn my face away to avoid getting any of the Rader clan's mutant bloodline in my eyes, I see J.T. on his cell phone calling in the tribal police and Kyle walking into the center of the pit toward Nokosee and the gator with a shotgun he pulled out of their airboat.

"Get your raggedy ass out of there, boy!" he yells over the long black over-and-under blue steel barrels.

Call me crazy-- you probably already have, maybe even worse than that-- but I jump into the pit and run after Kyle. It just comes natural. I didn't even think about it. I mean, that's a good thing, right? Anyway, I tackle the second drunken idiot from behind, knocking him to the ground and the shotgun into the air. Unfortunately, when it hits the ground, it discharges.

King Roar whips around, dragging Nokosee with it toward Kyle and me. We're struggling for the shotgun. Kyle curses and pushes me away. I see the gator coming and freeze. Although King Roar can barely see me, he can smell me. He stops. Kyle levels the shotgun on King Roar once again but before he can pull the trigger, my dad is on top of him, tackling him from the side and knocking him to the ground.

King Roar lunges for the new shadows rolling in the dirt but Nokosee holds on, calling it back and digging his faux moccasins into the sand.

Dad unloads a punch across Kyle's jaw, which makes him let go of the shotgun. Dazed, and with the fight taken out of him, he slumps to the white-hot sand. Dad falls on top of him, trying to catch his breath. Let's face it; my ol' man is not in shape. He looks around and sees J.T.

"J.T.," dad shouts, "what the hell is going on here?"

J.T. cups the cell phone and tells him what happened as he stands over Bart who is cradling his father, trying to stop the blood gushing out of the hole that once held the old man's arm.

Dad is trying to take it all in when Billy Joe rushes by screaming and trying to shake loose of Charlie's dead man's hand shake. Charlie sees his arm dancing in front of him and throws up all over himself and his son. Bart, grimacing, yanks his dad's arm out of Billy's hand where it lands in his dad's lap. The old drunk rolls his eyes upward and faints. Bart turns to my dad and yells, "You gotta kill it, Jones! You gotta kill it!"

"Symona!"

Mom arrives. She stops some distance away and yells across the space. "Come here!"

I ignore her and turn to my dad. "Don't do it, dad," I scream, "It wasn't the gator's fault! It could have eaten me a hundred times but it never tried!"

Dad can't turn away from me.

"C'mon, man," Bart shouts, "Kill it!"

Dad turns to Nokosee. Nokosee is looking at him and struggling to corral the beast. My dad turns to the TV cameras surrounding him, capturing every moment. He turns back to me.

"This one's for you, Stormy"

I feel like I'm in a beer commercial and wonder if this is how all men look at the world. But, for some reason, maybe because he's feeling guilty as hell for hitting me, this time I believe him.

"But you gotta kill it," Kyle says from the end of the long arm of the law, my dad's grip. "It's the law!"

"Turn around and shut up." Dad pushes Kyle around and turns to me. "Stormy, come here."

I crawl over to his side.

"Take this." He gives me the shotgun, turns and reaches into his pockets for a plastic wrist tie. "Keep it on him."

"Hey," Kyle says, straining to look behind him, "What are you doing?"

Dad slips the plastic cuff around Kyle's wrists and pulls it tight.

"I'm surprised you don't know since you know the law so well. I'm arresting you for public drunkenness and discharging a firearm in a public place." He turns to Billy Joe. "Throw me your snare and get me some duct tape."

Billy Joe is still looking at Charlie, still thinking that could easily be him a one-armed man squirting blood in rhythmic bursts from a jagged hole. Dad yells again.

"Billy Joe, throw me the snare and get some duct tape!"

This time dad's voice reaches past Billy Joe's morbid revelation and he hops to it. He grabs the snare lying on the ground, throws it to dad and takes off for the duct tape.

King Roar lurches with the sudden movement and follows the fuzzy object across the road with its one half blind eye and sees dad.

Dad shakes his head wearily. He knows he just lost any chance to sneak up on his quarry. He pushes off of Kyle and stands unsteadily. He extends the snare toward King Roar and starts circling the beast. He looks at Nokosee hanging across the back of the giant gator trying mightily to hold it back. Their eyes meet.

"Chin-ha-pal-teh," dad pauses, struggling with the Muskogee language he made an effort to learn when he was assigned to the park. "En-nok-a-chee-cha-tay-ko-mish." He hopes Nokosee understands that he means the gator no harm.

"Your Muskogee sucks big time. Try English," Nokosee shouts.

I don't know about you, but I was real surprised when Nokosee spoke English in front of everybody like that-- I even looked at my mom and she was just as surprised as I was-- but my dad never acted surprised. I guess he always knew.

King Roar follows dad's moving body and stands up on its feet. Nokosee and dad know the gator is about to attack.

Nokosee leans back against the gator and digs his mocs deeper into the sand, every muscle rippling and tensing in the effort.

But there is nothing Nokosee can do to hold back one hundred million years of savage pre-dinosaur DNA. King Roar leaps across the sand dragging Nokosee with it.

Before dad can take two steps back, before anyone can scream, King Roar grabs the snare and rips it from his hands. The gator's one thousand pound momentum reaches out of the paleontology books and becomes agonizingly real as it races over dad, knocking him onto his back with such force that his head bounces off the earth. Stunned, dad's body relaxes and is caught by the unexpected impact of the gator's driven fury when it steps on his diaphragm and forces the air from his lungs. He tries to push King Roar off but he can't. Sand is kicked into his eyes making it hard for him to see. He hears the crowd screaming in horror as King Roar rolls over his body one more time.

King Roar is focusing on the snare, whipping it back and forth across a bright sky full of smoke and ash when dad grabs the beast's leg and tries to push it off. He wants to breathe; to live but his struggle to free himself, which seems like an eternity, has no effect. He feels Nokosee's hand moving down the beast's leg and blinks through his tears to see the young Seminole burying his shoulder into the gator's rib cage just behind the front leg and, with an effort he later tells me reminds him of the George Bellows painting *Stag at Sharkey's,* of boxers trying to kill each other, of line and power firmly implanted in his brain. He watches Nokosee's outstretched body struggle mightily to lift the enraged animal, to topple it onto its back.

And it's all in slow motion dad tells me later, tapping memories of movies he thought he had long forgotten. He can hear Nokosee's long drawn out scream rising slowly from his gut and now he sees Bruce Lee in the middle of a long drawn out *kei*, both with sinews rippling and that force he equated with so much far Eastern mystical mumbo jumbo b.s. slowly lifting the gator off its feet.

The real world begins again with the sudden impact of sound and pain and motion in a real-time slap of the gator's tail in my dad's face and I think, just for a second, this is karma, dad, this is pay back for slapping me and the need for revenge on my part is all but gone.

Dad rolls away and when he comes up from the earth, his heart is racing at a frightening pace, his lungs are on fire, his chest is deeply heaving, trying to grasp all the air it can get. He sees Nokosee rolling with the gator over and over and over in the sand toward a perimeter of people who are screaming and running away. He can't believe the kid is still holding on and wonders how he can do it, to take the full weight of the gator and still hold on.

Dad struggles up to one elbow and watches in amazement as the gator stops rolling not so much because it's tired, but because Nokosee has its right front leg in some kind of half-Nelson and is pressing on an artery just behind the eye. He's cutting blood flow to the creature's primitive pea-sized brain and with one final Herculean effort, rolls the gator onto its back.

Dad can't believe it and neither can I. Nokosee, covered in fine white sand, his white shirt shredded and caked in blood, is putting the gator to "sleep."

Nokosee falls against the gator's stomach. Winded and struggling for air, he looks around and sees dad. He shouts across the bloody earth, "Let it go!"

Dad pauses to catch his own breath and to pull himself up to his knees. "I can't," he shouts back, "the law won't let me."

Nokosee looks for me. He sees me standing next to Kyle with the shotgun, crying, pleading with my eyes for him to stop and live. My mom is standing behind me, her hands on my shoulders and her eyes wide and frightened on Nokosee.

He turns away and looks at the crowd. They're taking pictures, video taping him from a safe distance. He knows he is going to be all over TV tonight. This is not what his father wanted. He turns back to me and then to my dad and asks, "What are you going to do with Haalpatee?"

"I'm going to cage it and return it."

"Give him to me now and I'll take him back for you."

"Can't do that, son. The state requires we tag and release each one we find."

Nokosee hears a siren and looks around. He sees a Fire and Rescue truck parting the crowd and four Seminole tribal police pushing through the crowd with their guns drawn, pointing at him and the gator. The siren frightens King Roar and Nokosee has to throw himself across the gator.

"Tell 'em to kill the siren!" Nokosee yells.

Dad shouts across the open ground and the siren grinds to a stop. Nokosee, struggling to hold the gator down, pauses to assess the situation before turning to dad.

"Tell these cop wannabes to holster their guns. We're gonna need them to help us." He turns away and adds, "Where's that crazy Seminole with the duct tape?"

On cue, Billy Joe honks his pick up truck's horn and emerges from the parting crowd. The truck has his name on the door panels promoting his gator farm, his post pro wrestling occupation, and the fact that he does parties.

The honking excites King Roar and he jerks free from Nokosee's grip and flips onto its stomach.

The crowd screams and scatters again.

Nokosee immediately throws himself over Haalapatee's still groggy head and tries to hold its mouth shut.

"Guys," dad yells at the tribal police as he hobbles toward King Roar, "put the guns away. This is where you're going to earn your big bucks. Let's catch this baby."

The tribal cops exchange dubious glances before J.T. jumps in behind dad and yells at them. They holster their weapons, part and close in on King Roar just as Billy Joe jumps from his truck and joins them on the run, unspooling the duct tape.

When dad jumps onto the gator's snout, six men join him, throwing themselves onto the gator. King Roar lifts its head and throws dad off as if he were nothing more than a pesky fly. The crowd screams and runs past a couple of TV crews who are backtracking but haven't panicked just yet because of the great Emmy quality footage they're getting.

King Roar's huge powerful tail sweeps the ground with two of the cops when dad jumps back into the fray, joining Billy Joe who is trying to wrap the gator's snout in duct tape, not an easy thing to do when you're digitally challenged.

But the gator won't have anything to do with that. Billy Joe throws his weight across the snout, and wraps the tape around the mouth using his own mouth as a substitute for a hand with an opposable thumb.

But the first two wraps are splitting as King Roar struggles mightily to open its mouth.

"Hurry!" dad yells.

A gator's strength is in its downward bite where it's needed to hold, submerge and drown its victim. Once the jaws are closed, a gator is at a surprising disadvantage because a lone brave-- or stupid--- man can easily hold the jaws together with his hands. Seeing the duct tape splitting is more than enough to make an expert gator wrestler like Billy Joe Cypress wrap it at warp speed because he knows this gator isn't like anything he's ever seen before.

When he's done, Billy Joe, ever the consummate performer, rolls away, jumps to his feet and throws his fingerless hands up in the air as if was trying to win points at a rodeo. That catches King Roar's attention and the next thing Billy Joe Cypress knows is that instead of being greeted with cheers from an adoring public, he hears frightened screams and finds himself on his back and the gator's muzzled mouth thrashing across his head.

Billy Joe grabs the snout and tries to push it away but the man just doesn't have any luck with these creatures because his right thumb, the last one he has, inadvertently slips into the side of the mouth, which causes King Roar to clamp down on it. When the gator twists its head, Billy Joe's thumb goes with it and blood squirts everywhere. Billy Joe's own gut-wrenching scream is drowned out by the crowd's audible revulsion and disappointment in the shared realization that some people just don't get breaks no matter how much you want them to.

King Roar, carrying seven men with it, rolls right over Billy Joe and leaves him clutching his hand and writhing in the dirt. Nokosee comes out of the roll with his torn shirt covered in more dirt and blood. Lying on his back, he pulls as hard as he can against the gator's momentum, leans close to its head and pushes harder on that artery near King Roar's brain.

King Roar stops rolling and the men find themselves struggling against nothing and falling over each other. Once they regain their positions, everyone tries to lift it from the ground.

It isn't easy. At one thousand pounds, even upside down and in its lethargic state, King Roar still has enough power to twist slowly from side to side to knock the men to the ground.

"Someone help them!" I yell at the people mulling on the perceived perimeter of safety but no one steps out of the crowd to help. I turn to my mom. "Hold this." I push the shotgun into mom's hands and run toward Billy's truck.

"Symona!" Mom holds the shotgun away from her body as if it were something disgusting and ugly.

"Point it at him!" I shout. "If he moves, pull the trigger!"

"No way, lady!" Kyle yells. He starts to back away from her. "Don't go pointing that thing at me if you don't know how to use it!"

"Then don't move, buddy!" mom screams back at a nerve jarring level that startles even her. She strains to lift the heavy double-barreled shotgun up to her shoulder and takes aim at Kyle's head. This scares him to no end and, with his hands cuffed behind his back, tries to duck and run.

"Please, mam," he shouts over his shoulder, "Please don't aim that at me!"

"Don't move!" mom yells back but Kyle keeps dashing about like a target in a carney sideshow. And so does the crowd; no one wants to be standing behind him.

I hit the brakes on Billy Joe's truck when Kyle runs across my path, bobbing and weaving and crying and looking back at his pursuer. When I see my mom chasing after him with the shotgun, I lean out the window and shout, "Mom, make sure the safety's on!" When mom shouts, "What's that?" I hear Kyle's stilted cry and turn to see him zigzagging across the ground like O.J. Simpson in his prime, heading for a chaotic mass of screaming cowards with mom in hot pursuit.

I fall back into the truck and drive it up to the guys struggling with the gator, jump out, run to the back and drop the tailgate. "C'mon," I yell, "put it in the truck!"

I grab King Roar's tail and together, with an extreme effort, we manage to get the biggest gator any of us will ever see into the bed of the pick up truck, sinking it under the weight of the gator and the men. Nokosee and dad stay with the gator but the rest are quick to jump out of the truck bed. Dad tells me to drive them back to the compound.

I look in the sideview mirror and see J.T. watching the truck limp away like an injured animal dragging its tail under the weight of the huge beast. He turns away and finds himself standing alone in the middle of the chaos. A Medivac helicopter is whipping up a dust cloud as it lands to whisk Charlie and his arm to the nearest hospital thirty miles to the east. When he shields his eyes and looks away, he sees two Miami-Dade County EMT's wrapping Billy Joe's hand in a gauze bandage. When Billy Joe sees a third man drop his sand covered thumb unceremoniously into a cheap Styrofoam cooler filled with ice, he starts crying. And I don't blame him; it's enough to make any man cry.

I hear the echoing ring of a shotgun blast and I'm left wondering if Kyle bought the big one.

Chapter 12

Sex, Lies, and Gatorbait

"You oughta arrest her too!" Kyle shouts over his shoulder at dad. "She almost killed me!"

"You shouldn't have tried to run away," dad says matter-of-factly.

It's an hour later. Dad is escorting Kyle by the arm through the compound office. Kyle's head is bandaged thanks to mom's errant shotgun blast. They pass J.T. He's smoking a cigar while sitting on the edge of the office desk, taking it all in.

"So what's with the gator?" Bart shouts from behind the Formica counter that separates the office from a standing-room-only public area.

Dad stops at the back office door that leads to our family living quarters and turns to him. "Why aren't you with your 'daddy?'"

"I can't do nothin' for him now while he's on the operatin' table," Bart continues, following dad through the office. "Momma and one of my brothers are with him if it's any of your gall damn business. So like I said, what are you gonna do with the gator?"

"Like I said," dad says while putting a key into the door lock, "No one's killing the gator."

"Dammit, why not? It tore off my daddy's arm for crise sakes!"

"It was provoked," dad says. "Damn." He can't find the key.

I hear all of this through my bedroom walls. I step out of my bedroom and head for the bathroom. I'm bathed and dressed and ready to go out for one final fling on the rez with Nokosee. Since I'm on a tight schedule to say the least, I have to skip taking time to dye my hair but thanks to my Hot Topic spray on hair color, my hair instantly has deeper pink highlights and is standing proudly around my head in a fashion my dad enjoys describing as "electrocuted." I've got on another pair of Brazilian-cut jeans only this time they're faded denim and I make sure to wear them as low as I can on my hips. I've got my favorite cork wedgies under my feet to make me look taller and to tighten my butt and thighs. I'm wearing a white t-shirt with the letters "CBGB" silk-screened across the front. I cut it in half so that it shows off my tanned bare midriff and pierced navel. Now I wish I had brought my tongue stud since it should come in handy later tonight. After today, I don't really care what my parent's think about me. I'm a new person. Braver. I cap everything off with my "Chiefs" gang jacket. I pause at the bathroom door to listen to the voices in the office and to adjust a small black leather bag that hangs from my shoulder at the end of a long black leather belt. A chrome plated Harley-Davidson derby cover is riveted to the front. The only thing missing is my cell phone with my "things to do with Nokosee list." I can't find it anywhere but that's no biggie. I know exactly what I'm going to do with Nokosee in the few hours we have left together and I don't need any reminders.

"If that's what they teach you at Ranger school," Bart continues, "there aren't gonna be any people left to protect."

"You guys got the police," dad replies, "The critters got me."

I smile, shake my head, open the bathroom door and fall back into the hallway. Nokosee is standing there, stark naked on the floor mat, frozen with only a towel around his shoulders. He lets out a yelp and covers himself quicker than I could have wished for.

"Shee-it!" Bart continues from behind the office wall, "I don't believe it. You've got to kill it! Its tasted human blood!"

Nokosee slams the door in my face.

"Rader," dad says, "the only thing that gator's gonna remember about human blood is that it tastes like Budweiser and comes with a hangover."

I hear the door to the office unlock, and swiftly tiptoe back across the hallway into my bedroom. I slide up against the wall and listen through a crack in the doorway.

"This is ridiculous!" Bart yells. "Here I am talkin' to a man more concerned 'bout protectin' some stinkin' gator's rights than my daddy's!"

When dad throws the door open and stops to look back at Bart another door opens at the same time. I hear my dad's bedroom door open and see mom walking across the hallway toward the bathroom with a towel wrapped around her and a makeup kit in her hand. I bite my lip when mom opens the bathroom door and takes a step into the bathroom. I hear her scream—and Nokosee too-- and watch her fall back into the hallway, dropping her things and watching the door slam shut behind her. Mom is leaning against the wall trying to catch her breath when she looks down the hallway and sees Kyle staring at her with eyes that could kill from across the living room.

"Oh my God!"

"Everything O.K back there?" dad shouts.

Mom pulls the towel tighter around her body and bolts for the bedroom, slamming the door behind her.

"I guess so," dad answers himself.

I have to force myself to keep from laughing out loud.

"You're forgettin' the gator never harmed the boy or my daughter," dad says to Bart, "and, from listening to Stormy, he had every chance to attack her and didn't."

"Who, the Indian?"

"Cute."

"Screw you, Jones!"

Dad stops and turns around. "Rader, I don't have to take any crap from you. Do you understand me?" When there is no response, dad asks him again. "Well, do you?"

"Yeah, yeah, I hear ya."

"Oh, and expect a subpoena in the next couple of days."

"For what?"

"Poaching and—"

"'Poaching'? You gotta be kidding me. Where's your proof?"

"And threatening to kill my daughter. I'm having one made up for Kyle and Dawson too."

This catches Bart off-guard-- and me too.

"She told me you bastards threatened to kill her."

"It's her word against ours."

"And the Indian's."

I hear Bart sputter for a moment and then some mumbled cursing before slamming the door behind him. I don't think he can get out of dad's crosshairs fast enough.

"Don't move."

I peek around the corner. Dad is walking back through the office when the sound of the bathroom door rattling back and forth gets my attention. I look down the hallway to see if anyone is around. I can't see anybody. I throw open my door, dash across the hallway and open the bathroom door for Nokosee. He's wearing a brand new white cowboy shirt. It's unbuttoned and he still can't figure out how to get the zipper up on a fresh pair of jeans, all compliments of J.T.

Maybe that's one reason I love him so much. *What a doofus.*

I reach down, yank it up, grab his hand and pull him across the hallway into my bedroom, quickly shutting the door behind us. I turn back to Nokosee, shush him softly and place my finger on his mouth to make sure he doesn't make a sound. I'm surprised, to say the least, when he sucks them playfully. He's looking at me with an excited, mischievous smile. Just when you think he's already stolen your heart, he just reels you in deeper. I want to kiss him and I do. It's our first real kiss. I have to tiptoe up in my wedgies to reach his lips. He grabs me so tightly I feel like I'm going to break in two. Our tongues are all over the place in each other's mouths and I gotta tell you, I'm thinking, is this how they kiss in the swamp? Holy cow, I can't wait for more. My heart is racing now after that first kiss and as much as I would love to throw Nokosee down on my bed and make love to him right then and there, I won't because I've got other plans. I push him away and try to catch my breath before slowly opening the bedroom door. I look around. The coast is clear. I grab his hand and lead him quietly as I can down the hallway and through the living room. When I see Kyle, handcuffed, staring at me from the nook between the office and our living room with hate-filled eyes, I'm at first surprised but then find myself sneering back just as quickly, even flipping him the finger before pushing Nokosee through the kitchen and out the back door.

We stumble behind a bush outside the compound kitchen window. It's nearly dark now but a full moon is rising in the east. King Roar is chained to a stake in the fenced-in back yard. He instinctively lunges for us, not knowing who we are. We press ourselves up against the wall as dad comes back and pushes Kyle through the back door and down the steps toward the gator.

"What are you doin'?"

"Despite working for the greatest government on earth, they can't afford to build me a jail, so this is going to have to do."

"Are you kidding me?"

We peek around the bush. Dad is marching Kyle across the backyard toward King Roar. The gator pulls at its chain to get to the men. Kyle jumps back.

"You can't lock me up out here like an animal. There's gotta be a law against it."

"Only if you're a terrorist."

We can't believe our eyes. Dad is padlocking Kyle to a chain wrapped around the huge front wheel of a swamp buggy only a few feet away from King Roar.

"Now if you remain quiet and don't move around too much, your cell mate will leave you alone. Otherwise, it'll probably eat you." Dad turns and starts walking back to the compound.

"How am I going to go to the bathroom?"

King Roar hisses at Kyle and yanks at its chain.

Dad pauses to look back. "Damn, there you go. I told you not to irritate the critter. Regarding bathroom privileges, just give a yell."

"'Give a yell'? And get him riled?"

King Roar gets riled, hisses and yanks at his chain.

Dad pauses at the back steps just as he opens the door and turns around. "Yeah, that's a problem. Hopefully your brother will have you bailed out by then. Talk to you later." Dad turns, steps through the doorway and slams the door behind him.

King Roar roars even louder and Nokosee and I have to laugh.

We hear J.T.'s voice as he looks through the open window just above our heads. "Kinda cruel and unusual punishment, don'tcha think?" He's so close we can smell the coffee he's drinking.

"Not if he don't bite the gator," dad replies. He's making himself a cup of coffee. I can hear him stirring in his cream and sugar. "Think I might have stepped over the edge here?"

"You've been way over the edge for as long as I can remember."

"Maybe I've finally had it with all these redneck dickwads."

"Whoe, Kemasabe," J.T. says as he turns away from the window. "What the hell do you think this is?"

We ease up toward the window and see J.T. leaning forward and pulling down his shirt collar. Dad shrugs.

"So what's gonna happen next?" J.T. asks.

"I don't know. I expect the ALCU will be all over my ass on this one."

A moment passes before J.T. asks, "Are you going to kill it?"

Dad pauses before answering. "Yes."

It's like I've been hit in the stomach. Sucker punched by my own dad. I collapse against the wall and look at Nokosee. He's not looking at me; he's straining to hear what the men are saying.

"I don't have much choice," dad continues. They're right. It's the law."

"It's a bad law," J.T. says. "Why didn't you kill it earlier?"

"Stormy. I couldn't hurt her."

"So you'll hurt her later?"

"She won't know what happened. By this time tomorrow, she'll be back in New Jersey with her mom."

I start to hyperventilate. I can't believe my dad is doing this to me. Nokosee looks at me. I can see the anger in his eyes.

"What about the kid?" J.T asks.

Dad pauses. "It's option two. He's going to Oklahoma."

I grab Nokosee to keep from falling over from the third sucker punch and sink slowly down the wall.

Dad pauses and with measured tones says, "I don't want him anywhere near Stormy."

I'm crying softly now, my head is rocking from side to side. Nokosee reaches out and touches my shoulder. I look at him through tears, take his hand and kiss it.

"I want a cultural anthropologist to study him until he's an old man," dad continues. "I don't want Stormy ever to see his face again."

I don't want to hear anymore. I grab Nokosee's hand and lead him away.

Chapter 13

Viva Las Everglades!

"Wanna dance?"

Yes. I wanna dance. I want to forget everything that has happened today. And everything that will happen tomorrow. The question, like so many things about Nokosee, surprises me. I had left him in a country and western dinner theater at the resort while I stepped away to take care of some business at the front desk. He can't wait to get back to the swamp but he's agreed to humor me because I think he knows—or hopes—I'm going to give him a going away present he'll never forget. And he's right.

"Are you tellin' me you can dance, pagan cave boy?"

"C'mon."

Nokosee takes my hand and leads me out onto the dance floor and away from my pain and the feeling that I have no control over my life. Despite my dad's betrayal, I'm following his advice to suck it up and make the best of it. Crybabies need not apply at the Joneses.

"I gotta tell you, Nokosee, I'm not really a country western kinda chick."

"Trust me, girl, it's evolved."

With the live band slinging rock riffs throughout the song, Nokosee takes my hand, puts his other hand around my waist and begins to lead me into the counter clockwise flow of cowboy couples in ostrich leather boots and big ol' hats and tourists in shorts and big t-shirts. By the time we are halfway around the floor, all eyes have turned to us not so much because everyone recognizes us from the day's events,

but because of the way we look dancing together. Despite
my position on country music, this girl can dance thanks to
another one of my dad's efforts to bond with me. But I've
never been inspired to dance like I am tonight. Nokosee,
with his long black hair flowing across the white cowboy
shirt down to his waist, is an inspiration. He doesn't see
anyone but me in his smiling eyes. And that, of course, is the
way I like it.

My God, I'm thinking as I look up at him as he leads me
backwards and then spins me under his arm, *is there
anything he can't do?*

The next song isn't any help in finding an answer. When
the band ends its set with a tune with more funk than twang,
Nokosee breaks from me and begins some exuberant free
style steps that end when he drops to a split with a snap up
to a twist that throws his long hair out in a wide circle
around him. Of course it gets a hand from everyone,
including me.

"Where'd you learn to dance like that?"

"Soul Train."

I laugh and shake my head in disbelief as Nokosee puts
his arms around my waist.

"'Course I never had a partner like you to inspire me
before, either. I mean, it sure beats dancing with your sister.
I hope I didn't embarrass you."

"You didn't embarrass me," I reply while looking up into
his eyes. I start taking in his face, savoring every handsome
feature because I know I may never see him again after
tonight.

"Stormy, I'm so happy right now."

"I can tell."

"But I think I may be tryin' a little too hard."

"What do you mean?"

"You know and I know this is probably our last dance."

"Aw, geese, Nokosee, you sure know how to kill a
moment." I put my head against his chest.

"I'm sorry, but you know I've got to leave tonight. Your
dad wants to ship me off to Oklahoma and you know I'm not

going to let that happen. And," Nokosee pauses, "you're leaving tomorrow anyway."

"I know," I say softly, looking at nothing.

"I think that's why I was dancing like some kinda 'Soul Train' fool. That, with a twist of Ghost Dancer thrown in. You know its Ghost Dancer tradition to keep on dancin,' to never stop until the Indian Messiah returns. Maybe if I dance hard enough, the sun won't rise and the night will never end. Or I'll never forget it."

"I know I never will." I tiptoe up and kiss him and we sway to the music. I don't want to stop kissing him and I can tell he doesn't want to stop either but I have bigger plans that go beyond kissing. I push away and look up at him. "C'mon, let's go." I take his hand and lead him off the dance floor.

"Where are we going?"

"You'll see."

As if on cue, our exit across the dark dance floor is caught under moving spotlights while Elvis' taped entrance music rises up from some soundboard.

"Ladies and Gentlemen," an announcer's recorded baritone voice echoes across the room, "welcome to *Viva Las Everglades!*-- A musical revue for the entire family! Please turn off your cell phones. Videotaping and still photos are prohibited. Now, settle back and enjoy our new show *Viva Las Everglades!* with your hosts, 'Brother Sun' and 'Sister Moon.'"

We stop on a landing and look back at the stage fronting the dance floor. A waiter wearing a patchwork Seminole jacket rushes by with a tray full of food and drink from the kitchen and climbs the steps toward another level of seating in the dinner theater. The digitally printed curtain of a painting of a Seminole camp by the master of the genre, the late Albert "Beanie" Backus, rises quickly up into the ceiling.

Brother Sun and Sister Moon are a Miccosukee brother and sister act. He's wearing a silk patchwork jacket and jeans; she's wearing the traditional two-piece woman's dress, but cut sexier. They're singing into small, nearly unseen wireless head mics. This allows them to pole out of a foggy swamp of cypress trees in two bithlos toward the audience. The festive vacationers, conventioneers and gamblers are amazed by the daring use of water on the stage and applaud appreciatively.

Sister Moon gets out, walks over to a chickee hut sheltering backup musicians and picks up a candy apple Fender StratoCaster electric guitar resting against one of the posts. Brother Sun pauses for a moment to mimic an Elvis pose from the King's late Vegas period-- and gets another round of applause and laughter for the effort-- before continuing on over to a Fiberglas cypress tree on the opposite side of the stage. He lifts another Fender from a branch and straps it on. This one is decorated in the Seminole patchwork design. They come together at the center of the stage to play and sing some hard driving rock and roll.

Nokosee is captivated by what he sees and hears. As much as I wouldn't mind seeing the show with him, we can't. As I said before, I've got other plans. I pull him away, tripping and stumbling, across the dark aisle and out the door.

When we get outside, I pull him behind a potted plastic palm in a large carpeted commons area filled with people and shove him against the wall. I look up at him and say, "I don't want to stop kissing you" and prove it by rising up and kissing him hard and long on the mouth before pushing myself away. With one hand against his chest to hold him back, I slip my hand into the top coin pocket of my jeans and pull up something that looks like a credit card. "Do you know what this is?" I ask.

Nokosee, breathless, speechless and wanting more of me, has a hard time focusing on the thing in my hand and shakes his head negatively.

"It's an electronic room key. Compliments of Stanlo Osceola."

"Who's he?"

"He's the top dog in our gang, the Chiefs. He works at the hotel. When I left you in the bar, I was with him getting this.

It's the key to the Presidential Suite and there aren't no presidents here tonight." My eyebrows dance up and down for emphasis.

Nokosee smiles and shakes his head in amazement as well he should but then he starts second guessing everything. "Oh, Stormy, it sounds great but why would this guy want to help me get--" He cuts himself off.

"Get laid?" I ask in mock surprise. "My, my, Nokosee, is that what you think is going to happen?"

Nokosee, my lean mean killin' machine blushing like only he can blush, starts stammering and turns uncomfortably away.

"It's such a great view, big guy, I thought we'd just go up there and snuggle before we say good-bye."

"I'm sorry," Nokosee says, looking at the potted plastic palm. "I'm kinda new at this. I didn't--"

I stop him with my finger on his lips. "So am I." I leave my finger lingering there wondering if he will suck it like he did before and hoping he will. He grabs my hand and I can feel it shaking. He pauses for a second and then, looking me unflinchingly in the eyes, sucks my finger-- no, makes *love* to my finger.

I yank it away and wonder if I'm really ready for all of this. I rest my head on his chest and feel his powerful heart pounding against my ear. I put my arms around him and squeeze him tightly. Nokosee can only see the top of my electric pink hair as I look to the side and catch the passing parade of families on vacation and gamblers on a hunch.

"I'm a 'Chief,' remember?" I say, still looking at the crowd. "It's one of the perks of belonging to the gang. I never used it but I want it tonight and we lucked out. That's all there is to it. Stanlo digs you. He wants to be your friend."

"Well, he's off to the right start," Nokosee whispers.

After a pause, I continue. "It pays to have connections, Nokosee. The Great White Father's daughter can get anything she wants here. Well, almost anything. She can't get love." I start to well-up and turn my face into his shirt to wipe away my tears. And then I think, *Oh, my God, my mascara must have rubbed off!* I look, just a smudge, it's not that bad. I turn around in Nokosee's arms, take his hands and draw him around me. With my back up against his chest, I look across the huge hotel lobby.

"Nokosee," I ask tentatively, "can you love me?" But before he can answer, I stop him short. "You don't have to answer that," I say while wiping away more tears with the back of my hand. "I didn't bring you here to see the show. I brought you here to say good-bye. Properly. Mom says I'm bad. Dad says I gave him his gray hairs. I didn't. But I will tonight. C'mon, time's a waistin'."

I turn and yank him stumbling after me across the wide lobby under the towering glass atrium. Nokosee is spellbound by the glass, chrome and height of the enclosed air-conditioned space. Looking up, he sees balconies spiraling upward into the night sky, eerily lit with the reddish glow of the Everglades fire.

We take the glass elevator pod and whisk swiftly upward through the atrium. The sudden rising movement catches Nokosee off-guard and he has to grab the polished brass rail encircling the elevator to keep from falling. When he looks down at the rapidly receding floor, he gets dizzy and nearly loses his grip.

"Look over there," I tell him. "That's the compound."

Nokosee looks across the wide expanse through the glass and is surprised to see the compound, its American flag hanging limply under a spotlight.

And then he sees the fire.

As we continue to rise, the Everglades reveals itself in an otherworldly reddish glow. Scattered lines of fire are crisscrossing each other towards the dark, smoky depths to become one single swash of flames dancing on the horizon. It looks like the whole Everglades is on fire.

He tiptoes up to see farther. He must be thinking about his family, I think, but I won't let him do that. When we hit our floor, I pull him away from the apocalyptic scene outside the windows, out the elevator and down a hallway. When I find the Presidential Suite and its double-wide entrance

doors, I stop and insert the key into the electronic door lock.
In the moment it takes to unlock, to find its magnetic code,
Nokosee grabs me by the shoulders and turns me around.

"Stormy," he says, looking at me with kind and loving
eyes, "how can I not?"

"How can you not what?" I ask.

"How can I not love you," he says. He bends down, gently
cups my face and wipes away my wussy tears before kissing
me softly on my eyelids.

At that moment, the door unlocks.

"Well, this is your chance to prove it," I whisper.

I grab Nokosee by his shirt and pull him into the room. I
stick my head out the door and look up and down the empty
hallway before locking it behind me.

"I would have taken you to my room back at the
compound but, as you know," I say while fumbling in the
dark for a light switch, "the Great White Father and his Not
So Great White Ex are waiting for me to return so they can
ship me off to New Jersey. Too bad. It was one of my
fantasies to do it with you in my own room."

I find the light switch and flip it on.

A moment passes as we take in the enormity of the suite
as it extends beyond the light into the darker depths of the
living room.

"Well," I say, "I guess this is just going to have to do."

"It sure beats a chickee," Nokosee says nervously.

I take Nokosee by the hand and lead him into the large
lushly appointed living room. I flip on another light and
before us over the sofa is one of the largest black and white
photographs of the Everglades Clyde Butcher has ever done.
His style has always been grand but this is monumental. The
size is so overwhelming it looks like you could step right
into it. "My, God," I say in amazement.

"I know where that is," Nokosee says. "It's near where I
live."

"It's beautiful." The photograph looks like it was taken
about as far away as you can get from civilization. "So what

Metro bus do I have to take to see you?" I ask while still looking at the photograph.

The question unintentionally brings up our unspoken apprehension about tomorrow when a thousand miles will separate us.

Nokosee squeezes me tightly and turns to me. "Try Greyhound."

We laugh uneasily. I turn and look up at him. "Where will I tell the driver to stop? By the second gator on the right?"

"The third gator on the Alley," Nokosee says with a smile. He's talking about "Alligator Alley," the road that stretches across the Everglades connecting Ft. Lauderdale with Naples. "The second gator will only get you lost. And don't worry about telling the bus driver where to stop. If I know you're coming, I'll stop him for you."

"I'm sure you will."

I take him by the hand and lead him toward another double-wide set of doors on the other side of the living room. I open it enough to slip my head in and say, "You gotta be kidding me." I push the doors open and there before us, perched on coral rock steps under the soft glow of a concealed light in the chickee hut canopy is the biggest bed either of us has ever seen; a four-poster with hand carved cypress trees as the posts supporting a thatched roof. The bedspread is a Seminole patchwork quilt.

Looking up, I'm surprised to see the full moon shining down on us. The bedroom's roof is framed in steel and glass and if it were not for the reddish glow of the smoke and ash wafting between us and the moon, the view could easily have been from a window on a space ship.

We turn to each other with incredulous smiles and shake our heads. We laugh nervously at this because we know where the moment is taking us.

"Must have had President Clinton in mind when they designed it," I say to relieve the tension while walking over to a cabinet hutch across from the chickee bed. I throw the doors open. "I wonder where the humidor is?"

"The what?" Nokosee asks.

I step back to admire the wide screen TV. "The cigar box."

The reference slips right by Nokosee thanks to his father. I learned while I was slapping mosquitoes in the Everglades with him that his dad censored a lot of the Outside world simply because he didn't want his kids growing up too fast. This from a man who wears the shriveled up blackened ears of Viet Cong he's killed in Nam. Who's to figure?

I open a drawer, pick up the remote and turn on the TV. The local news comes up. Because of limited visibility due to heavy smoke, the driver of a SUV lost control, flipped and burned on Alligator Alley. This is not the kind of thing you want playing in the background when you do it for the first time. So I start switching channels.

Nokosee silently steps up behind me and puts his hands gently on my shoulders. "I don't smoke, remember?"

"Neither did he. Would you believe," I ask while looking at the TV and flipping the channels, "I've never done this before?"

"I wouldn't care if you did. My mother says 'love conquers all.'"

I roll my eyes and step away. "Don't go thinking about your mom at a time like this."

I find MTV. It's a Red Hot Chilly Peppers Weekend. Anthony Kiedis, the lead singer, is jumping up and down in a desert somewhere, his long straight black hair bouncing behind him like the tail of a dragon in a Chinese New Year's parade.

"Hey, look, Nokosee," I say, pointing at the TV, "it's you!"

Nokosee turns and looks at the TV. He's startled by what he sees. He's never heard their music or seen them play.

"Separated at birth," I say. "Maybe you could get them to join up with your father's guerrilla group. They could become like, you know, the official band."

"We already have an official band," he says while watching the TV. "The Stones."

I'm not surprised; it's always about dad.

"Nokosee," I say. He looks at me. "Here." I throw him the remote and he catches it with one hand. "You know how to use these things, right?"

"What, do I look like I live in a swamp or something? Of course, I do. Dad only steals the best."

"Good. Find something romantic."

"This isn't romantic?"

"Funny. I'll be back in a sec."

I use the moonlight and the bluish glow from the TV flooding the bedroom to find my way to what I suspect is the bathroom door.

"You can take as long as you want," Nokosee offers.

I look back. He's mesmerized by the music video. Thank God his dad didn't let him play computer games or else he'd probably be a video junky by now. "Thanks, pagan cave boy," I say with a slight smile at the bathroom doorway, "but we're runnin' on borrowed time. I won't be long." I shut the door behind me.

When I'm ready, I open the bathroom door and stop at the threshold. He's still watching TV but the bathroom light falling across the screen makes him look around. I'm in silhouette but he can see enough to know that I'm not wearing anything except the Seminole jacket and the demure pose Botticelli gave Venus in the painting of her birth rising from a clam shell, a picture he told me he saw in an art book his mother gave him, an image now changed forever by a new punk goddess called Stormy Jones in an otherworldly vision that will remain with him even to his death bed. At least I hope it will because I know exactly what I'm doing. It's all planned. Even the pose. From the first time I heard Nokosee tell me about the painting, I knew it would be this way.

He jumps to his feet.

"Are you as scared as I am?" the punk goddess asks.

"Scareder."

I turn off the bathroom light. Except for the music of the Red Hot Chili Peppers, the bedroom is just the way I dreamed it would be, bathed in moonlight-- and yes, TV light, but if Nokosee likes the music playing, it's okay by me. Anyway, right now, I'm really not thinking about the music.

"Nokosee, can you come to me? I don't think I can walk across the floor." And that's the truth.

Nokosee throws the remote onto the carpet. His steps are faltering, unsure. He comes to me as a boy, not a man. He pauses in front of me, his eyes racing over my body. He sees my trembling hands and, thankfully, grabs them just in time because I swear they are about to shake right off of my body. And now I can feel him shaking too.

"Stormy, you're so bad."

"That's what you love about me, right?"

"That's what I *adore* about you. What am I going to do with you?"

"Unzip me."

Nokosee pauses and sees me looking up at him with unflinching, daring eyes; eyes my trembling hands betray, eyes I know he can't say no to, won't say no to. I take his hands and place them on the zipper between my breasts.

"You haven't forgotten how to use these things, have you?"

"If I have," Nokosee replies anxiously, "please take me out and shoot me."

Unzipping my Seminole jacket begins without a problem until I cup and lift my breasts and push them together. Nokosee forgets what he has learned and drags the zipper sideways, catching it in the cloth.

"Oh, no," he whimpers.

"You gotta be kidding me."

"I wish."

"Here, let me do it." I push his hands away and try freeing the zipper.

"I can do it," Nokosee says. He tries to grab the zipper.

I slap his hands. "Stop! This isn't the way it's supposed to happen."

"What do you mean, 'supposed to happen?'"

"Never mind. We don't have that much time."

"What, are you in a hurry?"

"Damn right."

I reach up, grab his shirt and rip it apart scattering buttons across the carpet and the bathroom floor. When I pull the shirt down around his arms, Nokosee tries to humor his goddess by speeding things up, by unbuttoning the cuffs on his long sleeves but he's not very good at that either. And, this being a western shirt, there are *way* too many buttons for me to be patient with.

"Stop it!" I yell. "You're making me crazy! Turn around!"

Before he's had a chance to turn on his own, I twist him around, grab his shirt and push him away. The shirt peels off his trailing arms like the skin from a banana and buttons fly everywhere. Nokosee stumbles away from me. I wait for him to turn around before I toss the shirt aside. Except for the stuck zipper part and the button cuffs, everything is turning out the way I dreamed it would. Well, maybe the music was different.

And maybe all girls are like this at this moment in this game of seduction, having planned it forever, even before knowing what having sex was, to live in this moment just once. And if they are like this, like me, then we are a blessing to all men whether they know it or not because, if for no other reason, we give them something to remember when they're old, to take with them to their graves.

Right now, I think Nokosee knows it. I *know* he's thinking he's never met anyone like me before and probably never will again.

Right now, my head is spinning, the room is spinning, and everything is so alien and new and dark. I clutch myself and stumble toward the bed to keep from falling.

Right now, I know he sees me standing before the sliding glass doors to the balcony, framed by the raging fire beyond, and is thinking *I'm* the thing he's always been looking for on his vision quest but didn't know where to find it, a punk goddess from New Jersey spending the summers with her lying father, a girl with an attitude and a spiked halo of fire.

He falls into this vision and holds on and wraps himself around it and won't let go. And the vision squeezes back. It wants to be kissed. He lifts her up and she wraps her legs around him and they kiss and they kiss and the fire continues to burn and Nokosee is spinning now, out of control and falling onto the bed. His vision rolls to the top and jumps off. She grabs one of his moccasins, pulls it off his foot and throws it away. When she throws the other one away and looks at Nokosee, she sees him lying prone on the bed, his head raised and peering down at his jeans, his hands working feverishly on the stuck zipper-- which isn't supposed to be happening. His vision doesn't hesitate or criticize but jumps onto the bed, grabs the metal fly and yanks it down. She jumps back off the bed, grabs his jeans and, with a little help from her own dream, rips them off as well as his boxer briefs and tosses them onto the carpet.

She can tell her dream is really glad to see her because now there is nothing to confine his desire. For a moment it looks like it is ablaze but it's only the reddish glow of the fire in the Everglades now penetrating the bedroom.

"Gee," I say, mesmerized by what I'm looking at. "Now I know why they call it a *gee*-string."

Nokosee laughs softly, nervously. He sees me hesitate. I realize what I'm about to do is the real thing and no longer a virgin's fantasy. He sits up and, with his hand extended, shifts across the bed. The thing I desire and fear so much is now hidden in the shadows of his body and I am drawn toward not it, but Nokosee's beckoning, loving eyes. I put a knee up on the bed and crawl toward him, leaving my childhood behind at the foot of the bed. I stop beside him and sit back on my calves. When he takes my hand and leans over to kiss it I pass something from my hand to his. He looks at it. I wish it could be something more romantic but it's a condom pack. He turns back to me and makes his eyebrows dance mischievously.

Thank you for doing that, Nokosee. Thank you for smiling, for making this moment easier on me, for making me think I'm doing the right thing. How can I not love you?

I smile and kiss his hand before letting it go. I won't say anything to spoil the moment, this moment I've been planning for so long. I won't take my eyes off of him as my hands slide toward the zipper on my jacket. I find the metal fly and begin to pull the zipper down and can see his eyes leave mine as they search for a sight of my hidden breasts.

And then it happens. The zipper gets stuck. Again. I can hear the romantic music on my dream record grinding down but I won't let that happen, can't let that happen. I yank at it and yank at it. I cut Nokosee's short nervous laugh off at the knees when, in frustration, I quickly pull the jacket up over my head and unsheathe each arm one at a time before balling it up and throwing it over the side of the bed.

Nokosee is looking at my young bouncing breasts when I quickly slip in beside him. He doesn't know it now, but he's looking at the face he will always love and never forget.

Nothing else is said from that moment on as we steer our course together away from our virginity with only the sounds of our lovemaking and the music of the Red Hot Chili Peppers to guide us.

Chapter 14

Escape!

I drift off to sleep wrapped up in Nokosee's strong dark arms, a hand holding mine. I remember him gently kissing my cheek but when I awaken, I find myself wondering *What is love? Did* we *make it--* I look at my watch-- *only a few hours ago? Was that it, or was I just mad at my dad?* To be honest, maybe it was a combination of both. I start feeling guilty but I stop myself. Despite the reasons, I know love had something to do with it and, despite my father's betrayal, I still wake up a true romantic and that, my friend, is remarkable. So, I can't be all bad. Still, I'm surprised and disappointed I'm thinking about my dad in any shape or form at this moment and that pisses me off.

"This ain't 'Romeo and Juliet,'" I say out loud interrupting my train of thought and the silence, the TV having been turned off a long time ago so we could concentrate on the moments-- and there were many-- at hand.

Nokosee squeezes my hand. "Excuse me?" he asks.

I turn from the fiery landscape burning outside the sliding glass doors to look at him. His face is alive with the fire's flickering, reddish glow. "We aren't going to die at the end of this play," I say with as much conviction as I can muster.

"Well," he says as he rolls over onto his back, "no one can ever accuse you of being a romantic."

I roll over and lie on my back next to him. I look at the thatched roof above our bed. "Think about it, Nooksy. We're just like them. Our parents don't want us having anything to do with each other and we're sneakin' around their backs for a kiss."

"Ah, Stormy, I think we're way past 'sneakin' around for a kiss.'"

I'm still thinking about Shakespeare which, I guess, is better than dad. "And there's no time for any of us." I turn to Nokosee. "You're taking that gator with you tonight, aren't you?"

Nokosee pushes my stiff but collapsed and flattened punk pink badge of courage away from my face. "If I could wish for anything, I would wish tomorrow would never come."

"But it is coming." I take his hand and kiss it. "I've got something for you. Don't move." I get out of bed and run quickly back to the bathroom.

"I like it when you run," he says.

"With or without my clothes?" I reply from the bathroom. I hear him laugh and settle back onto the bed. I return with my purse and pick up the gang jacket from the floor and stand next to the bed. I open the purse and pull out his Special Forces knife. "I thought you might need this. Daddy doesn't know I swiped it from his desk. By the time he finds out, it won't matter."

"Thanks," Nokosee says while looking at it and turning it over in his hands. "It's my dad's knife. He wants me to pass it on to my son." He looks back up at me with a case of dancing eyebrows.

"Keep dreaming, pagan cave boy," I say without a trace of humor. Focusing on releasing the stuck zipper on the Seminole jacket I say, "I also want you to have this. Mom thinks I earned it. I didn't. You earned it." It comes undone. "Turn around."

Nokosee doesn't say anything as I guide his arms into the jacket. I slip my hands underneath his long thick black hair and lift it out and over the jacket, spreading it across his broad shoulders. "A little tight, but it'll do. You're the real chief around here. The rest of us are impostors. Turn around and let me look at you."

Nokosee, looking at the colorful embroidery, slowly turns to me. I can tell he's pleased because tears are welling up in his eyes. *I swear if he cries I'm going to lose it.*

"Sorry 'bout the zipper," I say. We laugh uneasily. I try to remain strong. "Tomorrow I'll be in New Jersey and if you're not quick enough, my father will have you shipped off to Oklahoma to be poked and probed and scanned and God knows what. What are you gonna do?"

"I'm gonna miss you."

He takes my hands, this incurably romantic lean-and-mean-fighting machine, and kisses them.

"I'll go on living," he says, his voice faltering, "but there will always be something missing inside me."

I start crying. "Don't start, Nokosee," I sniff. "The last thing I need now is a tearful ending."

The phone rings, startling both of us.

"My God, who's that?" I rub the tears away from my eyes and start looking for the phone.

"You're not expecting any calls, are you?"

"Only if there's trouble," I reply while scooting up toward the headboard.

"What do you mean by that?"

I see a series of buttons above a console stretching across the width of the bed and push one of them. "Stanlo is supposed to call me if they find out where we are."

The whole bed is illuminated by track lights hidden in the thatched roof but the phone keeps ringing.

"Dammit!" I quickly turn the lights off and push another button. Opera, probably Pavarotti and the other guys, comes blaring out from the four speakers hanging on the posts surrounding the bed. "My, god!"

Nokosee is laughing.

"Stop it! It's not funny!" I shout. I can't turn the music off and try another button. A telephone answering system pops up from a hidden space on the headboard. *Finally!*

"Don't answer it," Nokosee urges loudly over the opera.

"Nokosee, I told you, it's probably Stanlo."

"I don't trust that guy. Let's just assume our gig is up and get the hell out of here."

Before I can respond, the answering machine kicks in.

"Stormy? This is your father."

Dad's voice shoots through us like a bolt of lightning.

"If you're there, pick up the phone."

"Oh, my God," I cry out. "How does he know we're here?"

"One word," Nokosee says matter-of-factly. "Stanlo."

"Don't make me come up there to get you," dad's voice threatens.

"We gotta get outta here!" I yell and jump off the bed before Nokosee can react. By the time he's out of bed, I'm in the bathroom getting dressed.

"Alright," the answering machine intones, "I'm coming up."

"Hurry!" I scream. "He's one tricky bastard! He's probably already in the elevator calling from his cell phone."

"I can't get my zipper up!" Nokosee yells.

"You gotta be kidding!" I stumble out of the bathroom with one cork wedgie on and the other being pulled on.

"Does it look like I'm kidding?" Nokosee replies hopping up and down in the middle of the floor while yanking on his zipper.

"Oh, my god! We don't have time for this! Forget your zipper and let's get outta here!" I run for the door.

Nokosee catches me at the door. "Don't open it," he whispers. He steps in front of me, places his ear against the door and listens for any sounds in the hallway. He doesn't hear anything. He turns the doorknob and can't get the door to open. He starts shaking the door violently until I jump in between him and the door and unhook the privacy latch. When I start to open the door, Nokosee pushes me aside and carefully peers out into the hallway.

No one's there.

He motions for me to follow him. Hugging the wall, we inch toward the cylindrical glass elevator tube when the car suddenly pops up.

"Oh, no," I sigh.

Nokosee looks for an escape but can't find one. He turns and pushes me back into the Presidential Suite.

"Leave the door open," he tells me, "and follow me." He leads me through the living room back to the bedroom.

"Are you crazy?"

Nokosee jumps up onto the bed and extends his hand to me. "Let's go," he whispers.

We hear voices in the hallway. Without further question, I take his hand and to my astonishment, find myself launched into the darkness of the thatched roof over the bed. Nokosee places me on one of the hand carved cypress log supports and pulls himself up next to me. I can feel the three tenors' voices vibrating up from the speakers through the cypress posts and wish we had thought to turn them off since the sound might draw my dad's attention upward to the speakers and us hiding in the rafters. But it's too late for that now.

The first voice we hear above the three great operatic voices is that one really bad voice that has always sounded to me like fingernails dragged across a chalkboard, my mom's.

"I bet she's with him now!"

It sounds like an army is marching through the living room toward the bedroom. I want to scream and almost lose my grip on the cypress log when I look down and see my purse and Nokosee's moccasins lying on the carpet.

The bedroom light comes on.

"Look, they *were* here!" mom shouts over the rising voices of all three tenors.

I see my dad's hand pick up the purse.

"Look at the bed, Sam!" mom shouts. "The little tramp was screwing his brains out just like she said she would!"

She throws my cell phone down on the unmade bed. I can see the last message I typed in all caps framed in the blue light of the phone's screen: FUCK NOKOSEE!

I want to die.

"Shut up!" dad yells.

Suddenly he's leaning over the bed and putting his hand on the sheets. My heart is about to burst. If he looks up, my goose is cooked. I look at Nokosee. He's drawn his knife. *My God! What's he thinking?*

"We probably just missed them. C'mon, let's go," dad commands and then, with a quick turn, vanishes from sight.

I strain to hear their footsteps rushing away and I'm about to let my breath out when I see Stanlo leaning over the bed. I stop short and pull myself deeper into the shadows of the thatched chickee roof. Stanlo looks up and starts to peer into the darkness when my dad's voice calls out from the hallway. "Stanlo, get your deceitful little ass out here right now!"

"Comin', Mr. Jones," Stanlo yells back. He pauses to pick up my cell phone. He looks at my last message and shakes his head knowingly before putting it in his pocket and walking out of the bedroom. I make a *mental* note this time to kill the smug jerk when I see him.

"You got Stormy into this mess," dad yells from the hallway, "and by God, until we find her, your ass is mine!"

After waiting about a minute, Nokosee slips down onto the bed. He sticks the knife in the waistband of his jeans, looks up and helps me down.

"You weren't planning on using that thing were you?" I ask loudly in order to be heard over the tenors.

"Once the hilt's in my hand, I'm committed," Nokosee replies.

"You should be committed! Are you crazy or something?"

Nokosee pauses, turns and looks at nothing as he ponders the question. "Probably." He catches himself and turns to me. "It's the downside of being a pagan cave boy."

I don't know what to think when he grabs my hand and leads me stumbling out of the bedroom. When we get to the hallway doors, I yank my hand away.

"Nokosee, you're scaring me. You're acting like this is some kind of war thing. Someone is going to get hurt."

"Well I can guarantee you it *isn't* going to be me or you."

I grab his arm. "Nokosee, stop this! Have you ever
listened to yourself? You're beginning to sound a lot like
that mass murderer Timothy McVeigh. You're both fighting
lost causes and you talk like you're at war!"

"Our targets aren't innocent people like his was. I'm sorry
if you don't like the way I approach the world, but that's
how my father raised me. I don't know how to see it any
other way."

I step back and look at him as if I'm seeing him for the
first time. "So, this is it? Is this where we part our ways?"

"I didn't want it to end this way. I was looking for
something a little more romantic."

"So was I. Nokosee, you really are starting to scare me. I
don't know if I should love you or run from you."

"Meaning?"

"I don't want to fall in love with someone who might get
killed."

Nokosee sighs. "Fair enough, Stormy, but you got to get
past this obsession you have with bad endings. Talk about
me scaring you…" He steps toward me. "I can't say good-bye
without one last kiss."

I don't respond right away but begin to rock back and
forth on the balls of my cork wedgies. "And neither can I."

I can't help myself. Call me a pushover for hunky bad boy
pagan cave men types, but I rock right up to his lips, throw
my arms around him and kiss him like it really will be our
last kiss. I can feel my breath being squeezed out of my lungs
and into his mouth and that too is frightening because it
seems I have lost so much to him tonight, including my
virginity, all of it falling into him and away from myself. I
hear the REM song in my head, "Losing my religion," but I
know I never had one to lose and quickly change the lyrics
to what I'm really thinking, "Losing my identity" and that's
something I'm not ready to let go of yet since I'm still trying
to figure out who I am. I push away to catch my breath and
my self. "You better go," I say and turn away.

Nokosee doesn't say anything but steps unsteadily
backwards, surprised that it has finally come to an end, this

dance with this extraordinary, unforgettable outsider-- me. (Yes, I know, it sounds like I have an incredibly huge ego but trust me, most of it is a figment of my imagination). He turns and stumbles through the doorway.

It's as if I've drained his grace with my good-bye. He looks up and down the hallway but doesn't see because he cannot get his mind off the girl he is leaving behind. He puts one foot in front of the other because it's expected of him, instilled in him by his Looney Tunes father. But his mind is on that crazy blue-eyed blonde with the spiked pink flamingo tipped hair he's leaving behind I tell myself and, although it may sound delusional and egotistical, I'm embarrassed to say it's also empowering and liberating.

I follow him out the door. We tiptoe down the hallway. Nokosee presses himself against the wall and when we get near the edge, he peeks around the corner.

He takes Stanlo's elbow full in the face.

"No!" I can't shout it fast enough.

Nokosee's perfect nose is broken and blood is squirting on the walls and carpet. He stumbles backward and raises his hand to ward off a second blow. He catches Stanlo's fist, twists his arm and directs Stanlo's head into the wall. Stanlo falls limp and slides down the wall leaving a trail of blood. Nokosee steps away and lets Stanlo fall forward onto his face. Dark red blood expands quickly out from under his head across the hall carpet.

"Oh, my God! You've killed him!" I shout.

But I'm wrong. I can hear him choking, crying. I rush over to him. He sees my cork wedgies, and rolls onto his side. He extends his hand for me to help him up. I take it and flip him onto his back, rifle through the pockets on his hip hop clown pants, find my phone, and leave him coughing and choking and begging for help with an outstretched hand.

"Stormy," he wails.

"My bad," I reply as I turn away.

That's when Nokosee, incensed, his eyes all ablaze with hate and anger, pushes me aside and jumps onto Stanlo's stomach with his knife drawn.

"No, Nokosee! Don't!" I shout. I try to pull him off.

"Stop him, Sam!"

I turn around. It's my mom. She's cringing, looking on in horror. And dad is racing towards Nokosee backed up by two security guards.

Nokosee looks back and kicks out. His bare foot catches dad square in the chest knocking the wind out of him. Mom screams. Dad falls backward against the wall and slides to the blood stained carpet and struggles to draw his gun.

"Dad, what are you doing?" I shout.

I jump between him and Nokosee and try to act as a shield but Nokosee pushes me aside and throws his knife. It sticks with a solid thud in the wall just inches from my dad's head. He freezes and, sweating, his chest heaving, looks at the knife before turning slowly toward Nokosee.

I whip around to Nokosee. "Nokosee, what are you doing?"

He doesn't see or hear me. His eyes are only on the gun. He pushes me aside.

"Nokosee, stop!"

Dad looks back at his holster and tries to remove the gun. I grab the sleeve on Nokosee's jacket to try to hold him back, but he shakes me loose and, walking purposively without urgency, walks over to my dad and yanks the gun out of his shaking hand just as he draws it from its holster. He cocks the gun and points it at him while backing away.

I run up and grab the gun. "Stop, Nokosee! This is crazy!"

Nokosee pushes my hands away and points the gun at the two security guards. "That's right, keep your hands up." He walks over to them and takes their mace canisters and throws them down the hallway. He then slips his knife under the coiled shoulder mics hanging from their epaulets and cuts through them. He tells them to get over and face the wall, hands against the wall. He comes back to my dad, squats beside him and doesn't take his eyes away.

"Kid," dad says, squeezing out the words, "you can't imagine the kind of trouble you're getting into."

Without saying anything and without taking his eyes off my father, Nokosee, points the gun toward the ceiling and releases the clip from the automatic's grip. He pockets the bullet clip and, still looking dad hard in the eyes, throws the gun away.

"You better turn yourself in before it's too late."

Nokosee doesn't say anything. Without taking his eyes off my dad, he reaches slowly for the knife next to his head, grabs it and works it back and forth until it comes out of the wall, dragging drywall, dust, and wallpaper with it. He draws it near my dad's face and holds it there for a moment.

"I know who you are, kid," dad whispers harshly over labored breath. He motions toward the knife. "We know all about your old man and what he's up to. You can run, but you can't hide. We'll find you sooner or later."

Nokosee points the tip of the knife right between my dad's eyes and pretends to twist it but Sam Jones won't flinch.

"Nokosee, stop it!" I cry. "Leave him alone!"

Nokosee smiles at dad and, without any urgency, lowers the knife and cuts through dad's coiled mic cord. He casually flips the knife backwards and catches the blade in his hand when the shot rings out.

The bullet catches Nokosee in the right shoulder blade knocking him backward onto his ass. The knife slides across the carpet.

I turn to the sound. Mom is pointing her small smoking designer handgun with both hands at Nokosee.

"Mom! What are you doing?"

"I'm protecting your father from this madman!" she shouts while walking toward us.

"Are you crazy?" I step between her and Nokosee. You could have shot dad or me!"

At that moment, dad makes a move for the knife lying on the carpet but Nokosee is more resilient than he expected. Nokosee, lying on his side, lifts his leg and with just a little snap of his barefoot, kicks dad's head back against the wall. Dazed, a stream of blood gushes from his broken nose. As

Nokosee grabs the knife, mom moves in closer with the gun and pulls the trigger.

A bullet pierces the dropped ceiling in the hallway because I've grabbed the gun and I'm wrestling mom for it.

The two security guards make a move to pull me off of mom but Nokosee grabs the knife off the carpet and stabs one guard in the thigh. The guard cries out and falls into mom and me knocking us to the ground. Nokosee uses that same circular motion he used to thrust the knife to roll with it and to bring himself to his feet. Holding his shoulder wound with one hand, he staggers against the wall and points the knife at the last guard who can't stop running toward him or raise his hands fast enough. Nokosee motions for the guard to come closer and when he does, he grabs the man's neck, exerts pressure and watches him drop to the floor unconscious. He's surprised to see his bloody hand print on the man's neck and collar. He looks at his hand and sees that it's covered in blood.

"Mother! Stop! What are you trying to do?"

I'm ashamed to say it, but I have to knee mom in the stomach to get the gun. She grunts and drops to her knees.

"I'm trying to keep you alive!" mom coughs. "That boy," she says, pointing at Nokosee for emphasis, "is nothing but trouble! I can't let you throw your life away for him!"

This is so surreal. I can't believe I'm pointing a gun at my mom. Or that I just rammed my knee into her stomach. All over a boy.

"Mom, *that boy* saved my life!"

"He's a loser! Look at him! What kind of a life can he give you?"

"I haven't asked him to give me anything!"

"Oh, no," mom snarls, "but you're willing to give him *everything* he wants! You're nothing but a whore!"

"Lisa," dad rasps through his broken nose and the blood in his mouth, "shut the hell up!"

Tears start welling up in my eyes. I can't believe my mom is talking to me like that. Maybe she's just angry because I kneed her. I know I would be.

I hear the elevator arrive. I turn and see four security guards through the glass. Nokosee is already waiting for them. Hiding behind a plastic planter next to the elevator, he trips the first one that steps out. The second follows the first to the floor and the third one gets kicked in the face sending him into the fourth guard who hasn't even gotten out of the elevator. With the third guard knocked out and impeding the progress of the fourth guard, Nokosee swoops swiftly down on the two guards on the carpet. The back end of the knife takes the fight out of one of the guards and the other opts not to continue the struggle. Nokosee cuts a mic wire and is about to cut through another when he hears my voice.

"Don't even think about it."

Nokosee turns quickly to me. He's thinking I'm talking to him and praying I'm not because I got mom's gun and I'm pointing it in his direction.

"Look behind you, Nokosee."

The last security guard was sneaking up on Nokosee, ready to pounce when I froze him in his tracks. Nokosee sees him standing there in a crouch, hands in the air. He turns back to me with a blinking surprised look on his face.

"Let's go, Nokosee. Let's get the hell out of here."

I aim my gun at the last security guard who is doing his best to stay out of my way, hands high in the air. I back into the elevator with Nokosee, push the lobby button and the doors start to close. I see mom through the glass walls. She's holding her stomach and hobbling up to the elevator, screaming.

"I'm sorry, Stormy! Please don't go down with him!"

"Too late for that, mom," I say, relishing the moment with naked hostility, "I already have." As I wave good-bye with the descending elevator I see my dad struggling to get up on his feet behind her. He's talking on his cell phone.

"My dad's calling somebody!"

Nokosee is looking down at the fast approaching hotel lobby, searching for escape routes. He sees more security guards gathering at the bottom. And cops; with guns drawn.

They're looking up at us, pointing their guns and circling the elevator.

"Stormy," Nokosee says without turning around, "tell me you can drive?"

"I can drive. Why?"

"We've got a little company downstairs."

I join Nokosee at the glass wall and see the hastily assembled reception committee, which is now also clearing the lobby of anybody who might get in the way.

"You're going to be my hostage. Give me the gun."   He doesn't look at me when he puts out his hand for the gun.

I put the gun in his hand. "And the plan is?"

Nokosee quickly grabs me by my cut-off t-shirt and pushes me up against the glass. "Pretend you're scared to death," he whispers in my ear.

Although his voice remains calm, I can hear his belabored breathing and smell his wound.

"That won't be too hard to do. Are you alright?"

"Considering I've just been shot, not bad."

I feel him moving around behind me. "What are you doing back there?"

"Removing the bullets."

I hear them drop against the floor and then feel the gun pushed up against my head. "And this is a *good* plan?" I ask incredulously.

"We'll soon find out. The last thing I want is to hurt you. When we get outside, we're commandeering a car. You're driving. Stop the elevator at the next floor."

"What? We haven't reached the lobby yet."

"Exactly."

Nokosee pushes me over to the control panel and I check the box illuminating the current floor. I push the button for the next one below and the elevator flies right by it.

"My God, it didn't stop!"

"Well, there goes that idea. I wanted to get off a floor or two above the lobby and then work our way out the back door, so to speak. Guess you can't have everything. Get ready to be scared."

Nokosee whips me around and forces my face up against the glass wall just as the elevator lands in the lobby. He puts the gun to the back of my head and looks at the cops on the other side of the glass as if he were completely insane. I see the crazed look in Nokosee's eyes reflected in the glass and wonder just how much of it is real. The elevator doors open and Nokosee whips me around, forcing me through the opening into the lobby.

"Don't shoot!" I cry. "He's got a gun!"

I'm surprised at how good I am at this. I see this as a sign that Nokosee and I would make a great team. I also discover I'm more excited than scared. I take that as a bad sign.

The cops back off enough for us to slip around the glass elevator tube.

"Start running for the entrance," Nokosee whispers. "It'll make it less easy for them to hit us."

We start running and Nokosee directs me like a puppet toward the main entrance. The cops and guards run along with us in a synchronized, sidestepping crouch that borders on the ridiculous.

"Zigzag," Nokosee whispers in my ear.

I zig when he wants me to zag but he quickly corrects that problem by pulling on the back of my t-shirt in the direction he wants me to go. With all the guns being bandied about, men, women, and children are screaming and running in all directions now as they realize they have stumbled out of their safe vacations into a life and death situation. This is a good thing for us because it makes the cops think twice before pulling a trigger and shooting an innocent bystander.

We burst through the glass entrance doors and keep running down the driveway, trailing a platoon of cops and guards. Nokosee directs me around a black Lincoln Navigator with tinted windows, putting it between us and the cops. He waves the gun at the valet who has just stepped into the driver's seat. The kid, a pimply-faced college student throws his hands in the air.

"Change of plans," Nokosee whispers to me. "Open the back door." He pushes me up to the huge SUV but I can't get the door open.

"Unlock the door!" I yell at the valet. He unlocks the doors and puts his hands back in the air.

Nokosee shoves me into the back seat and follows in after me, closing the door behind us. He keeps my head down and yells at the valet from behind the front seat.

"Drive us outta here or I'll kill you both!"

The valet whips around and pops it into drive and leaves a smoking trail of rubber and flat-footed cops and guards huffing and puffing down the ramp toward the street. When we get to a stop sign at the intersection, the valet, maybe only a year or two older than us, asks us which way to go and Nokosee yells at him to just keep driving. The kid, without being told to, honks his horn and blows through the intersection.

Unfortunately, it isn't done cleanly; a car clips our right rear end sending the SUV screeching sideways across the pavement. But the valet manages to maintain control and steers through the traffic.

Within a minute, the valet is standing alone on the side of the road with a great story to tell his grandkids and wondering what just happened as the SUV roars off into the night with its lights off and me at the wheel.

"Are you bored?" Nokosee asks in belabored breaths from the back seat.

"I'm scared shitless!" I yell back at him. I turn the wheel hard and hit the horn to avoid a car pulling into the intersection.

"My dad says that's better than boredom."

"Will you please stop quoting Chairman Dad?"

"I think this is how the revolution will be," Nokosee says while staring ahead.

"What are you talking about, you crazy Injun?"

"Never boring."

For some reason I laugh out loud.

##

I brake hard and slide over the parking space bumper, across the compound yard and into one side of the veranda, collapsing the aluminum awning on top of the Navigator, which is now belching hot steam like a volcano.

"So how long have you been driving?" Nokosee asks as we throw the doors open and jump out.

"Don't start," I warn him. I run around the front of the behemoth. "Oh, no, dad is going to kill me."

The wood veranda floor is crunched like an accordion. I turn and push Nokosee out of the way.

"I'm in *real* deep now thanks to you!" I backtrack around the SUV and yell back at Nokosee. "You know, they have a name for what we just did: Grand Theft Auto."

"I saw the movie," Nokosee replies, turning quickly to follow me. "Ron Howard was great in it. Who would have thought Opie would grow up to become this big shot Hollywood producer and director? Do you know he directed *Splash*? The mermaid movie with Daryl Hannah?" he asks between labored breaths.

"You know, *now* you're starting to scare me." I try to focus on the number of felonies I've committed in the last half hour and wonder how much prison time I'll have to serve. We have to bend down when we walk up the steps onto the veranda because of the collapsed roof.

"Unlock the door, Stormy," Nokosee says firmly. "I was just trying to get your mind off about what's going down."

"'*Going down?*' I think you gotta cut back on the *Miami Vice* re-runs back in the swamp." I insert the key in the lock and start to open the door but stop as another thought grabs me. "Kidnapping! We're kidnappers, too!"

"Stormy," Nokosee grunts as he pushes me aside to work the doorknob, "you're an innocent bystander. I kidnapped you, remember?"

"I'm innocent, all right. Go tell that security guard I pointed the gun at; see if he agrees."

"Now that was impressive." Nokosee starts shaking the doorknob. "You must be madly in love to do something like that."

I shake my head. "I must be mad. Period."

"Well, there's your alibi. Temporary insanity."

"And what's your excuse?"

"Permanent insanity," Nokosee replies. He can't get the door open.

I push his hand away from the doorknob and grab the key. I look at him and then the doorknob. "You gotta be kidding, right?"

He shrugs. "I was raised in a chickee, for crying out loud."

The door unlocks and we walk into the dark office.

"Don't turn on the lights," he says.

"Oh, I don't think we have to worry about them *not* knowing we're here."

We stumble through the shadows toward the door to the living quarters. I open the door and lead Nokosee toward the kitchen. "Talk about small towns where everybody knows everybody else's business, this is a freakin' *village* for crying out loud. Mom and dad, the police-- the media-- are all probably on their way."

I pick up a set of keys hanging from a nail on the back door. "Talk 'bout a lost cause, why are we even trying?"

"Stormy, stop." Nokosee grabs my hand. "I never asked you to do this with me. I appreciate the lift over here, but this is where we part company. I don't want you getting in any deeper."

King Roar growls outside the kitchen window. We look through the window into the backyard.

"Where's the redneck?" Nokosee asks.

"Your gator ate him."

"What?"

"Now we got a murder rap hanging over our heads."

"No way! We didn't kill--"

"Oh, Nokosee, you're *so* easy. I'm kidding. His buddies bailed him out."

"Who told you?"

"Stanlo."

"Whoe, talk about cold. Not even a helping hand for that guy when you got your phone back."

"You didn't give me a chance. Hell, what were you planning on doing to him? Scalping him?"

Nokosee looks away and pauses, it appears, to consider the question. Instead, he says this: "If you ever miss me, you'll know where to find me, right?"

"Yeah," I reply with an awkward smile and tears welling up in my eyes, "by the fourth alligator on the right--"

"The third." Nokosee doesn't let me finish. He grabs me and nearly crushes me in his arms, kissing me with more passion than I suspect I will ever know again.

Nokosee pushes away and with tears in his own eyes says, "My heart is breaking. Saying goodbye to you is the hardest thing I've ever done in my life. I'll always love you."

He lets me go, turns and runs over to the door and tries to open it. Of course, it won't open. He starts shaking it.

"Oh, my God," I laugh while wiping away my tears. "How are you ever going to lead a revolution when you can't even open a door for crise sakes?" I walk over, push him aside and unlock the door.

"Well, maybe if I had a key..."

"I doubt it. Just don't start the revolution in front of a door."

"Thanks for the advice," he says dryly before jumping down the steps. "I'll try to remember that."

I see the blood stain on the Seminole jacket as he disappears into the night. Without a moment's hesitation, I know exactly what I have to do. I turn and run through the living quarters to the bathroom, open the medicine cabinet and start looking for something to dress his wound. I hear the gator growl and look out the bathroom window. I can see Nokosee carefully approaching the beast, softly calling its name in Muskogee. The gator strains against its chain and tilts its head to the side to look at him with its one good eye. With King Roar at the end of its chain, Nokosee drops to his knees in front of the gator, extends his hand and pats the reptile on its long broad snout.

I have to turn away. I can't watch. That gator scares me. I find what I need in the medicine cabinet and run back to the kitchen. I grab a plastic grocery bag-- *What, not paper, daddy? Must be from mom*-- and fill it with the stuff. There's a loud knock on the back door. I nearly have a heart attack. It's only Nokosee.

"My, God, Nokosee! I thought it was the cops!"

"I hate to ask you to do this, but can you help me out?"

"Help you what?"

"Come here and I'll show you." He steps back from the door.

"Oh, my God, what happened now?" I open the door and walk down the steps.

"I can't yank the stake out of the ground. I need your help." He reaches out, grabs my hand and pulls me along.

"Are you crazy?" I shake loose of his hand. "That thing hates me!"

"No he doesn't. He's just jealous. I had a talk with him. Everything is okay."

"You had a talk with him?"

"Yes. Please, Stormy, help me yank the stake out of the ground. I promise you, it's the last favor I'll ever ask."

"Of course it'll be!" I throw my hands up and start pacing about. "I'll be dead! Tomorrow's big story! Stay tuned for live coverage of Stormy Jones' gruesome death!"

Nokosee grabs my arm. "Stormy, trust me. I won't let anything happen to you. C'mon."

I shrug, thinking how bad can it be compared to everything else that's happened to me today. "Okay, Dr. D, what do I have to do?"

"Act like bait."

"'*Act like bait?*' Are you crazy?"

"I'm surprised you have to ask. Just stand here." He lets go of my hand.

"What?"

"Stop yelling," he whispers as he walks toward King Roar. "It's scaring him."

"*Scaring him?*" I shout.

"Don't say anything," Nokosee warns me again. "Your English is confusing Haalpatee. The only people that sound like you want to kill him."

"Oh, great!"

He shushes me. I look at the gator. He's looking back at me with his one good eye, checking me out like some kind of rude boy only this one's sizing me up for snack food. I sigh. I can't believe I'm standing in the middle of the backyard pretending I'm lunch-- I check my watch-- no, make that a midnight snack for a monster alligator. Oh, the things you do for love. I really do need counseling.

"Now act like bait," Nokosee shouts across the yard.

"What?"

Nokosee is standing behind the gator, holding the heavy chain connected to the stake. "Jump up and down and start yelling how much you love me!"

"Are you nuts?" I scream.

King Roar hisses and pulls at his chain. Nokosee struggles to hold it back.

"That doesn't sound like a woman in love to me. C'mon, show me the *love!*"

I'm really losing it now. My boyfriend has turned me into *gatorbait!* I grab my head and scream, "You're making me crazy! You're *killing* me!"

The gator yanks Nokosee forward. "That's it!" he shouts, "But with more emotion."

I scream again and start running around in circles shaking my hands like Marilyn Monroe in "The Misfits" when she discovers the men she's been hanging out with—including Clark Gable—want to kill captured wild horses. I guess Nokosee didn't see that film on "Movie Night" because he can't appreciate the impersonation and instead criticizes me for my over-the-top "histrionics"—I swear that's the word he uses— and directs me to make the "bait" look more believable.

I must have pulled it off because a moment later the gator pulls the stake out of the ground and Nokosee with it. I look back. The damn thing is coming right at me. I run toward the back door, jump the steps and race through the kitchen screaming like a little girl. And trust me, you would too.

The stupid one-eyed gator follows me into the house. I don't look back but keep running out the front door. I hear it destroying the kitchen. I'm sure it's knocked over the refrigerator. I jump off the veranda and fall on the grass beside the smoking SUV. I hear the TV set crash on the floor. I look up. The giant gator is coming out the front door. He stops to look around to sniff the air and it seems he completely forgets about me because the next thing I know, he's running down the steps trailing the bouncing chain and its stake behind it. I never feel the gator as it races over me but the stake almost gets me. Nokosee has, of course, let go of the chain and picks me up on the run.

"Are you okay?" he asks.

I brush his hands away. "I can't believe you just used me for gatorbait!"

"You're fine," he sighs.

We hear sirens and turn to see the flashing red and blue lights of half a dozen police cars kicking up a cloud of dust as they race toward the compound. Nokosee kisses me and starts out after the gator. He shouts back, "I love you, Stormy! You're the best gatorbait a guy could ever want!" before disappearing into the night.

"Hold on!" the gatorbait shouts back. "I'm coming with you!"

I hear people screaming in the village. People shouldn't be screaming in the village. They should be applauding and whistling and having a good time since J.T. turned the faux Seminole village into a real SoBe style open-air nightclub. J.T.'s world is a 24-hour money making machine. I catch up to Nokosee who has stopped along the main road leading to the boat ramp.

"Nokosee, what's happening?" I ask with winded breath.

"Haalpatee. He don't dance."

I see what Nokosee is staring at. A souvenir chickee kiosk is racing through the village like a bat out of hell. Tourists and Natives are screaming and jumping out of the way. And then I see King Roar's tail. The giant gator somehow snared its chain on the kiosk and is dragging it behind him, leaving destruction and chaos in its wake. Nokosee starts after it, cutting across the village to intercept it.

From a distance, it has a cartoonish sensibility about it: a boy chasing a chickee without any apparent means of locomotion across the pavement with people screaming and running in all directions. But when the chickee crashes into a parked car and shatters in an explosion of splintered wood and sharp-edged thatched palm fronds, carpeting tourists and Natives alike with slivers of stabbing glass and wood, it loses its punch line real fast. I start after Nokosee.

Nokosee jumps over the broken detritus of the new trying to make a buck off the old and doesn't stop until he sees himself on TV. He's fighting King Roar in living color on the eleven o'clock news. He's stunned. He's never seen himself like this before, outside of his body from a different time. The TV, a small battery operated model, is sitting on top of a folding metal TV dinner table outside a chickee. An old Seminole couple is watching it from their Barcaloungers, also dragged outdoors. Now they're fearfully watching Nokosee and expecting the worse.

It comes without any announcement.

One moment they're looking at each other and in the next moment the old Seminole couple is scooped up by King Roar's chain, slammed together and taken on a joyride across the grass in their matching Barcaloungers.

The old man catches the TV in his lap and holds on for dear life before being flipped over one of the many logs the village uses as parking space bumpers. His wife lands next to him and when they look up from their upside-down

positions like astronauts waiting to be launched from Cape
Canaveral, Nokosee is looking down at them. He asks if
they're all right in their native tongue and, instead of
replying, they turn slowly from him to the TV. The old guy
shifts the TV a little so Nokosee can see it better. It's still on
and Nokosee is still on it. It's too weird for everyone.
Nokosee turns to watch himself on TV when I run up to him.

"Nokosee," I yell, "you don't have time for this. The cops
are right behind me! Let's go!" I tug at the sleeve on his
Seminole jacket and have to drag him away from the TV.

"Hey, that was me!" he says excitedly. "I'm gonna be
famous like you!"

"Oh, Lord," I sigh. "I hope not. I don't think that's what
your father had in mind. Aren't you supposed to be like
clandestine or something?"

Nokosee slaps himself aside the head as we start running
again and pretends to be surprised. "Oh, right, I knew I
forgot something! Man, is he going to be pissed."

"Welcome to the club. 'Course I wouldn't blame him. I
can't believe you told J.T. about the New Seminole shtick
your father dreamed up."

"I can't either. Ply me with enough Cokes and I guess I'll
tell you anything."

"Cokes?"

"I love 'em but dad won't let me or my sister drink 'em
because he thinks we'll cross over to the Outside and he'll
lose us for the cause. At least I didn't tell 'im about my old
man's other idea."

"About takin' back Florida?"

"Yeah, that one."

"You are one tough nut to crack-- Look!"

Billy Joe Cypress has lost control of his pickup truck and
is careening through the screaming crowd. This probably
wouldn't have happened if A), Billy Joe had listened to his
doctors and stayed in the hospital so his thumb might have a
fighting chance at getting reattached and B), he had found
someone to take care of his gators while he was laid up and
C), he hadn't just seen the thing that had taken his thumb

off in the first place running hell-bent-for-leather across his path. To say that King Roar scared the living bejesus out of him would be putting it mildly. Billy Joe overcompensated by turning the steering wheel a wee bit too hard and when he tried to correct himself, his thumb brace got caught in the steering wheel spoke which redefined at that exact moment the meaning of the word "pain." It's when he let go of the steering wheel to cup his dangling thumb with what was left of his digitally challenged other hand that he crashed into the chickee.

We run over to the smoking truck to see how Billy Joe is doing. He's moaning pretty bad but at least he's alive. And then we see the gators and stop in our tracks. The impact has unlocked the tailgate and Billy's cargo of performers are making a break for it by scrambling over each other and across anything that comes into their path like misplaced tourists or my cork wedgies. I scream. Nokosee slowly reaches out and finds my hand to steady me. "Don't move," he whispers.

"Don't worry," I whisper back, "I'm too scared to move."

"Stormy!" It's my dad.

I look back. "Oh, no." Mom and dad and the cops are catching up.

"I'm outta here!" Nokosee turns and takes off across the grass.

"Don't leave me!" I run after him, lifting my feet as high as I can as if that will help should a gator cross my path.

King Roar hits the water running down the boat ramp and disappears beneath its black surface. When four firefighters sitting in an airboat nursing a few brewskies after a hard days work turn from a TV to the sound, the only thing they see is the chain and stake sliding rapidly into the water. The thing that gets them on their feet however are the gators diving in behind it.

"Holy crap! Look at that!" one of them yells, pointing at the boat ramp. "There's freaking gator's all over the place!"

At this point, the nightly fireworks go off filling the sky behind the boat ramp with shooting stars and Roman candles, explosions and the shimmering rain of sparkling sulfur.

We stumble to a stop beside the fire fighters and join them looking at the booming pyrotechnics.

"Hey, it's them," one of them says.

A fire fighter is looking at the TV and pointing at us. His buddies turn to look.

"Get in the boat!" one of them shouts. The airboat tilts under the fire fighters when they rush to the side and extend their hands to us.

"C'mon, hurry up before a gator gets ya."

"Look out, here comes one now!"

I turn just in time to see a gator scrambling down the boat ramp toward me. Without missing a beat, I lift my leg for it to crawl under.

The guys in the airboat can't believe what they just saw.

Nokosee sees his bithlo lying on the grass embankment and runs across the boat ramp to get it. He looks around quickly for his sea turtle shield but can't find it anywhere. He picks up the pole lying beside it, throws it into the dugout and starts pushing it into the water.

"Nokosee, wait!" I run up and stop at the water's edge.

"Are you coming?" he asks.

I shake my head 'no.' Tears are streaming from my eyes.

"I thought so," he says. "If you ever change your mind, you know where I am."

"Third gator on the right?" I ask softly.

"You got it."

He turns, steps into the water, pushes his bithlo off and hops in. He picks up the pole and, standing, looks back at me until he is enveloped by the night.

I try to keep him in sight, using the bursts of fleeting light from the fireworks to follow him along the embankment but I soon lose him to the dark and stop running. No matter how hard I peer into the shadows, I can't see him and, finally accepting the fact I may never ever see him again, turn and begin to climb up the embankment.

I hear Bart Rader's deep ugly voice and stop short. He's talking to Kyle and the two younger brothers, Clint and Dawson, are trailing them. Hearing him talk sets my heart to racing and sends a chill through my body. I can't move and don't want to. I don't want them to see me. They are walking toward some airboats tied up on the sloping canal bank. Everyone is carrying a shotgun or a rifle sealed tightly in what looks like oversized Tupperware. Bart has a .44 magnum strapped to his side, a gun Clint Eastwood informed us "is the most powerful handgun in the world".

I try to make myself invisible behind the embankment and drop slowly to a crouch. I turn around and, hoping for a miracle, try to see if I can see Nokosee one more time but the only thing I can see is the night and the fires on the Everglade horizon. When I turn back, Bart is standing above me. I gasp and catch myself.

"Looking for someone?" he asks with a sneer and a flick of his head toward the darkness.

"I know what you're trying to do, you bastard!" I shout up at him.

Bart sees the four firefighters in the airboat looking over at him. He steps in between them and me.

"Well, my goodness, little girl," he says with a smile and the sound of surprise in his voice, "we're only going fishing."

I point up at him and wave my finger. "I swear to God, if you try to kill that gator or hurt that boy I'll have my dad all over your ass so fast you won't know what hit you!"

"What's going on?"

It's Kyle. He's sitting in the driver's seat of one of the airboats. He's allowed it to drift over to us. Before anyone can answer, three rapid gunshots echo across the boat ramp from the village followed by a loud familiar voice shouting the obvious.

"My God! They're all over the place!" mom yells.

It's mom and dad. The Raders see his Smokey the Bear hat bobbing and weaving in the mob of frightened tourists and Natives. He's shooting at the gators. When Bart sees the four beer-drinking fire fighters jumping out of their airboat and running up the boat ramp toward all the commotion, he uses that moment to draw his big gun and point it at me.

"Get in the boat."

I can't move and realize that all the fear I felt in the last thirty minutes pales to what I'm feeling right now. But then, the threat of death has a way of doing that to you.

"Now," Bart adds with a quick glance back over his shoulder to see if anyone is watching. He pulls back the hammer for emphasis.

I raise my trembling hands and slip down the embankment toward the airboat. When I step into the airboat, Bart slides down the embankment and jumps in behind me. He looks back at the village to see if anyone is watching.

The place is in chaos, no one is watching. More shots are heard among the firecrackers and the loud booming sounds of the skyrockets. I see J.T. pull up at the edge of the boat ramp on his black custom chopper and think, "Osceola's spear" won't be going into the swamp tonight. J.T. gets off and kicks a passing gator with his boot. He's got a shotgun strapped diagonally across his back. Bart looks at Kyle sitting in his perch above the deck of the airboat.

Kyle turns on the muffled airboat engine and we ease out into the canal. As we and the other airboat pull away from the village and are enveloped by the night, I wonder how these redneck poachers of all things alive and wild in the world now turned kidnappers are going to get out of this without murdering the only one who can identify them: me.

Chapter 15

What are you, the fucking Statue of Liberty?

Nokosee told me later that King Roar led him back into the burning Everglades, that it was waiting for him in the canal. He followed the giant gator's undulating moonlit tail and wake toward the west and then, surprisingly, past some sawgrass and out of the canal into a shallow pool of water that stretches across the horizon. The surface of the wet prairie is shining dimly, reflecting the moonlight through the pink-gray smoke and dust.

It's an eerie world just beyond the sawgrass. A smoldering cypress stand is not far away. It seems to be rising out of a cloud on the water, a cloud teasing him and later us with its lazy undulating billowing puffs that squeeze outward from between the trees and then return on a beckoning finger of smoke.

We enter this same burning cypress stand. The air is heavy with smoke and ash and it's hard for us to breathe. My eyes begin to water and I start coughing. Bart tells me to shut up and tapes my mouth and hands with duct tape. It's like he's on another poaching mission, only this time I fear it's a human he's after and not some helpless animal.

As we glide deeper into the swamp, Bart orders Kyle and Clint to cut their engines. For the first time I hear the sounds of a dying world, the crackling and snapping sounds of wood and bark and twig being consumed by heat and flame.

I see Nokosee in the distance, silhouetted against the burning Everglades. I try to scream to warn him but I only succeed in tearing my lips and making a weird sound.

But it's enough to get Nokosee's attention before Bart hits me.

Nokosee, seeing our black airboat framed against the burning cypress stand, turns and begins poling with all of his might. Bart tells Kyle not to rush it, that they have all the time in the world. "He ain't going nowhere," he laughs.

Dawson, armed with a shotgun, jumps into the water from the other airboat which has slipped silently in front of Nokosee blocking his escape. Nokosee turns to the splashing sound, sees Dawson running through the water and aiming the shotgun at him and tries to change course but he doesn't see the cypress knees jutting up out of the water and runs the bithlo aground, jamming its bow between the knees. Nokosee is thrown forward. I want to scream, but I can only cry and feel so very helpless.

That's when Bart orders Kyle to gun the airboat, banking at the last second to hit Nokosee just as he gets to his feet with a wall of water that knocks him backward out of the bithlo.

Nokosee pops up into a blinding light and has to shield his eyes. Kyle is pointing a rotating searchlight mounted next to the driver's seat at him.

"I thought you'd come back this way," Bart says. "Look who came along to say goodbye. Cut the light."

Kyle turns the light off and Nokosee is left blinking and trying to see. When he regains his vision, he sees Bart standing in the bow pointing the Dirty Harry gun at my head.

"Did you think you could get away with it, boy? Well, did ya?"

Nokosee doesn't say anything.

"My daddy got his arm ripped off because of your pet gator and I owe you big time for cutting me up like I was nothing more than a side of beef."

Nokosee barely acknowledges Dawson's noisy arrival when he suddenly backkicks and catches Dawson in the stomach, knocking him in the water. The shotgun goes off, blowing a hole through the hull of the bithlo. Bent over now from the kicking position, Nokosee dives into the water and disappears.

Bart fires into the water. "Turn on the light!" He yells. When it comes up, all we see are a trail of bubbles and blood leading to the airboat. Bart pushes me aside and walks along the airboat, shooting into the water. We hear Nokosee's body bouncing off the bottom of the flat hull and Bart races over to the other side and starts looking for him again. Meanwhile, Kyle has jumped down from the driver's seat, picked up his shotgun and stuck it against my head. He pulls me up closer to him, stretching my t-shirt and choking me in the process. He's looking for Nokosee on our side of the airboat when he hears a splash and turns around. Bart's gone. He pushes me forward to look over the side of the airboat and we can't see anything in the dark coffee colored water.

"Bart!" Kyle cries. "Bart, where the hell are you?"

"He's occupied," the voice whispers in Kyle's ear.

Kyle whips instinctively to the voice and sees Nokosee standing next to him dripping wet, the gunshot wound in his shoulder now peppered and bleeding from buckshot. Nokosee's hand goes for the shotgun, grabs the barrel and points it away from my head. Kyle pulls the trigger and blows a flaming branch off a cypress tree over our heads. I scream like a bloody maniac, tearing my lips again against the duct tape.

An angry sneer grows across Nokosee's face as he grabs the shotgun with his other hand and, with a quick twist, turns it under Kyle's grip catching the man's finger between the trigger and the trigger guard. Kyle lets go and lets loose a loud, piercing scream. Nokosee silences the scream with the butt end of the shotgun into Kyle's mouth, knocking the man and his separated teeth into the water.

Nokosee whips out his knife, turns to me and cuts the duct tape from my hands. When I turn around and rip the duct tape from my mouth, the first thing I say is: "Look out!"

Nokosee turns to see Bart rising out of the water behind him with the .44 magnum pointing at his head.

"Don't," Bart says between heaving breaths.

Nokosee does. He grabs me and pushes me down with him as his foot shoots out over the water towards the gun and makes contact. A hole the size of a man's fist materializes in one of the airboat rudders. Before Bart can squeeze off another round, Nokosee is on him and both are tumbling backward into the water. Nokosee grabs the gun barrel under the water and turns it away just as Rader pulls the trigger. It misses its target.

"One bullet left," Nokosee says matter-of-factly.

Nokosee is counting the shots, trying to remain objective and dispassionate from the action as his father taught him. But it isn't easy. He strains against Bart's heavy bulk and, using the arm which hasn't been shot up, manages under excruciating pain to lift Bart high enough out of the water to head butt him across the nose. The cartilage crumbles, blood gushes out, pain rushes to the brain on an express train and Bart falls back into the water cursing God and man. He lets go of the "most powerful handgun in the world" and Nokosee, as taught by his father, saves the Outside's technology for the cause by sticking the gun in the waistband of his jeans. He lifts Rader just far enough out of the water so that he can hit him again but as much as he wants to, he can't punch him because it's impossible for him to make a fist without feeling the pain in his shoulder. He grimaces when he tries, starts to shake, and falls into the water on one knee.

"Forget about him, Nokosee!" I yell, "Help me!"

He looks back and sees me trying to push the idling airboat back off the cypress knees. Seeing the airboat reminds him there's a second one he has forgotten about. He rises clumsily to his feet and starts looking for it.

It's heading straight for us and the guy driving it is firing a handgun at us.

The first bullet whizzes past Nokosee's head and he knows the guy is either one hell of a shot or too damn lucky. Either way, Nokosee doesn't wait to find out. Dodging another bullet, he runs in a crouch through the water over to me, throws his back against the hull and, with a loud painful groan, uses his powerful legs to help me dislodge the airboat.

A third shot ricochets off the hull just as I jump onto the airboat and climb up into the driver's seat. Nokosee rolls across the bow and falls into the hull as I throttle the engine and turn sharply into the night. I look back and see the three broken, bleeding, cursing, and moaning men trying to find their balance as they get up only to get hit with a one hundred mile-per-hour gust of wind and a shower of stinging wet needles that slap them back into the water. I like that. A lot.

The second airboat stops to pick up the Raders and I know it isn't over yet. I glance down at Nokosee and see him looking up at me. He seems impressed and he should be. Despite the fact that I'm *really* pissed off with my dad right now, I'm also *really* thankful too he taught me how to drive one of these things. It's not easy "manhandling" this piece of big, awkward machinery through the cypress trees-- especially at night when you can't see the cypress knees sticking out just above the water. I'm sure this isn't something Nokosee can do having been raised by that Luddite nutcase father of his. I like the idea I can do something better than my lean-mean-fighting-machine-macho-pagan-caveman-boyfriend.

This little self-serving, imaginative interlude on my part is quickly knocked asunder when I sideswipe a cypress tree. The glancing collision shakes loose Nokosee's grip on the gunwale and he finds himself sliding most unexpectedly across the aluminum hull. He catches himself beneath my feet and looks back through the propeller cage to see if he can see the other airboat. He can't because they aren't behind us; they're next to us. A shotgun blast gets our attention.

I hit the rudder hard to the left and the airboat banks so quickly and steeply that Nokosee suddenly finds himself almost vertical and sliding head first across the hull.

When I come out of the steep turn, a quick glance behind tells me all I need to know: they're faster and they're trying to kill us.

I gun the airboat for all it is worth, slipping and sliding between the cypress trees while trying my best to keep the prop wash between us and them.

Bart can barely focus but, of the injured, he's the only one capable of firing a weapon as he unloads another round of buckshot. His driver, however, more than makes up for what the others are lacking. Clint Rader, the youngest of the clan with "a hankerin' to kill somethin,'" had joined the Army recently to go off and kill some Arabs. He must be back on furlough or something. I guess this will just have to do until he gets back to Iraq.

Clint tries to swing around my airboat but I slip out wide with him, blinding and buffeting him with a torrent of stinging water droplets. He eases up and tries to slip around on the inside but I block his move again.

By this time, Bart Rader has been knocked backward onto his butt far more times than he cares for and instead of cursing me and the Indian, he's hurling invectives toward his little brother. Clint tells him where he can go and, with a quick snap on the rudder stick, sends Bart crashing back into the hull again.

Clint fakes left but tries the same side again and, despite my efforts at blocking his path and swamping him with water, it appears the craziest of the Rader maniacs won't back off. Although he can hardly see in the prop wash, he's beginning to close the gap between himself and us. Talk about tenacious, I can't believe this guy.

When I turn around to see where I'm going I'm shocked to see a fallen cypress tree in my path. The branches that are above the water are still burning. Without any time to study the situation, I opt to jump the tree where there are fewer branches by turning into that direction and gunning the airboat.

"Hold on!" I yell.

When Nokosee looks around there is barely enough time to grip the frame before the bow strikes the fallen tree with a bang that pushes us into the air. The flat bottom catches the air and stays aloft for what seems like an eternity before crashing back into the water and skipping across the black surface. The impact knocks me out of my seat but I grab it and hold on. When I pull myself back into the chair, Clint is riding parallel to me once again, swooping in and then away to avoid the cypress trees in his path.

Bart fires another round and the shotgun pellets bounce off the steel prop cage in a spray of sparks and shrapnel. I catch some of them in my back and cry out.

Nokosee looks up and sees me slumping over in the driver's seat and struggling to control the rudder. The airboat starts to bounce and slide across the water and when I finally regain control, the Rader airboat is banging up against our side. Nokosee sees Bart trying to aim his shotgun at me and without thinking, jumps across the water into the Rader airboat and falls against Bart. The shotgun blasts buckshot into the bottom steel plate of Clint's chair and, although his ass is really sore right now, it could have been much worse if he hadn't been wearing a seatbelt because he would have been propelled through the smoke and ash into the darkness.

Kyle jumps on Nokosee punching and kicking. The punches to Nokosee's wound are enough to make him faint from the pain and he loses his grip on the shotgun. When he looks up, Bart is backing away and telling Kyle and Dawson to get out of the way so he can kill him.

Nokosee doesn't wait for Rader to get a good bead on him; when Kyle jumps away, Nokosee slides on his back toward Bart and kicks him in the kneecap, shattering it and bringing all 250 pounds of screaming angry redneck down on top of him.

Bart pulls the trigger as he collapses and the shotgun blast nearly strikes Clint Rader again in his perch above the action.

Kyle reaches across his fallen screaming brother and tries to punch Nokosee but instead gets kicked in the head. He falls backward onto the hull, stunned and disoriented.

Clint looks down and sees this Indian whom he's already been told is "one dangerous son of a bitch," who "isn't afraid of nothin'," who could probably "kill him with his little finger," who is now standing in his own airboat and looking up at him with such undisguised malice that the fact he's also pumping another shell into the shotgun is anticlimactic.

"Screw you," Clint yells down at him and with a quick flick of the rudder stick, Nokosee is bouncing his head off the hull, dropping the shotgun and lying between Bart and Dawson.

Both guys take a swipe at him. Bart's elbow opens Nokosee's broken nose and I'm sure the intense pain is blinding. Bart, whimpering, trembling from the pain of his shattered kneecap, rolls on top of Nokosee and starts slapping him with highly inaccurate girly man punches across the face. Nokosee manages to knee Bart in the balls, which drops him again in a moaning heap of blubber on top of him.

Despite the pain in my back from the shotgun pellets, I can still manage to drive the airboat and avoid crashing into anything. I'm parallel with them now and I can see Nokosee push Bart off and, disoriented, rise unsteadily to his feet. He can't find the Clint Eastwood gun he stuffed in his pants and starts looking for it in the hull just as Dawson buries his shoulder in his stomach. The impact sends Nokosee crashing against the steel propeller cage. Clint reaches out, grabs Nokosee's long hair whipping back and forth in the slipstream and slams him hard up against the steel frame.

"You, bastard, are going to die tonight!" he yells over the roar of the engine. He bangs Nokosee's head against the steel frame one more time just to make his point. "Do you hear me? Die!"

Maybe somewhere down the road, but not just yet because I'm not going to let that happen. I slam my airboat against Clint's and only his seatbelt keeps him from flying into the swamp.

And Nokosee's grip.

Nokosee is holding onto Clint's wrist. As Clint struggles to steer the airboat, Nokosee twists his wrist and, I swear, I hear it snap across the water and hear his scream scrambled and echoed through the propeller cage.

Dawson punches Nokosee in the stomach and doubles him up. He loses his grip on Clint's broken wrist and slides down the propeller cage.

"Get out of the way!" Bart yells.

Dawson turns and sees Bart lying prone against the bottom of the hull pointing the shotgun at Nokosee. He rolls quickly away.

"Look at me, boy!" Bart shouts. "This is what the face of death looks like!"

I'm closing the gap now and I see Nokosee raise his head slowly and when he sees the shotgun pointing at him what does he do? He smiles. This must really piss Bart off; he can't even scare the guy.

"You think it's funny, hunh? Let's see you laugh at this!"

I tap their airboat on the backside and it starts fishtailing across the water. Everyone standing in it falls into the hull. Including Nokosee.

You know how they say things come in threes? Well this time Bart's errant shotgun blasts finally finds its target hitting Clint in the chest and killing him instantly.

The flat-bottomed airboat starts spinning in a circle. Centrifugal force pushes Nokosee up along the propeller cage and he has to insert his fingers through the wire cage to hold on. Dawson, fighting that same force, grabs the metal tubing of the driver's perch and crawls up the side, one hand over the other. He tries to grab the rudder stick to regain control but Clint's limp body is blocking his reach. To get his dead brother out of the way, he unsnaps his seatbelt and physics takes over from there: Clint's body is launched from the airboat into the night and right at me. I duck, and the rag doll body bounces off the propeller cage behind me and disappears into the fire's raging hungry open mouth leaping out of the night to devour it.

"Clint!" Bart screams over the roar of the engines.

The out of control airboat is coming right at me. I bank hard to the left and swamp their airboat with a deluge of water. Their engine sputters and almost dies. I look back. The water on the hot engine is causing their airboat to trail a smoking cloud of steam.

Dawson climbs into the driver's seat, grabs the rudder stick and guns it through the burning cypress stand back toward the Seminole village.

Bart is livid. He sees Kyle coming to and tells him to get Nokosee, that he's killed Clint and throws Kyle the shotgun

Kyle manages to crawl back across the bouncing flat hull toward the propeller cage, grab the wire frame, and pull himself up. He aims, pulls the trigger on the shotgun and nothing happens. There's no shell in the chamber. It hasn't been cocked. To cock it, he has to let go of the wire frame surrounding the airboat engine and propeller, not the most prudent thing to do. He opts to take a wild swing at Nokosee with the shotgun. It strikes Nokosee's hand and he loses his grip, rolling further backward along the propeller cage. He's holding on now with one hand. I can tell from his expression that the pain must be unimaginable.

Kyle can't be stopped. Filled with anger and rage, he tosses the shotgun onto the airboat hull and pulls himself up to Nokosee. He grabs Nokosee's head and pushes it through the tight opening toward the spinning propeller.

Nokosee's long hair is getting sucked into the machine. Just as I try to close in to help him, Dawson hits the rudder hard and sends their airboat into a spin. I can't react quickly enough and continue racing forward.

I look back and see Nokosee, holding on with just one hand, kick off from the propeller cage and use the momentum of the turn to roll onto the top. He's now over Kyle's head-- and upside down.

Holding on with his one good arm, Nokosee twists around and delivers a short, snapping weak eye thrust. But it's enough to make Kyle let go and grab his eyes- which is probably not the thing you want to do when you're riding the side of a spinning airboat and holding on with one hand.

Kyle tries to grab the bar again but his timing is off because they're just coming out of the turn and losing the physics that made it possible for Nokosee to roll to the top of the cage. Kyle overcompensates and misses the bar and his arm passes through the cage right into the path of the propeller. Inch by rapid inch, bits and pieces of Kyle's hand and wrist and forearm are thrown across the swamp and Nokosee's body in a slapping rat-a-tat-tat of flesh, bone, and blood.

When parts of his brother hit him in the back, Dawson looks around and is shocked to see the bloody stump and the final expression of wide-eyed disbelief on Kyle's colorless face just before he lets go of the speeding airboat and falls backward into a burning cypress tree. Kyle spins in the night sky like an exploding galaxy spitting off body part stars before crashing into the water.

The Raders see it too and both brothers call out "Kyle!" in unison, their voices distorted in a trailing mournful echo through the propeller cage.

I'm circling around when I see Dawson bank hard to go back. Nokosee is holding on with one hand, his body swinging out at a right angle from the propeller cage before the airboat changes course again and he's thrown violently back against it.

Nokosee loses his grip and slips back along the propeller cage. He catches himself with a last minute grip on the metal frame before falling over the side. His one handed grip is the only thing that keeps him from falling into the whirling propeller.

I try to stay with them, to match Dawson turn for turn when my airboat broadsides another burning cypress tree.

The last thing I see is Nokosee looking back at me across the dark moonlit waters as I'm catapulted through the air into what appears to be a pool of fire.

Dawson, who had been looking back over his shoulder at Nokosee, also sees the crash and laughs heartily. He pulls his foot away from the accelerator and fans the rudders to brake the airboat as quickly as possible.

Nokosee, to his horror, finds his feet swinging toward the wooden, steel-tipped propeller blades. He pulls his legs in as tightly as possible and, hanging on the cage with one good hand, kicks out and straddles the waving rudders.

Whether by accident or on purpose, King Roar swims across the path of the airboat. The airboat strikes its huge body with such force that it raises its bow high enough to catch enough air, and with Nokosee's weight on the stern, to flip it over.

Nokosee tells me later that he will always remember it in slow motion: he's airborne holding on with one arm wrapped around the propeller cage and his legs are trailing behind him like an egret flying through the air before the huge black airboat begins to twist and fall back on top of him; he can see Bart falling head over heels with shotguns and plastic containers into the water and his younger brother Dawson snapping his seatbelt and bouncing off the propeller cage and falling past him and, finally, the big square craft coming down on him-- and that's when he lets go.

What he remembers next is tasting the tannic water, feeling the pain in his broken fingers, the pain in his broken nose, and the pain in his shoulder wounds and coming up for air through no choice of his own. He will always remember the sound of that gasping breath, so loud, so desperate and so long, and the truth it brought with it that, despite his efforts to the contrary, he wanted to live-- even if it meant living without me.

This is not something he likes about himself and I'm not so sure I do either. I mean, wouldn't you give up all reason for living if you saw the one you loved the most in the whole wide world just die in a pool of fire? I know I would. Anyway, he's been conditioned by his psycho pop to accept death as part of the package that goes with the honor of being the first of the New Seminoles. It's with this sense of loss of honor and the loss of his first true love that Nokosee, on his knees in waist deep water, begins to cry uncontrollably in deep, body shuddering spasms (which kinda makes up for wanting to live without me). His inconsolable stomach wrenching sobs rise above the background noise of the crackling and popping sounds of the burning cypress trees and the burning airboat, giving a surreal voice to the spent lives of flora and fauna, man and beast.

Struggling to his feet and, cradling his broken hand, he turns and stumbles through the tears and the shallow water past the burning airboat wreckage, back toward the place where he last saw me alive.

"Where do you think you're going?"

Nokosee stops short. He can't believe Bart Rader is still alive, still hasn't given up. When he turns to the voice, Rader reaches up out of the water and pulls Nokosee down, slamming his head against a cypress tree. Dazed, he turns and sees Bart sitting next to him, lying up against the same cypress tree, and bleeding from the forehead. He's holding a shotgun on him.

"I know," he stammers, "You're wondering if I have any shells left. Well, punk, why don't you take a chance and find out?"

Nokosee wonders if anyone *hasn't* seen that Dirty Harry movie. He can't tell if Bart is bluffing but he also can't make a move for the guy. It would be cool to die honorably, to die for love, but he can't make himself do it.

And that surprises him (and me much later).

"What a wuss."

Bart jams the shotgun under Nokosee's throat.

"Boy," he says evenly as he fumbles for Nokosee's knife beneath the water, "if I can't have your gator, I'm still gonna have you."

Bart rolls to the side and grimaces from the pain of his shattered kneecap. He fumbles underwater for Nokosee's knife, finds it and, without pausing, jabs the tip into the center of Nokosee's chest and starts to cut through the skin.

Nokosee cries out and tries to squirm free but he just doesn't have the strength to fight back.

"How's it feel, you little prick?"

I hear Nokosee's scream echoing across the moonlit, burning cypress stand. I want to believe in retrospect that as the knife pierces his skin, it's also cutting through Nokosee's anguish and his knowing loss of love and will.

"You carved a big 'N' on me, boy, well, I'm gonna carve my whole goddamn name on you! That's Bart Rader with a capital 'B'."

Something floats up and bumps Bart's elbow. He looks back and screams.

Clint's dismembered head is staring up at him with eyes forever frozen in horror.

Bart recoils and slaps it away only to discover that a metal stake has been driven up through the neck and into the skull. Nokosee sees it too but it makes no sense to him as Bart slides off and kicks at the head.

Bart's foot catches the chain and he knows what that chain is fastened to. He can feel the links pulling rapidly against his boot and knows that the biggest gator he ever saw in his life is on the other end of the chain and it's coming for him.

But from where?

The splash is the only giveaway. He turns to the sound and sees the gator moving swiftly through the water toward him and before he can do anything about it, the gator has taken him into its mouth and is crushing his chest. He tries to scream but the air has been forced from his chest. He's dragged underwater and shaken back and forth like some kind of a monster's plaything. He lashes out desperately with Nokosee's knife and slashes the gator's only good eye.

King Roar spits Bart out of his mouth and backs away thrashing his mighty head back and forth in a terrible fury. Bart's head is barely above the churning water when he squeezes the shotgun's trigger below the surface.

The blast lifts King Roar out of the water. Nokosee sees his old friend's stomach has been ripped open; blood and intestines are trailing into the water. He throws himself onto Bart's back and tries to strangle him but Rader rams the shotgun into his side and he falls away with a new kind of pain and the thought that his ribs are broken.

When Nokosee tries to suck in air and life and the pain that comes with it, he sees King Roar coming back, charging in a blind rage at Bart and chomping down on his massive upper body. Bart cries out, twists around, and hacks away at King Roar again with Nokosee's knife but the gator twists, wraps the chain around Bart, and rolls them under the water. Bart's broken leg swings up out of the water like a limp rope and Nokosee is sure he can hear the man screaming under the water.

"Bart!"

Nokosee turns to the voice. It's Dawson Rader. He's limping out of the fire consuming the overturned airboat and falling into the water. He's bleeding too and he's got a double barrel shotgun and he's trying to get off a shot.

Nokosee struggles to throw himself against the man but he can't move quickly enough. Both barrels are unloaded into the gator's chest as it breaks the surface of the water killing it instantly. Bart falls away from the gator's terrible mouth, unpeeling from the limp jaw one jagged tooth at a time.

Nokosee, sucking in air in sharp, fast breaths, wants to scream but his broken ribs won't give him that favor.

Dawson stumbles across the water and falls beside his brother. "Bart? Are you all right?" He turns him around.

"What do you think, man?" Bart spits out in an anguished, coarse whisper. "I was in the mouth of a giant goddamn gator for crise sakes!" He looks around anxiously. "Did you kill it?"

"Don't worry. It's dead."

"Where is it?"

"Look behind you."

Bart turns around and recoils. King Roar's lifeless body is floating right beside him. He hears Nokosee's quickened breaths. He turns to him.

"This little Indian has caused us a whole lotta grief," Bart says between his own heaving breaths. "He's killed two of us and now we're going to take our time killing him. Take the kid's knife," he commands weakly.

Dawson steps up and tries to take the knife out of Bart's hand but he won't let go.

"Give me your snake gun."

Dawson pulls out a handgun no bigger than a derringer from his pocket and slaps it into his brother's hand. Double-barreled, twin triggered, and only slightly longer than the two shotgun shells it's carrying inside, it's built to kill anything up close and personal.

Bart lets go of the knife, takes the gun and jams it under Nokosee's jaw. "Now," Rader says through clenched teeth and a whole lot of pain as he pulls Nokosee's hair back, "take the kid's knife and skin that gator."

Nokosee's head is slowly rolling back and forth in fevered pain but his eyes widen for a moment when he hears Bart's plan.

"That's right, you little red bastard, you're gonna watch us skin your pet with your own knife."

Nokosee tries to struggle free but Bart presses the snake gun tighter against his throat and pulls back the double hammers.

"Don't even think about it, you half-breed punk. If you're dead you won't be able to save that little whore you've been screwing."

Nokosee stops struggling and turns quickly to Bart.

"That's right. You can hear her moaning back there. She probably doesn't look like much right now, but that's okay; my brother and I aren't too particular when it comes to fresh meat."

It's strange how sound can travel across the water but I can hear their voices. And yes, I was moaning and coughing up water because I just had the wind knocked out of me when I belly-flopped at fifty-miles-per-hour, skipping across the water like a stone.

Nokosee can't tell if Bart is lying or not but he tells me later—much later-- the thought that I might be alive is enough to give him pause to play by their rules.

Dawson rests the shotgun against the cypress tree and turns to King Roar's lifeless body.

Unable to move his head in Bart's tight grip, Nokosee shifts his eyes toward King Roar and when he sees it floating on its back in the shallow water, the moonlight glistening off its white underbelly, his eyes well up. That gator was his friend and protector, a living talisman that saved his life more than once growing up in a world of poisonous snakes, panthers and bears, and yes, even Bigfoot. And now Nokosee sees an Outsider straddling the creature, holding its lifeless lower jaw out of the water and, when the man is sure he's watching, plunging Nokosee's own knife through the animal's throat and slitting it cleanly from side to side to release the blood and primeval DNA back to the earth where most developers and homeowners living on freshly drained Everglades land think it should have stayed in the first place, fossilized and without rights.

Nokosee sighs and lowers his eyelids but Bart won't let him turn away.

"Keep 'em open!"

Bart pulls Nokosee's hair and the pain is enough to throw Nokosee's eyes wide open. He watches-- but he's seeing King Roar alive and well and younger and with two good eyes and he's seeing himself as a young boy playing with the gator and being happy. And, he tells me later, he sees me too, and wants to see me again and, if it's true, that I'm alive, he will wait for the moment, a moment he prays to his mother's God will be given to him so he can save me and kill anyone who gets in his way who tries to stop him.

Dawson Rader is good at what he does but then he has had lots of practice in and out of gator season. Although it is a repulsive thing to see, when done properly, the skin is literally peeled away from the body as if it were a banana.

Nokosee can hardly breathe. King Roar's blood is floating all around him. It surprises him that he's acting this way, that he feels faint, but then again, he's never hyperventilated before either so this is all new to him.

When Dawson is finished, he sloshes through the water back to them, sticks the knife in the cypress tree, and drops the skinned gator hide next to Nokosee.

"So what do you think of your pet now?" Bart asks.

Nokosee won't look at it. Instead, staring straight ahead, he asks without any sign of emotion, "Where's Stormy?"

"I knew she'd get this little numb nuts to talk."

"Where is she?" Nokosee asks again, this time looking Bart in the eyes.

"You know, for a guy in your position, you sure have a lot of attitude."

"Watch him," Dawson warns as he grabs his shotgun.

"'Watch him?' What can he possibly---"

Bart stops in mid-sentence, his eyes widen and he begins to moan.

"What's wrong?" Dawson asks while backing away and aiming the shotgun at Nokosee's head.

Nokosee grabs Bart's hand holding the snakegun and twists it toward Dawson. He answers the question without taking his eyes off of Bart.

"I've got your brother by the balls and if I squeeze too hard he's going to shoot you. So one more time, where is she?"

"I d-don't know. I d-don't think she made it."

"Wrong."

It's me and I'm limping out of the darkness and the fire and waving the missing .44 magnum at the brothers.

Dawson swings the shotgun around at me and Nokosee squeezes Bart's balls as hard as he can. The snake gun fires and the momentum from the shotgun pellets striking Dawson in the back sends him careening toward me. I try to get out of the way but stumble over a submerged cypress stump and fall into the water just before Dawson Rader's lifeless body falls on top of me.

In a rage, Bart shakes loose of Nokosee and rises unsteadily and painfully onto his one good leg.

"Dawson!"

He turns and aims the snake gun at me while I'm struggling to get out from under Dawson's dead body and pulls the trigger.

Nothing happens. He's pulled the trigger on the empty barrel.

"Goddammit!"

Before Bart can aim and pull the other trigger, Nokosee kicks out and catches him just below his last good knee. Bart cries out and falls into the water. He twists to his side and turns the gun on Nokosee.

Nokosee watches Bart's finger start to squeeze the trigger and expects to die. When the shot is fired he snaps his eyes shut and opens them just as quickly when he realizes he's still alive.

Bart is still pointing his arm at him but his hand is missing. The man's heart is pumping blood out of the stump in a quick rhythmic stream. Nokosee turns to Bart's face. The man is staring in horror at where his hand used to be. He turns slowly like one of those oscillating sprinkler systems, pumping out blood in long streams over the water and onto the cypress tree with each beat of his heart. He holds out his butchered arm toward me and says, "Look what you've done!"

I'm lying in the water and trying to back up but my legs are caught under his brother's body. And I'm pointing the "most powerful handgun in the world" in both of my hands at him and the barrel is smoking and I'm still pulling the trigger over and over again and nothing is happening. The gun is empty.

"You bitch!" Bart cries as he crawls through the water toward me, his eyes large and maniacal. "You stupid little bitch!"

Suddenly the airboat explodes behind us and when we all turn to look at it, to watch the fiery gasoline fueled mushroom cloud rise into the air, no one sees a hand grab

Nokosee's knife or the man behind the knife who is thrusting it through Bart's back and out his stomach.

Bart turns to the new pain rising like a rocket from his stomach and is surprised to see the knife sticking and moving upward through his tank top and the blood and the bile pouring out of the gaping hole in his gut. He turns his head to look at his killer and is surprised to see that it isn't Nokosee.

"This is for my son," the man whispers in his ear.

Bart feels the knife and sees his intestines pulled backward through his body and feels himself falling into the water. The last thing Bart sees in life as he looks up through the dark water is a ghost from the past. The longhaired Seminole standing above him is wearing war paint and the knee length patchwork shirt-dress the tribe use to wear a hundred years ago. And he's coming down to get him, to scalp him. Bart feels his head being yanked out of the water and the last thing he hears is my scream.

"No!"

"Father!"

Busimmanolotome, Nokosee's father-creator, is on his knees in the water, cutting away Bart Rader's scalp. "This is the first one. There will be more to come."

"Nokosee, make him stop!" I scream as I try to get up.

"'Nokosee, make him stop!'" Busimmanolotome says mockingly. "Is this the best you could do, my son?"

"Father," Nokosee replies as he struggles to his feet, "She saved my life."

Busimmanolotome stops cutting for a moment to look at me. He's not impressed. Without turning away, he rips the knife through the last piece of flesh holding on Bart's scalp and pulls it away from the exposed bloody skull.

"Oh, God, Nokosee, what's wrong with him?"

"'Oh, God, Nokosee, what's wrong with him?'" Busimmanolotome echoes in a high-pitched voice. He gets up with Rader's scalp in one hand, the knife in the other and walks low in the water like a samurai toward me while whistling a happy tune.

Although the tune is familiar to me, I can't put a finger on it until he starts singing the chorus and then I know its *Good Morning Starshine* from *Hair*. I try to back up but can't. I point the gun up at the man. He stops singing.

"Put it away, little girl," he says disdainfully while lifting Dawson Rader's body off of me. "There isn't a bullet made with my name on it; and besides, it's empty."

He throws Bart's scalp on a cypress knee next to me and proceeds to scalp the younger Rader.

"Gliddy glup gloopy, nibby nabby noopy, la-la, lo-lo."

While he's singing and working the knife through Dawson's scalp, I struggle to my feet and try to step widely around the still bleeding scalp on the cypress knee and the man who put it there when he reaches out and grabs my wrist with his bloody hand. Horrified, I look down to see him looking up at me with a kind but very insincere smile.

"Thanks anyway for not pulling the trigger. You never know. It's not like I'm infallible or something."

I recoil and he lets me go with a laugh and I stumble past the bodies to Nokosee.

Busimmanolotome laughs again. "Nokosee," he says casually while continuing to scalp, "see if you can find that guy's head. It'll look good on a pole outside our chickee. Maybe we could shrink it." He turns back to scalping Dawson. "Tooby ooby wala, nooby aba naba, early morning singing song."

I fall into the bloody water beside Nokosee. "Nokosee," I say in whispered disbelief, "tell me he's kidding, right?"

"Does it look like he's kidding?" Nokosee sighs. He starts moving toward his father and stumbles. I take him under one arm and help him walk unsteadily through the water.

"You've been trailing me all along, haven't you?"

"Since before you were born," Busimmanolotome says while cutting away at the scalp. "Can't let anything happen to my one and only."

He cuts through the final piece of flesh holding the dead man's scalp to his skull and yanks it away. He rises and turns toward us with the scalp held high in one hand while singing another selection from *Hair*.

"I got my hair, I got my head, I got my brains, I got my ears." He holds the note surprisingly well and pauses to wiggle his shriveled, sun-blackened Viet Cong ear necklace for emphasis before continuing the song. When he gets to the part about his ass, Busimmanolotome turns around, bends over, lifts his knee-length shirt and shakes his bare ass about. Gerome Ragni would have been proud.

Nokosee pushes away from me and staggers toward his father. "I could have used your help a little earlier, dad."

Busimmanolotome stops shaking his ass and drops his shirt. "Watch the attitude, boy. Me thinks you've been hanging around that Outsider too long. Besides, those airboats were a little too fast for my bithlo." He shows Nokosee the scalp. "Here's something for you to remember them by. Not a bad start, eh? Sure beats a wussy little merit badge, doesn't it?"

Nokosee turns away and stares into the night.

"Now don't get all weak on me, son. This is what we do. And remember, we take no prisoners." He thrusts the scalp into Nokosee's hand.

Nokosee looks at the bloody scalp and then turns and looks at his father and sees the man searching his eyes for a clue to his resolve. Nokosee tells him point blank: "Don't touch her."

Busimmanolotome pauses to study his son's face before finally saying with great disappointment, "How could you even think I would hurt her. Am I that much of an enigma?"

"Yes you are."

His father sighs and shakes his head sadly. "I blew up the airboat so they could find her. Make it a quick goodbye. I can see the choppers coming now."

He turns, grabs up King Roar's hide and Clint's head and disappears into the cypress stand, crouching and splashing into the darkness with *The Age of Aquarius* on his lips.

Nokosee turns and looks behind him. He sees the bright searchlights of two helicopters approaching from the south.

And two airboats with spot lights sweeping the cypress stand. He turns and sees me looking at him like I did the first time we saw each other: in horror and in fear. Tears start flowing from his eyes before he lifts the scalp defiantly high over his head and lets loose a long rhythmic and painful war cry. When he's done, and breathing heavily, he looks at me for one last time.

But I won't look at him now.

"What are you?" his father shouts from the dark, "the fucking Statue of Liberty?"

A moment passes and, to my relief, I hear him limping away, splashing through the water

When I finally turn around, I can't find him anywhere. I hear the familiar soft sound of a small electric motor and see Nokosee's father sitting in the back of a bithlo, holding onto the small electric outboard's tiller and steering them into the shadows of the cypress stand, taking his son-- and the boy I will try hard to forget but will fail to do-- into a past that probably never existed and into a future that his father hasn't finished inventing, a future that leaves me filled with dread.

I run through the swamp to get a last glimpse of Nokosee and stop short beside a smoking cypress tree where I can see him better. He's riding slumped over in the bow, resting on his sea turtle shield, saved from prying eyes by his father. A heavy-duty mounted machine-gun is set in the bow. It reminds me of a dragon's head on a Viking ship. His father has jammed a stake with Clint's head on it through the machine-gun's tripod so that it's staring ahead with wide-open haunted eyes. When I see Nokosee look back, I quickly slide behind the still hot cypress tree and burn myself. I cry out and know he heard me and wish he hadn't, wish I was more courageous, wish I knew what I wanted at seventeen and wonder if I ever will.

I hear the copters, look up and find myself walking into a clearing and waving so they can see me. I feel self-conscious about that and wonder if Nokosee sees me. I hope he doesn't because I want to believe that Nokosee is proud of me and that somewhere in his heart he can forgive me.

But how can he? I ask myself while standing in the middle of the clearing with the searchlights crisscrossing my body. *If I didn't choose the Outside because of all of its hypocrisy and betrayal, what am I doing here?*

I hear my dad calling my name. By the time I run out of the light toward the edge of the clearing, yelling "Nokosee, stop! Don't leave me!" it is, of course, too late.

Notes

For those who want to protect the Everglades, check out **Friends of the Everglades (FOE)**. This non-profit grass roots organization is dedicated to protecting and restoring this fragile ecosystem. It was founded in 1969 by **Marjory Stoneman Douglas**, the pioneer conservationist and author of *The Everglades: River of Grass* (1947), to stop the jetport's construction. Although one runway was built, the group was able to convince Congress to stop further funding of the project. Today that lone 10,500-foot runway—long enough to land the space shuttle—is used only for pilot training and emergency landings. You can find their website at **www.everglades.org**.

To see pictures of the jetport runway sitting in the middle of the Everglades please go to: **www.airnav.com/airport/TNT**.

The small plane that spots Stormy and Nokosee in the Everglades is a Micco. It was once manufactured by the Seminole Tribe of Florida. You can learn more about it at **www.miccoaircraft.com**.

To see the Albert "Beanie" Backus painting reproduced on the curtain in the hotel dinner theater go to: http://entertainment.webshots.com/photo/2423232650040331057PkZjCv

To see the Everglades picture Nokosee and Stormy saw in the hotel room, the one Nokosee said is close to where he lives, go to: http://www.clydebutcher.com/clyde-butcher-larger_image.cfm?largephoto=BilliesBay_L.jpg